QUESTION: What had the colonel taken with him?

ANSWER: Gold, the gun, the blueprints.

QUESTION: How did these fit together?

ANSWER: Think. Gold is money, good any time, any place. When McCulloch arrived back in 1858 he would dive into Dixie, good old slave-holding Dixie. He would be right at home there.

But he had taken the gun. The approaching war—and the deadly submachine gun. They went together.

The psychiatrist's report had suggested that McCulloch was a paranoid with criminal schizophrenic tendencies. And his idea was as insane as he was. Just about the most insane idea that a certified nutcase had ever dreamed up.

Colonel McCulloch wanted to alter history so the South would win the Civil War.

QUESTION: Who could stop him?

ANSWER: Only you, Troy Harmon. Only you.

A REBEL IN TIME

Harry Harrison

A TOM DOHERTY ASSOCIATES BOOK
NEW YORK

A REBEL IN TIME

Copyright © 1983 by Harry Harrison

A TOR Book
Published by Tom Doherty Associates, Inc.
49 West 24 Street
New York, NY 10010

Cover art by Tom Kidd

ISBN: 0-812-53967-2   Can. ISBN: 0-812-53968-0

First edition: February 1983

Printed in the United States of America

0   9   8   7   6   5   4   3   2

ONE

The Capital Beltway wraps Washington, D.C. in a concrete noose. Its six lanes of traffic swing wide through the forest land of Virginia, brush the outskirts of the dormitory town of Alexandria, then cross the Potomac into Maryland. Land is cheaper than in the District so that office buildings and pollution free factories have been located here, appearing suddenly in forest clearings. Exit 42 branches off in this area and leads to a divided highway. But just before the stop sign there is an unmarked country lane that disappears away among the trees.

The old Pontiac rumbled out of this beltway exit and turned down the lane. Just around the first bend there was a large, white and windowless building. The driver took no notice of this nor of the sign above the entrance that welcomed him to

Weeks Electronics Laboratory 2. He drove past it and continued along the lane until he was out of sight of the building. Only then did he pull off into a roadside clearing and kill the engine.

After emerging from the car he carefully pushed the door shut behind him, instead of slamming it, so that it made no sound. Then he stood with his back to the fender, looking at his wristwatch, oblivious to the first glorious russets and golds of the autumn foliage around him. He was single-minded and intense, with all of his attention concentrated on the watch. A casual observer would have seen a man who was a bit over six feet tall with a not unhandsome face, although his nose was perhaps a little too sharp for his features. However his smoothly tanned skin, his brown hair just touched with gray at the temples, gave him a most distinguished air. His forehead puckered as he stared intently at the watch; a familiar expression that had left a permanent cleft between his eyes. He was dressed in a nondescript trenchcoat, dark blue trousers and black shoes.

He nodded with sudden satisfaction, pressed a button on the watch, then turned and walked off among the trees. He moved quietly, but swiftly, until he reached an oak tree that had been blown down by a storm; quite recently because the leaves were just beginning to drop. Then he eased himself down onto the ground and crawled for at least fifteen feet in the shelter of the tree before climbing to his feet again and hurrying forward.

Less than twenty yards further on, the grove ended in a grassy ditch that ran along the base of a chain-link fence. Beyond the fence was green parkland interspersed with occasional clumps of trees; a corner of the Weeks Electronics building was just visible through the foliage. The man started down into the ditch—then drew back quickly to the cover of the trees. A moment later a uniformed guard holding a German Shepherd on a short leash walked by on the other side of the fence. As soon as they were out of sight the man hurried forward again, down into the ditch, pulling on a pair of leather gloves as he went. Without stopping he swarmed up the fence until he stood, balancing on the top, just below the double strand of barbed wire. He flexed his knees, extended his arms to keep his balance, then jumped smoothly over the wire to land on the other side.

Then he ran, head down, fast, aiming for the nearest clump of trees. But before he could reach it a jeep raced into sight, cutting sharply across the grass, braking to a skidding stop before him. The guard seated beside the driver had his carbine raised and aimed at the intruder who stopped, then turned slowly to face him. The guard looked on in silence as the tall man lifted his arm slowly, glanced at his watch, then pressed the button in its side.

"Exactly six minutes, nine and three-tenths seconds, Lopez," he said. The guard nodded expressionlessly and lowered the gun.

"Yes, colonel," the guard said.

"That's not good, not very goddamned good at all." He climbed into the back of the jeep. "Let's get to the guardhouse."

They drove around the laboratory to a low building that was concealed from the road by the larger building. A group of uniformed men stood beside it, watching in silence as the jeep arrived. A gray-haired guard with sergeant's stripes on his sleeves stepped forward when the vehicle ground to a stop. The colonel stepped down then pointed to his watch. "What do you think of six minutes, nine and three-tenths from the time I went into the woods from the road until the time I was intercepted?"

"I don't think very much of that at all, Colonel McCulloch," the sergeant said.

"Neither do I, Greenbaum, neither do I. I was halfway to the lab before the guard turned up. If I had been an intruder I could have done a lot of interesting things in that time. Do you have anything to say?"

"No, sir."

"Do you have any questions?"

"No, sir."

"None? Aren't you interested in how I got as far as the fence without being detected?"

"I am, sir."

"Good." Colonel McCulloch nodded as he would at an idiot child. "But your interest is a little late, sergeant. Exactly one week too late. That's how long ago I noticed that a newly fallen tree had blocked part of the field of vision of one of the remote TV cameras. I waited one week for you or one of your men to notice it. None of you did. I therefore arranged this demonstration to show just how lax security is around here."

"I'll see that it's tightened up, colonel . . ."

"No you won't, Greenbaum. Someone else will. You are losing those stripes, taking a salary cut to match, and a reprimand goes into your record . . ."

"No it doesn't, McCulloch. Because I'm quitting this job. I'm through."

McCulloch nodded agreement. "Yes, you are through. And you have just described yourself as well. A quitter. You quit after serving twenty years in the Army too. Now you're quitting—"

"Bullshit, colonel, if you will excuse the expression." Greenbaum glowered in anger, fists clenched. "I got out of the service to get away from chickenshits like you. But I just didn't get far enough away. You're in charge of security at this lab. Which means you got responsibilities too. If you gave a shit you would have reported that tree. We're supposed to be in this together, you're supposed to help us. Not pull this boyscout and indian crap. Well I'm getting just as far away from that kind of stuff as I can. Beginning right now."

He turned and stamped away. McCulloch watched him go in silence. Only when Greenbaum was out of sight did he turn to the silent guards.

"I want a written report on this exercise from each one of you. On my desk in the morning." He waved Lopez out of the jeep and took his place. "Get me back to my car," he told the driver, then turned to the other guards as the engine started up. "Every one of you is expendable. Screw up like Greenbaum and you go just the way he did."

McCulloch did not look back as they drove away.

At the car he unlocked the trunk while the jeep turned and vanished back down the lane. He took off his coat and threw it into the trunk. He was wearing his uniform underneath. It was empty of all decorations and identifying insignia, other than the silver eagles on his shoulders. He reached into the trunk again and took out his uniform cap, settled it firmly on his head, then took out a black attache case as well before slamming the lid shut. A few minutes later he was on MacArthur Boulevard driving south towards the District.

It was a short ride. A few miles down the road he

turned into a large shopping center, where he parked close to a branch of the D. C. National Bank. He locked the car and went into the bank, taking the attache case with him. It was a brief visit. He emerged less than ten minutes later, got into his car and drove away.

He was watched most carefully by the man in the black Impala that was parked two rows away. The man raised a microphone and spoke into it.

"Able One to Able Two. George is now leaving the lot and turning south on MacArthur. He's yours now. Over."

"Will do. Out."

The man replaced the microphone on the dash and got out of the car. He was lean and blond and unremarkably dressed in a gray suit, white shirt and dark tie. He entered the bank and crossed to the receptionist.

"My name is Ripley," he said. "I would like to see the manager. About some investments."

"Of course, Mr. Ripley." She picked up the phone. "I'll see if Mr. Bryce is free."

The manager stood up from behind the desk and shook his hand when he entered the office. "Mr. Ripley. Now just what can I do to help you?"

"This is a government matter, sir. Would you please look at my identification."

He took a leather wallet from his breast pocket, opened it and passed it across the desk. Bryce looked at the gold badge and the accompanying card behind the plastic window and nodded. "Well, Mr. Ripley," he said. "How can I be of aid to the Federal Bureau of Investigation?" He started to hand back the ID but the agent stopped him.

"I would like you to authenticate the identification, sir. I believe that you were given an unlisted number for use if the occasion should arise?"

Bryce nodded and opened the top drawer of his desk. "Yes, I've used it once before. Here it is. If you will excuse me."

The bank manager dialed the number, then identified himself to the party at the other end. He read off the ID number from the wallet, then placed his hand over the receiver.

"They want to know the case reference."

"Tell them Investigation George."

The bank manager repeated the words, then nodded and hung up. He passed the ID back to the FBI agent. "I was instructed to cooperate with you and to give you any information that you might need about one of our clients. But I must say that this is not a normal practice . . ."

"I realize that, Mr. Bryce. But you are now involved in a security investigation with a top priority. If you refuse to cooperate I must go to your superiors and—"

"No, please! That's not what I am suggesting. Please don't misunderstand me. You have my cooperation, of course. I was just saying that information about our clients is always confidential—in the normal course of events. But in a matter of national security, very different, naturally. How can I be of aid?"

Bryce was talking rapidly, unaware when he took the handkerchief from his breast pocket to pat his suddenly moist forehead. The agent nodded, unsmiling.

"I appreciate that, Mr. Bryce. I hope you understand that your voluntary cooperation makes you liable to prosecution for violation of national security should you mention this to anyone else?"

"Does it? I didn't know—but of course, I'll speak to no one."

"Very good. A few minutes ago a man left this bank after transacting some business. His name is Wesley McCulloch and he is a colonel in the United States Army. No, don't write that down. You won't have any difficulty in memorizing this information. You will find the bank employee he dealt with and bring back the record of any transaction or transactions the colonel may have made. You will tell no one the reason for your interest."

"Of course not!"

"We appreciate that, Mr. Bryce. If you don't mind I will wait here until you return."

"Yes, please, make yourself comfortable. This should not take a very long time."

The manager returned in less than five minutes with a file folder in his hand. He carefully closed and locked the door, then opened the folder before him on the desk.

"Colonel McCulloch made a purchase . . ."

"Did he pay by check or with cash?"

"Cash. Large denomination bills. He purchased gold and paid for it in cash. Eight-thousand, five hundred and thirty-two dollars. He took the gold away with him. Is that the information you wanted, Mr. Ripley?"

The agent nodded and smiled, ever so slightly.

"Yes, Mr. Bryce. That is exactly what I wanted to find out."

TWO

Sergeant Troy Harmon rode the Metro in from the Pentagon, wondering just what the hell this assignment was all about. It was so hush-hush that he had been told nothing, absolutely nothing about it. Other than to get over soonest to this address on Massachusetts just up from Union Station. Transportation was not provided. He rode the Metro, looking down at the thick, sealed envelope he was carrying. His own records, the history of his nine years in the Army. Decorations, promotions, goof-ups, Fitzimmons Hospital records when they dug the shrapnel out of his back. Two years in Nam without a scratch—then a short round from his own supporting battery. A Purple Heart from a chunk of Detroit steel. Then a transfer to the MP's, then G2, military intelligence. The records were all here. It would be inter-

esting to look at them. And military suicide if he
were to open the envelope.

And what organization was he going to on Massachusetts Avenue? He knew most of the spook
outfits, starting with the CIA out in Langley right
on down. But he had never even heard of this one.
Report to Mr. Kelly. And who the hell was Kelly?
Enough. He'd find out soon enough. He looked up
to check the station, McPherson Square, then
looked back down just in time to catch the eye of
the girl sitting across from him. She looked away
quickly. A very foxy girl, what they used to call a
high-yellow when he was a boy. She glanced back
again and he gave her his toothpaste commercial
smile; lips pulled back so his white teeth showed
in nice contrast to his dark-brown skin. This time
she raised her nose slightly and sniffed as she
turned away.

Rebuffed! He had to smile. Didn't she see what
she was missing? Five foot ten of handsome, clean-
cut soldier.

The train slowed as it entered Metro Center.
Troy was the first one off and he stayed ahead of
the pack as they rushed for the escalator to the
Red Line. He rode up into the indirectly lit cavern,
more like a futuristic spaceship hangar than a
subway. It made the old Independent in New York
look like the filthy hole that it really was.

There was a cool, autumn bite to the air as he
walked down Massaschusetts checking the numbers. There it was, a tall, brownstone house,
just across New Jersey. No name, no identifying
plate, nothing. He climbed the steps and pressed
the polished brass button, well aware of the fish-
eye of the micro TV camera above it. The door
buzzed and he went through into an airlock ar-

rangement, with another door ahead of him that did not open until the outer one had closed. Very neat. And another TV pickup here as well. Inside was a marble-floored lobby with a desk at the far end. His heels clacked as he walked the length of it. The receptionist, a very cool redhead in a very tight sweater looked up at him and smiled.

"May I help you?"

"Sergeant Harmon. Mr. Kelly is expecting me."

"Thank you, Sergeant Harmon. If you will take a seat I'll let him know that you are here."

The couch was too deep and soft to be comfortable, so he sat on the edge of it. There was a copy of Fortune and a copy of Jet on the low table in front of him. What was this—catering to his special needs? He tried not to smile as he picked up Jet. Maybe they were trying to tell him something. If so he had got the message a long time ago. Pics of a big party at the Hotel Theresa, then babies with rat bites in the slums just a few blocks away. It was a different world to him. He had grown up in Queens, in South Jamaica, a nice, secure middle-class area of frame houses and green trees. He knew as much about Harlem as he did about the back of the Moon.

"Mr. Kelly will see you now."

He dropped the magazine, took up his envelope, and appreciatively followed the receptionist's sweetly rotating bottom into an adjoining office.

"Come in, Sergeant Harmon. Pleased to meet you," Kelly said, coming from behind his desk to take Troy's hand. The way he pronounced *Harmon* was positive proof that he was from Boston. His elegantly tailored three-piece pinstripe suggested Back Bay and Harvard as well. "I'll take that envelope, thank you."

Kelly took the folder of military records and added it to the file on the desk before him, tapping the edges until all the papers were neatly in line. He looked at the sergeant as he did this, noting what he saw. Late twenties, good service record, he could read that from the ribbons without looking at the file. Not too tall, but solidly built. Jaw like a rock, face expressionless. Eyes black and unreadable. Sergeant Troy Harmon was obviously a professional soldier and a man very much in charge of himself.

"You've been sent over here on temporary assignment from G2, because of your specialized knowledge," Kelly said.

"Just what would that be, sir? I fired sharpshooter on the M16."

"Nothing quite that deadly," Kelly said, smiling for the first time. "We understand that you know a great deal about gold. Is that true?"

"Yes, sir."

"Good. That particular knowledge will be most helpful to us since we are predominantly headquarters staff here at QCIC. We depend on the other security services for field personnel." He glanced at his Rolex. "You'll be seeing Admiral Colonne in a few minutes and he will explain the operation in detail. The admiral is the man who directs this agency. Now—do you have any questions?"

"No, sir. I don't know enough about what is happening here to think of a question. I was given this address and told to bring my records to you. You just mentioned that this department is QCIC. I don't even know what those initials stand for."

"The admiral will explain all that to you as well. My role is strictly liaison. You'll file all reports with me." He wrote quickly on a piece of paper and passed it over. "This is my twenty-four hour phone number. Keep track of expenses and let me have the slips once a week. Also contact me for any equipment or specialized assistance that you might need. The admiral will brief you on this operation, which is code-named Subject George."

Kelly hesitated, tapping his fingers on the edge of the desk, before he spoke again. "The admiral is old Navy, Annapolis, been around a long time. You know what that means?"

"No."

"I think that you do, sergeant. When he was on active duty during the Second World War, Blacks were called Negroes and they weren't allowed in the Navy. Other than as mess attendants."

"Say mess boys, Mr. Kelly, that was the term. And my father was in the Army then, fighting to make the world safe for democracy. Only the Army was segregated and, since the Blacks couldn't be trusted to carry guns, they drove trucks and dug ditches. But that was a long time ago."

"For us, maybe. Let's hope it is for the admiral too. But this is a hundred percent WASP outfit. It couldn't have got that way by accident . . . hell, sergeant, maybe I'm talking too much."

Troy smiled. "I appreciate the thought, Mr. Kelly. I'm a firm believer in field intelligence. I'm not too worried about the admiral."

"You shouldn't be. He's a good man. And this is a damned important job." Kelly picked up the file as he stood up. "We'll go see him now."

The roar of the traffic outside on Massachusetts Avenue was muted to a distant hum in the large conference room. Heavy drapes covered the

windows; floor to ceiling bookshelves lined the
walls. The admiral sat behind the long mahogany
table, carefully loading tobacco into an ancient
briar pipe. He was suntanned, and almost completely bald; his blue uniform smooth and un-
wrinkled, the rows of ribbons on it impressive. He
waved Troy to a chair opposite, nodded at the file
that Kelly placed before him, then struck a
wooden kitchen match and puffed the pipe to life.
He did not speak until Kelly had gone out and
closed the door.

"You've been seconded to us by military intelligence, because of your specialized knowledge, sergeant. I want you to tell me about gold."

"It's a metal, admiral, very heavy and people set
great store by it."

"That's all?" Admiral Colonne scowled from
behind a cloud of blue smoke. "Are you being
facetious, Harmon?"

"No, sir, I'm telling you the truth. Gold is an
important industrial metal, but that is not what
most people care about. They buy it and steal it
and hide it, because other people prize it highly. In
the west we treat it as a commodity—but the rest
of the world sees it as a safer investment than
banks or bonds. Gold purchased legally here is
worth twice as much after it has been smuggled
into another country, say India. That's how I got
involved with it. The US Army has men stationed
right around the world. The temptation to turn an
easy buck by selling gold is something a number of
grunts just have not been able to resist."

The admiral nodded. "All right, that's one
aspect of gold. What about the industrial use you
mentioned? Other than jewelry—what is it good
for?"

"Electronics. It's malleable, does not rust or tarnish—and is a good conductor. All of the contacts in computers are plated with it. You'll also find that it is used in windows to cut down on the amount of sunlight that is allowed to pass through . . ."

"None of this has any goddamned relevancy to the case we have here!" The admiral slammed the file on the table before him. "What we are interested in are the reasons why a certain Army colonel is buying a lot of gold. I know that it is all perfectly legal, but I still want to know why."

"May I ask what 'a lot' is, sir?"

"A little over a hundred thousand dollars worth, as of yesterday. Do you know what the initials QCIC stand for?"

Troy accepted the abrupt change of topic without comment. "No, sir, I don't. Mr. Kelly said that you would explain."

"*Quis custodiet ipsos custodes.* Do you know what that means?"

"I should. After two years of Latin in college. A literal translation would be—who shall keep watch over the guardians?"

"Right. Who shall watch the watchers? That little problem has been around for a very long time—or it wouldn't have a Latin tagline attached to it. Policemen who take bribes are bad enough. But what about the people who are entrusted with the security of our nation? Someone has to keep an eye on them. Well—we're the people who have to do just that. That's what this agency is here for. You must realize that what we do here is vital to the security of this country. Without any conceit, this is undoubtedly the most important security operation in the land. We cannot afford to make mistakes. As the old saying goes, the buck stops here. We have the ultimate responsibility in assuring this nation's security because we must watch *all* of the other security operatives. That is the reason why I approved your assignment to us. There are three things in your record that I like. First, you know all about gold. Second, your security clearance is Top Secret. Can you imagine what the third reason is?"

Troy nodded slowly. "I think I can. Is it the fact that I blew the whistle on my CO when I caught him on the take?"

"It is. A lot of soldiers would have looked the other way. Did you expect some special reward for doing what you did?"

"No, admiral, I did not." Troy held his temper under careful control. "If anything I expected the direct opposite. I am pretty sure that the Army doesn't like enlisted men taking potshots at the officers. But this was special. If he had been pocketing officers' club funds or something like that, well maybe I might have thought twice. But this was in an MP outfit where we were working full time trying to keep drugs out of the barracks. Our problems were not just with grass or uppers and downers, but the hard stuff, H, and it was getting in. When I found out that my own commanding officer, the guy who was supposed to be stopping the stuff, that he was getting payola from the pushers, well that was just too goddamned much." Troy smiled coldly. "The last I heard he was still in Leavenworth. I was pulled out of my outfit, I expected that, but I didn't expect to be bumped two grades and transferred to G2."

"That was my doing. I overruled some of your officers who were thinking of doing just what you said they would. No one has ever lost money underestimating the reflex thinking of the military. I have been keeping a watchful eye on your career ever since. Because men like you are rare enough." He caught Troy's expression and smiled. "No, sergeant, that is not an attempt at flattery but the honest truth. When I say that I mean that I value most highly men who put their oath of loyalty before personal friendship or job security. We need you here. I hope that after this operation is completed, that at that time you will consider a permanent transfer. But that is still in the future. Right now I want you to turn your attention to this operation. It is code-named George."

He opened the file and took out a sheaf of papers, then leafed through them.

"Operation George began as a routine check. This sort of thing takes place on a regular basis, all of the time, a routine surveillance of people with high security clearance. The subject of this particular investigation is an United States Army colonel named Wesley McCulloch. He has a fine military record and first class security clearance. Unmarried but, if you will pardon the expression, not unlaid. He keeps fit, skis in the winter, surf-boards in the summer. Owns a small house in Alexandria and only has a few thousand more to go on his mortgage. All of this very dull and ordinary stuff . . ."

"Except that the colonel has been buying a lot of gold."

"Correct. It started quite recently, just a little over six months ago. At that time he had some money invested in gilt-edge stock, plus a little more in a savings account. He cleared everything out and bought gold. Sold some bonds that he had inherited as well. Now we both know that all of this is completely legal. But I still want to know why."

"May I see the file, admiral?"

Troy flipped through it quickly but methodically, then held it up. "There's no mention in here of the colonel's duties."

"There wouldn't be. The FBI agents who make up these reports operate on a need-to-know basis. McCulloch is in charge of security at one of our most important and secret laboratory facilities. His work there cannot be faulted in any way—he's doing an excellent job. That's not what is bothering us. It's the gold. It doesn't, well . . ."

"Smell right?"

"Correct. Call it a hunch, call it anything. It is just too much out of the ordinary—the only unusual thing that McCulloch has done in his entire lifetime. That's your assignment. Find out why he is buying the stuff."

"I'll do that, admiral. I'm intrigued by it as well. I can't think of any possible reason for a man in the colonel's position to be doing this sort of thing. Legal reason, that is."

"You think that it could be illegal?"

"At this point I think nothing, sir. I have an open mind. What we need are some hard facts before we can decide anything."

THREE

The rain thundered down in a heavy tropical downpour. Although it was the end of October the air was muggy and stifling, one of the main reasons that Washington has the dismal nickname of Foggy Bottom. Troy Harmon sat behind the wheel of the Pontiac, slumped down in the seat with his hat tilted over his eyes. It was no accident that the hat, as well as the raincoat, closely resembled those worn by Colonel McCulloch when he had left his house about thirty minutes earlier. The colonel had also been driving a vintage Pontiac—the same color and year as this one. The sound of the rain hammering on the metal roof almost drowned out the sudden beeping of the radio. Troy lifted it to his ear and thumbed it to life.

"George Baker here," he said. The earphone rasped in reply.

"George is parking in his usual place in the lot now."

"Thanks. Out."

Troy turned the ignition key and switched on the engine. It had taken four days to set everything up, working slowly and carefully so that there could be no mistakes. He did not believe in rushing into a case before he was completely prepared. But now, with the preparations completed, he was looking forward to the next part of the operation. All of the details concerning Colonel McCulloch's daily and weekly routine had been in the FBI reports. Troy had studied them closely and made the most of the opportunity. The FBI had supplied him with a guest membership to the athletic club where the colonel played squash three times a week. He had made a single visit there—and it had taken him less than a minute to open McCulloch's locker and make impressions of all of his keys. The duplicates were in his pocket now as he drove the old Pontiac slowly down the tree-lined street. It was hot and stuffy with the car windows closed—but he liked it that way. All of the glass was now completely steamed up. He had to lean over to wipe a clear patch on the windshield so he could see out.

As he turned the car into the driveway of the colonel's house Troy pressed the button on the radio-operated garage opener, now set to the same frequency as McCulloch's. The door swung up and he rolled under it. Any casual observer would assume automatically that this was the colonel coming home. Since McCulloch had no friends or acquaintances in the neighborhood the chance of his finding out about this unscheduled visit were very slight. Troy waited until the door was completely shut behind him before he got out of the car. He left the raincoat and hat on the seat, clipped the radio to his belt then reached over for his attache case. Instead of turning on the garage lights he used the flashlight from his jacket pocket.

The burglar alarm box was next to the door that led from the garage into the house. The QCIC technician had identified the key for him and told him just what to do. Insert, rotate one full turn clockwise, then remove. He reached up and did just that. The blue light on the front of the box went out. When he left the house he would have to reverse the procedure. He found the correct door key on his second try, unlocked it and was about to pull the door open when he stopped. It was too easy. If McCulloch had anything to hide—wouldn't he take some more precautions than just the burglar alarm?

Troy ran the flashlight along the top of the door, then down the sides. Nothing seemed to be protruding. But it was very easy to leave a small piece of paper jammed into the door, that would fall out when the door was opened. He bent over—and there it was!

A burnt matchstick just under the hinge, its blackened head barely visible. When he opened the door it dropped onto the sill. Very good. He leaned close with the light and saw the tiny groove it had made. It would be going back into that groove when he left.

Then he swung the door wide and let himself in. It was cool and quiet in the hallway. The door at the far end opened into the kitchen.

Troy had all the time in the world.

He was going to use it wisely, taking as long as

he needed, rushing nothing. McCulloch would not be home for eight hours in the very least. He was being watched and there would be plenty of time to get out of the house should his routine be changed.

"What I want to do with you colonel," Troy said to himself, looking around the room, "is to find out just what makes you tick."

He took off his sports jacket and hung it on the back of a kitchen chair, then loosened his collar and tie. The breakfast bar was clean and polished. Troy spread his pocket handkerchief on it, then opened his attache case and took out the thermos of coffee. After pouring himself a cup he placed the thermos on the handkerchief. He sipped and looked around.

Very GI. The place was clean as a BOQ. It should be, considering the fact that McCulloch had been in the military most of his life. From VMI he had gone right into the Army. A clean record, plenty of combat experience, a good soldier. Then OCS— and on to a lifetime career. It showed. Breakfast dishes rinsed and drying on the drainboard. Even the frying pan washed and put away. Eggs and bacon for breakfast, shells and wrapper in the otherwise empty garbage can. Milk, butter, more eggs, bread, an unopened sixpack in the refrigerator.

Slowly and carefully, Troy went through the rest of the house. Room by room. There was a desk in the living room, but all of the drawers were locked. That would require special attention later. Some magazines in the rack next to the couch. Army and sports magazines, some well-thumbed copies of Newsweek and the Readers Digest. A few shelves of books. Old texts and military manuals from OCS. Some newer ones still in their dust-jackets. Popular novels, engineering texts, some historical studies, a guide to western ski resorts. He wanted a record of the titles to look at later.

One thing about QCIC, they had some interesting gadgets. The small Japanese camera was completely electronic. Instead of film it recorded pictures on an electronic card—up to ten exposures a second. It could also be adjusted to any range of visible or invisible light. He set it now to ultraviolet. The UV flashgun emitted only a weak blue glow that he could see. It was a brilliant flash to the camera. He photographed the spines of all of the books, then stowed the camera away again.

It was in the main bedroom upstairs, under the rug beside the double bed, that he found the inset panel. The floor was made of polished oak boards and the wooden panel had been set into them, flush on all sides. There was a small indentation on one edge that his finger just fitted into. When he pulled, the panel opened like a door on its concealed hinges. Set into concrete beneath it was a combination safe.

"Now isn't that nice," he said, rubbing his hands together in appreciation. "A really big one. Too big just for his medals and checkbooks. It would be very interesting to find out just what it does contain."

He used the phone beside the bed to dial Kelly's number. It was picked up on the first ring.

"Harmon here. I've found a floor safe, a large one. I wonder if you can help me."

"That's very interesting. I'm sure that we can. Did you notice what make it is?"

"Yes. An Atlas Executive. No keyholes. No

hinges visible. A single dial with numbers running up to ninety-nine."

"Very good. We'll have someone there in under an hour."

While he was waiting, Troy went back downstairs and looked into the desk; a picklock opened it quickly. There was some correspondence, the usual collection of bills and receipts, canceled checks and checkbook stubs. He made no attempt to examine the contents in detail, but photographed it instead. It was a quick job and he had put everything in order and locked the desk again when the well-worn truck pulled up less than forty-five minutes later. The sign on the side said ANDY THE PLUMBER—24 HOUR EMERGENCY SERVICE. Andy was dressed in workclothes and carried a large and battered toolbox. He locked the truck and strolled, whistling, up the walk. Troy opened the door, just before he pressed the bell, and let him in.

"I'm Andy, just like the truck says. I hear you got a problem with some financial plumbing." He took the toothpick from his mouth and carefully put it into his pocket. "Where's it at?"

"Upstairs. I'll show you."

Andy knew his job well. The battered toolbox was pristine inside, with tools and equipment set into shaped niches in the velvet lined trays. He knelt and admired the safe.

"Nice," he said, rubbing his hands together. "Very secure. Fireproof, good for a couple of thousand degrees for a couple of hours. Impossible to crack."

"Then you can't open it?"

"Did I say that?" He took a metal box with a wire antenna from its niche and switched it on. "I mean your run-of-the-mill safecracker couldn't do a thing with it. He would just walk away. I can open anything. But let's first see if there are any electronics or alarms wired to it. No, it's clean. Now let's listen to it sing. No tumblers, so you can't hear them fall. But there are ways."

Troy didn't ask what they were. It wasn't his business. Andy was using supersonics, something, to probe the guts of the safe. A number of small battery powered devices were attached to the knob and the front plate. The largest of the gadgets had solid state circuitry and a digital readout. It took Andy less than fifteen minutes to work his electronic magic. Then he whistled as he detached all of his machines and put them away.

"Aren't you going to open it?" Troy asked. Andy shook his head *no*.

"Not my job. I'm a technician, not a law-breaker." One of his compact instruments looked like a printing calculator. Andy tapped out a series of instructions; and it buzzed and ejected a slip of paper. He handed it to Troy. The paper had a short list of letters and numbers printed on it.

"R means right," Andy said. "And as you might have guessed L is left. Turn the knob a couple of times counterclockwise to clear it before you start, then just set the numbers in the order the ways it reads. The door is spring loaded, it'll just pop open at the last number. After you close it again give it a couple of more spins, then set it to fifty-six which is what it was at when I came in. Someone might remember that number. Have a good day now."

Troy watched him drive away, then went back to the bedroom. Andy's electronics had done their job well. When Troy had set the last number he

felt the safe door push up against his hand. It
opened about an inch, leaving more than enough
room for him to get his fingers under the edge to
open it all the way. He looked inside and saw that
the safe contained only one thing.

Neatly stacked ingots of gold, gold sheets and
gold wire.

It was very attractive indeed. The more he
worked with gold the more he admired it. There
really was nothing else like it in the world. Reaching down into the safe he lifted off the top ingot
and weighed it in the palm of his hand. It was solid
gold all right. Nothing else, not even lead, had that
massive feel to it, the dense weight-to-size ratio.
He started to put it back in its resting place—then
stopped, his eyes narrowed in thought. Something
here was just not right.

Troy placed the gold ingot onto the carpet, then
bent over the safe, making a rough count of the
rest of the ingots. He could not see them all, but he
could make an estimate. A moment's work on the
calculator verified his suspicion. But he had to be
sure.

He opened his notebook beside the safe, then lay
flat on his stomach. He wasn't much of an artist,
but a rough sketch would be good enough. With
careful strokes he drew the pile of ingots, then
outlined the positions of the wire and sheets of
gold. When this was done to his satisfaction he
laid aside the notebook and carefully, piece by
piece, removed the gold from the safe, pulling it
onto his closed attache case. When almost a third
of the gold had been stacked on the case he stood
and went into the bathroom to get the spring scale
he had noticed there earlier. It would be accurate
enough for a rough count.

Troy stood on the scale. One seventy-five fully dressed; the thing was at least five pounds off. That wouldn't matter. He made a note of the weight in his notebook then stepped back onto the scale holding the attache case with its burden of gold. He did this three times, making careful record of the total weight each time. When he was finished he replaced the gold exactly as he had found it.

The mathematics were simple indeed. His weight, along with that of the unburdened attache case, was one-hundred and eighty three pounds. He multiplied that by three, then multiplied his fully laden weight by three, and subtracted the smaller number from the larger.

The result was just over thirty-nine pounds.

Thirty-nine pounds of gold.

That was an awful lot of gold. A moment's work with the calculator verified that. The last time he had looked, gold was around four-hundred and thirty-six dollars an ounce. But a Troy pound was only point eight-two-three of an Avoirdupois pound. He fed this correction in, then divided by twelve since there were only twelve ounces to the Troy pound.

Troy stared at the final figure and nodded his head. Yes indeed, yes indeed! This was something that the admiral would have to hear about at once.

It was a quick phone call. Kelly put him right through to the admiral when he said that he had urgent news.

"Admiral Colonne speaking. Is that you Sergeant Harmon?"

"Yes, sir. I've found the safe where the colonel keeps his gold. Before I closed the safe I weighed the gold, roughly, but accurate enough so that there is probably no more than a five percent error either way. It appears that the colonel is a sharper operator than the FBI realized. He has more gold here than the hundred-thousand that they reported."

"More? How much more?"

"I would say that the colonel now has over two-hundred and fifty thousand dollars worth of gold in that safe, admiral. A quarter of a million dollars."

FOUR

"I prefer a verbal report," the admiral said. "You can write up your conclusions later on. But for the moment I just want to hear what you have found out."

Troy nodded and spread his notes out on the conference table before him. The room was the same as it had been on his last visit; the curtains drawn, a hushed quiet, just the two of them present. He tapped the figure on the first sheet.

"You know, of course, that the colonel has at least two and a half times as much gold as we thought he had?" The admiral nodded grimly as he spoke.

"That is indeed relevant—but it just raises more questions. How did he get that much without the FBI noticing it? And it also adds additional force to our original question. What does he want it for? Have you come up with any answers to that one yet?"

"No, sir. But I do have some leads." Troy pulled over the next sheet of paper. "Colonel McCulloch has shown some remarkable changes in his behaviour patterns during the last year. He has been buying books, going to libraries and museums, things that he never did before. I've had all of his school records checked, right back through high school in fact, while the FBI has interviewed a number of his military instructors. Under the guise of a routine security check. His new interests just don't fit his normal behaviour pattern."

"What do you mean?"

"For all of his life, as far as I could discover, McCulloch has never had any intellectual interests whatsoever. That doesn't mean that he is a stupid man. His classwork in school was good enough when he wanted it to be. But he had to study hard in order to get his grades above average. After leaving school he apparently put away all of his books and as far as I can determine appears to have never voluntarily opened one ever again. This is confirmed by men who have served with him. And he has never even been known to go to the movies. If he watches television it is only when in company with others, and usually only a ball game. He does not own a television set of his own."

"What does he do with his spare time?" the admiral asked, digging at the dottle in his pipe with a penknife. "Don't tell me he just sits and looks at the wallpaper when he goes home?"

"No, sir. He works out in the gym very often, plays squash, golf on weekends as well. Physical things. He is sociable, drinks with friends at least once a week, but always in moderation. And he dates very often. Dinner and drinks, dancing afterwards, then into the sack. He leads a busy life, keeps fit. But he doesn't *read*. That's what I find so disconcerting about his new interests. And they seem to overlap, this period of gold buying and book buying."

"Do you think that there is a connection?"

Troy pushed the papers into neat rows, silent for a moment before he answered. "On the surface I guess that I don't have any evidence at all to say that there is any connection. But I have to think of Occam's razor."

"Wasn't that something about entities not being multiplied forever?"

"Yes, sir. If there are a number of possible answers, why then it is usually best to settle for the simplest. There have been two abrupt changes in McCulloch's life, and they both began at roughly the same time. Which leads me to believe that they must be linked together by something more than coincidence. That's what I must find out next. I think the time has come for me to meet the colonel. I've done what I can from the records. Now I want to get to know him, to find out what makes him tick."

"Perhaps. Do the books he has been buying give you any leads at all?"

"None that make sense." Troy read from another sheet of paper. "Here's what was on the shelf above his desk, in the order that I found them. *The Encyclopedia of Military History, One Bridge Too Far, The Gatling Gun, Stress Analysis in Alloys, The Horse Soldiers, Gone with the Wind, Ordeal by Fire, The Ninja, The Alteration* ..."

"That's enough. I'm beginning to see what you mean. A mixture of fiction and non-fiction, varied, all jumbled together as if they were on a shelf of bargain books."

"Not completely jumbled. If there is one thread of interest that a number of them represent, why then it is military history."

"Agreed. But the colonel is a military man. That is his life and his career. We can't make too much of that. All that we really have now are clues and hints—and a quarter of a million dollars in gold. All right. I'll back your plan to get closer to McCulloch. What do you suggest?"

"You told me that he is head of security at a government lab. Does he have any Army troops under his command there? I couldn't find anything about that in the FBI report."

The admiral blew through his pipe and, satisfied with his cleaning, began to repack it with tobacco. "The FBI never went near Weeks Electronics. Not their job. But as I recall he has some armament technicians there, as well as a few specialists in electronic security. Perhaps some others. Why do you ask?"

"I would like to look at the men's records. Find some reason to run a security check on one of them."

"They're all clean or they wouldn't be there. That place is top security. They do research of some kind, death rays for all I know. Anyone stationed there would have to be as clean as a hound's tooth."

"I'm sure of that, admiral. And I don't really care what kind of research they are doing there, it's of no importance. Nor do I really want to investigate the security of the men. I just want to get close to McCulloch, to work with him, to suss him out. And there isn't a joe in the Army that you can't investigate for some reason or other. Maybe he loses a few bucks gambling, goes to a whorehouse that the mafia has a part of—or has a girlfriend who has an ex-boyfriend with a police record. I just need some kind of hook to hang a security investigation on. I can make it look real, I did work of this kind for years."

"I'll go along with that," the admiral said, pressing a button under the edge of the table. There was a knock at the door and Kelly came in. The admiral waved him over.

"Get on to the Pentagon and have them dig out copies of some enlisted personnel files. The sergeant here will tell you what we need. If they ask why we want them just say security investigation for QCIC and they won't ask twice. Sergeant Harmon, I want you to report back to me as soon as you have found what you are looking for."

It was work that Troy knew well, that he had done often enough before. In the third folder he found just what he was looking for. It was only three in the afternoon and the admiral should still be in the building. Yes, the secretary called back, in five minutes in the conference room. The admiral must have an office, Troy thought—he certainly had a secretary—but Troy had no idea where it was or why they always met in the big room. A puzzle, but not a big puzzle. He looked at his watch, then picked up the file and headed for the stairs.

"This is the one, sir," Troy said, sliding the file across the shining surface of the table. "Corporal Aurelio Mendez. Everyone calls him by his nickname, Chucho. He's a whiz kid with electronics, but very unmilitary. He comes from Baltimore and goes back there every weekend when he is off duty. Drinks and plays a lot of pool with the gang he grew up with. Nothing wrong with that—except he is one of the very few who got out of the Puerto Rican ghetto there. Which means he knows a good collection of pimps and numbers runners, petty criminals of all types."

The admiral scowled at the folder. "Do you mean that you have uncovered a real security risk? The Weeks lab has a top secret security listing."

"There is no security problem at all. An undercover agent, also Puerto Rican, spent almost a month on this clearance. His friends respect Chucho and they have learned to let him alone. He's also a very tough cookie, even though he is always on the carpet for an overweight problem. One of his drinking partners tried to rib him about' his military career. Chucho got him over the head with a billiard cue. Knocked him clean out and they had to put seven stitches in his scalp. No official report was made of the incident and the two men are still buddies. But all of his friends know that Chucho has plenty of macho and they have learned to leave him alone. But this kind of thing is more than enough grounds for me to run a clearance check on."

"Then let us arrange it. The sooner the better. The deeper we get into this problem the more questions we get—and we still don't have answers for any of them. Then there is something else that we have to consider. When you get to the laboratory you will have to associate with a full colonel. In which case you are going to have to have a little rank. We better give you a temporary promotion to lieutenant. Wait, belay that order, no one respects lieutenants, it's a lower rank than sergeant.

You'll have to be a captain. I hope you won't mind being an officer for a time?"

"No, sir. I've used a lot of different ranks in G2 work. And I'll settle for lieutenant, if it's all right. Too much power might go to my head. But I'll need a letter of authorization to get a new uniform. And the same goes for the new dog tags."

"Of course. I'll see to that right now. I'll have the entire matter arranged by late this afternoon."

At ten o'clock the following morning Troy Harmon drove the military jeep off the Beltway at Exit 42, then turned into the broad driveway that led to Weeks Electronics Laboratory Number Two.

FIVE

"Morning, lieutenant, can I be of some help to you?"

The uniformed guard was well into middle-age, pot-bellied—and unarmed. The casual visitor might therefore assume that security was lax here, that there might not even be any secrets worth protecting. However there was a second guard in the security station behind the first one, heavily armed, looking out through thick glass that was almost certainly bulletproof. The laboratory was well guarded and securely protected. Troy took out his ID and handed it over.

"I'm here to see Colonel McCulloch."

"Sure enough. Is he expecting you?" The guard passed the ID into the building behind him through a steel security slit.

"No, but I have orders to report to him."

"You've got a winner then. If I could see the orders, please."

The guard also slipped the orders through the slot then, still smiling, stepped to one side. There was a TV pickup in the guardhouse behind him that now had an unobstructed view of Troy. Not only was he on Candid Camera, but his picture was surely being recorded at the same time. All of the procedures here were first class; the security was really very tight. McCulloch was a professional. Troy knew that he was going to have to stay on his toes at all times. A phone began to ring; the outside guard turned to open a metal door in the wall behind him. He picked up the receiver, listened, then held it out to Troy.

"For you, Lieutenant Harmon."

Troy turned off the engine and climbed out of the jeep, then took the handpiece from the guard.

"Lieutenant Harmon."

"This is Colonel McCulloch, lieutenant. What's this all about?" His accent was deep South—born in Mississippi, Troy recalled.

"Security, sir."

"I know that," McCulloch's voice was very cold. *"I asked you what was the nature of this visit."*

"Security, sir. I'll give you full details when I see you."

The line went dead. Troy's expression did not change, but he smiled to himself as he hung up the phone. First point scored. The colonel was pissed off. Good. Maybe he might even lose his temper. There was the distant sound of the phone ringing inside the security booth. The guard picked it up, spoke briefly, then disconnected. He pressed a button on the phone and his amplified voice came from a speaker under the roof.

"You can go in now, Lieutenant Harmon. The guard will show you where to park." Troy did not move.

"Thank you. You have my ID and orders there."

"They'll be returned when you leave."

"Sure. Except I'm not going inside until I get them back."

The guard gave Troy a long, cold look, then passed the documents back through the security slot. Troy slipped them inside his jacket and climbed back into the jeep; the outside guard joined him. The heavy metal gate swung slowly open and they drove through.

"Just follow this road around to the right of the big building, then hang a left at the first junction," the guard said.

"I got you. Your colonel sounded peed off at me."

"No reason for you to think that," the man said placidly. "There's your turn."

"Maybe not. But he sure sounded like a hard man to get along with."

The guard gave him a quick look, then turned his eyes back on the road. "The world's a hard place, sonny, and jobs aren't that easy to get during a recession. Not when you're my age."

"I read you, pops. The colonel is really a sweety."

"You said it, I didn't," the man answered in a noncommital voice. "Pull into that slot there, number eight, and I'll take you in."

The guardhouse was clean and uncluttered and very GI. When they passed an open door the two clerks working inside did not even look up. The guard knocked at the unmarked door at the end of the corridor, then opened it.

"Thanks," Troy said, braced his shoulders and walked in. The colonel sat at his desk, writing. Troy stood at attention until he looked up, then he saluted. The return salute was slow in coming, a bare lift of the hand.

"I'll see your orders, lieutenant."

"Yes, sir."

McCulloch skimmed through the papers quickly, then threw them onto the desk. His face was expressionless but there was the cold bite of anger in his voice.

"There's nothing in here about the reason for this call, just an authorization. What do you want?"

"May I stand at ease, sir?"

"Yes. What are you here for?"

"We had a request for a security check on one of your men, a Corporal Aurelio Mendez."

"Mendez is clean. All my men are clean. Who initiated this request?"

"The Baltimore Police Department. May I sit down, colonel?"

"What the goddamned hell do you mean, lieutenant? Walking in here like this, your attitude . . ."

"Listen, colonel, I'm not in your outfit and I'm not assigned to you. I'm here to get your cooperation in this investigation, nothing else. If you don't want to give it I'll just get back to the Pentagon and tell General Brownlee what occurred. You did recognize his signature on those orders?"

Just to drive it home, Troy turned his back on the colonel and pulled the wooden chair away from the wall and sat down on it. He could see the color rise in McCulloch's face and he waited for the blast. The colonel had a very short fuse.

The explosion never came. McCulloch's clenched fists relaxed and he spun about in his chair to look out of the window. When he turned back he was in complete control again.

"All right, lieutenant, let's get on with it. What do you want to do?"

"I would like to talk to Corporal Mendez, just informally. If there is a room I can use . . ."

"No. Permission refused. If you are going to question him I must be present. I am in complete charge of security at this laboratory, and that includes the security of my own men."

"This is contrary to regulations."

"Not to *my* regulations. You will do as I have instructed or I will arrange for Mendez's transfer out of this outfit right now."

Troy shrugged. "Whatever you say, Colonel. You've got the rank. But I will have to report this infringement of my orders."

"You just do that you n . . . lieutenant, just do that."

McCulloch's temper was barely under restraint again. What was that he had almost said—then changed his mind? Before Troy could goad him even further the Colonel had seized up the phone and was punching in a number. When there was no answer he stalked out of the room without another word. Troy went and looked out of the window, not bothering to touch anything in the room. This was one place that was sure to be clean.

Almost a quarter of an hour passed before McCulloch returned. He threw open the door and stood aside in order to let a rotund corporal wearing greasy fatigues enter the room. Then he came in himself and closed the door.

"Corporal Mendez, this is Lieutenant Harmon from the Military Police. He wants to ask you some questions."

"What's up, lieutenant?" Chucho asked, chomping slowly on a wad of gum, his dark indian features smooth and unreadable.

"Sit down, Chucho . . ."

"My friends call me that. My name is Mendez, Corporal Mendez." He remained standing, staring at Troy with cold contempt.

The colonel has talked to him already, Troy thought, walking over to his own chair and sitting down again. What could he have told him? Could there be a possible connection between the two men, something that didn't relate to the security work? He could only try to find out.

"What's the problem, Chucho?" he said. "I haven't even talked to you yet and you got your back up. Is something bothering you?"

"Nothing bothering me except I don't like cops. Army kind or any kind."

"I'm sorry to hear that. Because the police are involved in this. That's the reason I'm here. It appears that there is a Baltimore Police investigation. The way I understand it there has been a report that one of your friends . . ."

"What my friends do got nothing to do with me. I don't know nothing. Look, I'm busy, if that's all you want—"

"No, corporal, that's not all that I want. This matter must involve you or I wouldn't be here, would I?" Troy was looking straight at Chucho, but had a clear view of McCulloch at the same time. The colonel was playing it cool now, his expression as impassive as Chucho's. "You have a friend—an acquaintance then if you don't like the word friend—someone that you have been seen playing pool with . . ."

"What kind of shit is this? I played pool with half the spics in Baltimore."

"Just hear me out. This matter is serious. An acquaintance of yours by the name of Paco Collado has jumped bail. When your name came up in the investigation it was bumped to my department . . ."

"Colonel, do I got to listen to this crap?" Chucho said, turning his back on Troy. "Wasn't this all settled once and for all when I first came here to clean up the bugs in the security network? Do we gotta do it all again?"

"No we don't," McCulloch said firmly. "You can get back to work, corporal." He walked over to the window and stood, looking out, until he heard the door close, then spun about to face Troy. "The corporal is right, this matter has been gone over before and is now closed. If your people feel it has to be opened again, then have him transferred. But I will not permit this interference in the operation of my unit. Is that clear, lieutenant?"

"Very clear, sir. I'll report back to the general everything that you have said."

"Do that, Lieutenant Harmon, just do that. Now get out."

Troy left. He was no wiser about the gold—but at least he had met the colonel and knew at least one thing about him. They were not destined to be bosom companions for life; he smiled at the thought as he got into the jeep and gunned it out of the lot. He had no love for the colonel, who appeared to be a thoroughgoing military son-of-a-bitch. And for some reason McCulloch had taken an instant dislike to him as well. That had been obvious from the moment he had walked into the room. Then, when he had lost his temper, the colonel had been about to say something—but had stopped himself. What had it been?

SIX

Nigger! Colonel McCulloch said as the door closed behind Lieutenant Harmon's back. He breathed the word so quietly that it could not have been heard a foot away, but there was still a terrible viciousness to its sound.

I almost called him that, he thought, almost said it out loud. But I didn't—and that's what counts. He irritated me, that's what he did, got under my skin. The bastard couldn't have bugged me more if he had been doing it on purpose . . .

He stopped, frozen at the thought, then turned to the window, watching the lieutenant emerge from the building and climb into his jeep. Was there any chance—any slight chance—that it *could* it have been done on purpose? Were they finally on to him? Twice in the last two weeks he had suspected that he was being followed, but neither time had he been able to make sure. Each

50

time that he had driven away from his normal route the car that he had spotted behind his had turned off. But that meant nothing. Two or three cars in radio contact could easily leapfrog one another and trail him without his knowledge. And his house, when was it?, four days ago, when he had had the feeling that someone had been there, that papers had been moved. No real evidence; just the sensation that things had been taken out and put back. All three of the matchsticks had been in place, in the front and back doors, and the one into the garage. Yet he had still felt that someone had been there.

Or was he getting just a little bit paranoid with the deadline so close? No, he had better be paranoid, that was the only way to stay ahead in any matter involving security. Believe that the worst was going to happen—then take every precaution to see that it didn't.

So—what if someone *had* been in his house? What if he had been followed and they now knew he had been buying gold? What would their next step be? The answer to that one was very obvious; he had been involved in this sort of operation often enough himself. The normal procedure would be to initiate an in-depth investigation of the suspect. And to have an operative meet him under some excuse or another. There was a chillness on the back of his neck at the thought; he rubbed it unconsciously. Could this jig lieutenant have been the one? Could the investigation of Chucho just have been a front for the real reason —which was getting into this office, getting to talk to him? Well why not? Maybe the black boy was smarter than he had looked.

But it doesn't matter, he said to himself, it

doesn't matter at all. He was just going to have to forget that it had ever happened. Even if his suspicions were true there was nothing at all he could do about it. He had to act normal, he must follow routine. There were only a few days to go now. He must not do a thing to draw any further attention to himself. He had to make a positive effort not to vary his lifestyle in any way. It was almost time and he was not going to let any hitches occur at this late date. If all that they had were suspicions, why fine, let them have them. As long as they could be kept at bay until it was too late for them to do a thing.

McCulloch turned sharply away from the window and sat down at his desk. He had a dinner date this evening and he was going to keep it, whether he felt like it or not. But he was going to make one improvement; he smiled at the thought while he dialed the number.

"Marianne, is that you? Right, Wes here. All set for dinner this evening? How's the appetite? It is? Best news ever. Listen, instead of knockwurst at the Old Europe one more time, what do you say to a decent steak at The Jockey Club? You say yes? I thought you would. And I liked that squeak of joy. Of course it's expensive—but have I ever denied you a thing? I'll call now for reservations. Seven on the dot. If I don't call you back it's all set. See you there. In the bar."

He made the reservations, then spent the rest of the afternoon doing mind-numbing paperwork, keeping doggedly at it until exactly six o'clock. Discipline, that's what made all of the difference. Plus the fact that staying at work filled his mind and prevented him from worrying.

As he went through the offices checking that the

lights were all turned off, he saw that most of the staff had gone home. One of the typewriters had been left uncovered, and he called out to the girls who were just going out the door.

"Whose machine is this?"

The three of them turned around, looking at him silently, until Daisy finally spoke up.

"That's mine, that one there."

That moronic little bitch. "Haven't I spoken to you before about leaving the machines uncovered at night?"

"Yeah. So I forgot."

"Did you? In that case there will be five dollars docked from your next pay envelope for causing excessive wear and tear on government property, by permitting it to be exposed to overnight dust. Do you think that will help you remember?"

"You can't do that!" she squealed.

"I've just done it."

That might make some impression on her dim little brain. She would complain to the union about it, but that wouldn't be his problem. He watched them leave, then turned off the lights and locked up. He hummed to himself as he drove back to the District.

He was just sipping on a second drink when Marianne came in. He signalled to the bartender.

"Another one of these for the lady."

"Bombay martini on the rocks with a twist. On the way, sir."

Marianne swept up, smiling, wearing something long and silky, cut fascinatingly low in the front. She put her cheek against his, she knew how he hated the taste and feel of lipstick, then made a kissing sound in the air.

"You look a million in that dress," he said.

"Something new?"

"No. But this is my super-special, only once-a-year dress. Your call really knocked me over. The Jockey Club, wow! I checked out early and went home to change. A special occasion, special dress." They clinked glasses and she took a deep swig from hers and laughed. "Honestly, Wes, I don't think I'll ever figure you out."

"Then don't try."

"We go out, have fun, no complaints. But then all of a sudden out of left field you come up with *this*." She waved her hand in a circle. "And this must be the most expensive place in town."

"One of them. Don't worry. It goes on the credit card." He burst out laughing at that, for no reason that she could tell, but she smiled and laughed along with him. This was going to be an evening to remember.

It was, in every way. When she couldn't make up her mind between the steak and the lobster he ordered her a surf-and-turf, then a bottle of French champagne which, as he explained, was the only wine that could possibly go with both dishes. She had a quick look at the price of the wine and couldn't believe it. Maybe she had been wrong about Wes, that he really did like her more than just as a fun date. Stranger things had happened in Washington before. When the crepes suzette were served she was so full that she could only peck at hers, but watching them being made was exciting, with all the brandy burning and everything.

"Happy?" he asked as he lit one of the black cheroots he had been smoking of late. She laughed and reached out and squeezed his hand.

"That's too tiny a word for it. I don't think I ever

enjoyed a meal more. Not since I've been in Washington."

"Didn't you eat this well back in St. Louis?"

"Are you kidding? In St. Louis if it's not a steak as big as a manhole cover, why then it's not a meal. I was almost a vegetarian by the time I got here six months ago. No, honestly, this has just been too much."

"Good. You deserve it. What about dancing afterwards, work off some of the calories?"

"What about working them off at your place instead?"

She held his hand even harder when she said this, then slowly licked her full red lips with the tip of her tongue. He responded to the excitement of the invitation. She was a sensual woman and there was an open promise in her words that he knew she would fulfill.

"Wicked girl," he said and she smiled in return and nodded enthusiastically. "But have an armagnac first while I finish my cigar. Anticipation is many times the better part of pleasure."

She leaned her head against his shoulder when they drove away. He found some light music on the radio and she sang along with it. At his place he drove into the garage as they always did. He turned off the burglar alarm and unlocked the house door before he came around and opened the car door for her. She never noticed the sideways glance he gave to see if the matchstick was still in place.

"Drink?"

"Yes, please. Some more of that heavenly cognac, whatever you called it."

"Armagnac. Which is brandy from Armagnac, just as cognac is brandy from Cognac. Only this is better."

"I never argue with the experts."

Marianne knew that she was a little bit tipsy—and she liked it that way. It made it easier to keep the mood going. Which mood was really an incredibly wonderful one. How long had she known Wes? Almost four months now. An occasional date, dinner, theatre sometimes, dancing, then to his place and to bed. Not that she really minded this very much. Except that she always had the feeling that this was all part of the package deal. No sex, no date. He had never said this in so many words, or even hinted at it. It was just a feeling that she had. A feeling she might have been very wrong about. Oh, how she hoped so.

And it was good tonight, better than ever. So natural and wonderful. They were on the couch and he had said something funny and she had laughed, then he had kissed her. And it was different, like the first time. Then, when he had let his hand slide gently onto her breasts she had actually gasped with pleasure. Even more so when he had cupped them to his mouth, his lips on her nipples.

It had happened then, on the couch, her clothes crumpled in all directions, like it was the first time happening all over again. Only later did he carry her, her warm naked body held close to his, up to the bedroom. Again, and still again. Sensations possessed her that she had never experienced before.

Then she screamed, he had hurt her, bit into her flesh, but he kissed and hushed her and she soon forgot it. He was just strong, too strong, but it was really all right.

For the first time ever she had actually dozed off after their passionate lovemaking. Everything was so different. She blinked her eyes awake as she felt him get out of bed and go into the bathroom. Marianne heard the sound of the shower running, like it always did after they had been in bed, but this time it lulled her to sleep again. She awoke suddenly with the bedside light in her eyes. He was standing over her, wearing his robe now, his hair still wet from the shower.

"More armagnac?"

"God, no. I have the strong feeling that it would simply destroy me."

"Whatever you say. Gin and tonic like always?"

She nodded, watching him leave, her thoughts, emotions, wheeling around and around. The little routines were still the same. The shower to wash away the lovemaking, the drink, then the drive home. But tonight had been so different. She reached down for the robe he always left on the foot of the bed, but it wasn't there.

Had he forgotten—or were things really going to be different? She refused to let herself hope. It was the old joke, all the single girls streaming into Washington from all over the country. Work in the office, meet the boss, get acquainted with a handsome officer, romance, marriage, then back to Peoria or Macon—or even St. Louis!—the envy of every girl who had stayed at home. But a joke, a dream that rarely worked out that way. Yet she still hummed as she kicked back the covers and went to the closet. You never knew, you just never knew. The air was cool; she liked the long wooly bathrobe of his that went right down to the ground. She pulled at it and it fell from the hanger and slipped to the floor. When she bent to pick it up she saw that it had fallen over a pair of saddlebags, the kind motorcyclists used. One of the bags was open and some papers were sticking out, blue-prints, the identification clear on the corner.

She straightened and put the robe on and was back in bed when he returned to the room.

"Thanks," she said when he handed over her drink. "Yum, good."

He put his glass down on the bedside table and went to turn off the bathroom light. "Those bags in the closet," she said. "I didn't know you were riding a motorcycle now."

His back was turned to her so she could not see his sudden hesitation, the quick widening, then the narrowing of his eyes. He threw the switch and turned back to face her.

"What about the bags?" he asked, working very hard to keep the cold anger from his voice.

SEVEN

"Nothing," Marianne said, squinting down into her drink as she tried to squeeze some more juice out of the wedge of lime with her swizzle stick, not seeing the sudden fierce intensity of his gaze. "Only there are some Department of Defense blueprints hanging out of the bags, weapons, marked classified. I didn't know that you took your work home with you."

"I told you I was in security. We never sleep."

"I can believe that. I know what you do in bed!"

She laughed at her own boldness and he smiled, walked over and bent and kissed her. The bags, the blueprints, were forgotten on the instant.

"Finish up that drink," he told her. "It's time you were getting home. Or you'll be sleep-walking at work tomorrow."

"Mmm, you're right. But don't call the cab until I get dressed."

"I don't know about the cab. Too many muggers and rapists around these days. I'm beginning to feel that even the cabs aren't safe anymore. I'll take you home. See you safely to your door."

He was turning away as he spoke and he never saw the sudden light of hope in her face. She gulped the drink, then ran downstairs to get her clothes. This was the first time he had even suggested taking her home! It had always been a cab, every other time. Control yourself girl! Nothing had been said so far, just hints. But what hints! She sang sweetly as she dressed.

Washington retires early and they made good time driving in from Alexandria, across the Potomac and right by the White House. It was lovely and sparkling in the searchlights. A perfect end to a perfect evening, Marianne thought. This city really could be beautiful. There was no traffic at all on Connecticut Avenue and her apartment was just ahead.

"Going to ask me up for a cup of coffee?" he said as they passed the Zoo.

"I'd love to Wes, but one look at you and afterwards the night doorman opens his big mouth, the word gets around and life would be unbearable with the bluerinse set who fill the building."

"What about the back way, through the parking lot?"

"Of course! I forgot about it, never use it at all."

The apartment house had been built into the side of a hill, which meant that when they entered at ground level by the lower lot entrance they were in the lowest part of the building, the subbasement. The little lobby was quiet and the elevator was empty. So was the hall on the twelfth floor. "You've got enough keys there," he said as she inserted the third one that opened the Fox lock.

"The insurance company made us put them in. There used to be a burglary a week in this building. We even had a mugging on the third floor—someone got in through the basement. That's why the double lock on the outside door that we came in through. Washington really is something."

"And getting worse."

"You can say that again."

The bar of the Fox lock rasped up in its street eyelet when she pushed the heavy door open.

"Get comfy," Marianne said. "While I put the water on. Instant okay?"

"Sure," Wes called after her as she went into the tiny kitchenette. "Won't we wake up your roommate?"

"Tricia? No way. Her door's open which means she's not home yet. She's got a real heavy thing going with her boyfriend. She never gets back until after one at night when he's in town. After that she sleepwalks in the morning. She's going to get fired if she keeps it up."

"Only twelve-thirty now. We have time to enjoy the coffee."

He walked around the living room as he talked, looking at the furnishings. He stopped in front of the fireplace.

"Does this thing work?"

"What?" She leaned out of the kitchen, looked, then laughed. The kettle hissed as it boiled over and she turned back. "Ornamental. I wish that it did work, like the one we have at home. I love an open fire. And it helps during the energy crisis. But not on the twelfth floor. Sugar?"

"Just one. And cream, not milk, if you have it."

He bent over and looked at the andirons; decorative imitations for a fake fireplace. Stamped brass that had never been used. But the poker had a solid steel shank. He picked it up and weighed it in his hand. Heavy.

"Here's your coffee," Marianne said, coming into the room. "If you're going to stir the phony fire with that thing you'll break all the little light bulbs and stuff."

"Yes, I would, wouldn't I," he said, turning to face her, the poker still in his hand. "Where's your coffee?"

"In the kitchen. Too hot yet . . . Wes, what are you doing?"

Her eyes and her mouth opened wide, but she never uttered a sound as the steel bar of the poker caught her across the throat. Crushing her larynx. She dropped heavily, like a bag of sand, the coffee cup falling from her hand. The blow was a destructive one and the chances were that she was dead before she hit the carpet. But he did not believe in taking chances. He struck again and again at the top of her skull until he was absolutely sure.

Wes was not surprised to find himself breathing heavily when he was done. Killing like this was not quite the same as firing an M-16 at a gook. This was more personal. But just as important. He stood there for a long minute, until the rapid beating of his heart had slowed down, forcing himself to remember what he had touched in the room. Nothing, yes, he was sure of that. Other than the poker. He took out his handkerchief and wiped the poker carefully, as far down as the mess of blood, hair and bits of scalp. He dropped it onto her body.

Then he took the thin leather gloves out of his

pocket and put them on. It was just twenty to one. Unbelievably, only a few minutes had passed. Seemed like an hour. He went to examine the windows, carefully, one by one.

The curtains were all closed and he was careful to open them just a slit when he looked through. He found the fire-escape outside the bathroom window.

"Just perfect, Wes," he said to himself, then turned off the bathroom lights. The window was over the bathtub so he put the bathmat inside the tub before he stepped into it. Be careful, think of everything. No fingerprints or footprints that might identify him. This was going to be a burglary by person or persons unknown.

But the window had not been opened for years and it refused to budge even a fraction of an inch after he had unlocked it. He hammered at it with the heel of his hand until, finally, it squeaked upwards. It stuck again, only half open, but that was good enough. A slim burglar should be able to wriggle through an opening that size. He groped for the towels in the darkness and found the largest one. It was big enough to drape down over the inside of the window, with still enough left to bunch up over his fist when he poked his arm outside. The glass broke with the first hard punch, a few shards tinkling down into the tub, a sound that had to be too small to be heard by anyone outside the room. He stepped carefully back out of the tub, kicking the bathmat to one side, before he lowered the towel and shook its load of broken glass into the bottom of the tub.

It was all very logical; he put the mat back on the floor and dropped the bath towel into the tub. An intruder had broken the window and climbed through. The towel was there in the tub, sloppy girls, that would explain the shards of glass in it. Now he was in the apartment. What would the intruder do next?

He would go into the living room. Search for valuables. Very quietly because the walls were like paper in some of these buildings. Ease the drawers from the desk, dump them silently onto the rug. Then the books. He stepped over the corpse, scarcely noticing it, as he systematically destroyed the apartment. There was some jewelry in a dresser drawer, not worth a lot, and he stuffed it into his jacket pocket. Burglars need money. In the drawer, further back behind the jewel box, he found her diary.

It was fun to read. But how could anyone write such stupid stuff? This guy and this girl and I saw someone else and I got a permanent today. He flipped quickly through the pages until he noticed his name. He scowled as he read her secret thoughts. She had her goddamned nerve. Pennypinching, him! She had really got what she deserved. He slipped the thin book into his pocket. Her purse was on the bed; he stripped the money from it then threw it onto the kitchen floor. It was only then that he noticed the cup of coffee cooling on the counter.

Christ, he was being stupid! She was out there in the other room, lying on top of one cup. So why coffee for two? Had she been getting chummy with the burglar or something? The police would not ignore a clue like this. He cursed himself for forgetting such an obvious thing as he carefully poured the coffee down the drain, then rinsed out the cup, saucer and spoon, drying them and putting them away.

It was almost one before he was finished. It took an effort, but he forced himself to ignore the time. She had said Tricia would not be back until one at the earliest. He had to be thorough, had to check carefully, then check everything again. He went through the apartment slowly, room by room, until he was absolutely sure that there were no clues present to mark his presence. This had been a simple break-in, a robbery, then murder on the spur of the moment when the girl suddenly appeared. With no evidence to the contrary. It was perfect.

The fuse box was in the kitchen, behind the door. He twisted the main fuse until all of the lights went out. The apartment was pitch black and he had to use his lighter to find his way back to the living room. He pulled the armchair over, out of line of sight of the door, then sat down in it in the darkness to wait.

Time stretched out, slower and slower, as he thought of all the things that might still go wrong. Normally he was not a man with much imagination, but now he began to shift and turn in the chair. Was there a chance that someone might have seen his car in the lot downstairs, and noticed that it didn't belong there? They could have written down the number—or even worse—called the police. Or Tricia might not come home, maybe she was going to shack up for the night with her boyfriend. He could still be there at dawn. Or . . .

The key turned in the lock.

On the instant he was up, careful, no rush, walking quietly to stand against the wall. Three keys, plenty of time. Two. Then the scratch of the bar, three. Light streamed in from the hall and he had a quick glimpse of her silhouette as she stepped through.

"Marianne," she whispered. "Are you home honey? Asleep?"

A New York accent. Another Yankee bitch.

She closed the door and groped her way down the wall in the darkness for the light switch. She clicked it back and forth.

"Shit. Burned out," she muttered. He slid along the wall towards the sound.

He had been in the darkness longer; his eyes were more adjusted to it. He could see her outlined against the streetlight that filtered through the drapes. He reached out for her.

She had time for only a single, choked-off gasp before his fingers locked tight. After that she had no chance. She was young and strong, but not strong enough. He had come up behind her so that there was no possibility that she might scratch or kick him. He pulled her body close to his and bent backwards, lifting her free of the floor.

She writhed and kicked, slower and slower. His arms were tired but he still held her, his fingers dug deep into her flesh long after he was sure that she was dead. But he did not take chances, he never took chances. Even when he released her neck he still made sure. Grabbing her full breasts and squeezing as hard as he could with both hands. Not a sound out of her. Just perfect, that's what it was, just perfect.

The phone began to ring as she slipped heavily to the floor.

What was it? Who could it be at this time of night? Could it be a neighbor who had heard something? No, impossible; he had been careful, quiet.

Wes stood in the darkness, paralyzed with indecision. He couldn't answer it—but he didn't dare open the hall door while it was still ringing. It was too loud. Should he take it off the hook? No . . .

It stopped ringing and he let his breath out in a rush. Time to get out of here. He felt his way to the door and stepped on something that crunched underfoot. What was it? It hadn't been there before. He kicked it ahead and opened the hall door a crack and peered through. The hall outside was empty. He opened the door a bit wider and looked down.

It was a woman's purse that he had stepped on; he smiled into the darkness. All contributions to the cause were gratefully accepted. He fumbled her wallet out, fingers clumsy in the gloves, and extracted the bills. Her lipstick fell onto the floor and rolled close to the full-length mirror by the entrance.

It gave him a very good idea. A little more distraction for the police. With the hall door open a crack there was just enough light for him to see what he was doing. Printing on the mirror with the lipstick, great sprawling illiterate letters. A work of art. He threw the lipstick aside and let in a bit more light to admire it.

OAFFEY PIGS DIE

That would put them off the scent all right! Now —it was time to go.

At one-thirty of a weekday morning, in a DC apartment house, there is very little stirring. The indicators on both elevators were unmoving; one of them still standing at this floor. He went right by them to the emergency stairs. No chances, take no chances. He walked all the way down, as quietly as he could, to the sub-basement. He pushed the door open slowly but the hall here was also empty. The lights were dim in the tiny lobby by the rear entrance; the lot outside was empty and dark. A fine rain was beginning to fall. Wes let himself out and, head tucked down, hurried to his car. The engine caught on the first turn; he used only his parking lights as he drove out of the lot. Then he turned on his low beams—and just caught the green as he turned onto Connecticut. Not a pedestrian or another car in sight.

He had driven two blocks before he remembered that he hadn't gone back into the kitchen to screw the fuse in; a sudden fear dragged at him. It was too late, impossible, to go back. What would the police make of it? He had no idea—but at least it didn't link with him in any way. It would be all right. He laughed, shakily, as the fear ebbed slowly away.

Rock Creek Park was deserted as he drove through it, then back along the Potomac. No one was in sight when he stopped and threw the jewelry into the river. He was afraid the diary might float, so he tore it up and poked the bits down into a rubbish basket among the newspapers and sandwich wrappers.

The drive home was uneventful and he was whistling happily between his teeth as he drove into the garage.

EIGHT

Troy Harmon had filed his final report, yet he still wondered if he would ever hear about Colonel Wesley McCulloch again. He had added, at the end of the report, the request that he be notified if there were any further developments in the case. There had to be a reason for the purchase of all that gold and he dearly wanted to know what it was.

But as far as he had been able to determine there was no case at all. Yes, the colonel had been buying a lot of gold. But no, there was no reason why he shouldn't. Since the law had been changed gold was freely available; it was not necessary to produce identification to buy it, nor were records necessarily kept. Nothing that McCulloch had done was illegal. Just very interesting. He had purchased gold with all the money that he possessed—then stowed the gold away in his safe. He

had used his savings, sold his new car and bought
an old one, got a second mortgage on his house.
And had bought gold and still more gold with it all.
What he had done might be considered eccentric—
but it still wasn't against the law. Troy had reported this in great detail, made a copy of the
report for his own files, and delivered it to Admiral Colonne's secretary. Sorry, the admiral
would be out of town for two days, but he will contact you upon return. Fine. Troy could use two
days off as well. An old friend was getting married
in New York. He had already made his excuses—
but it still wasn't too late to phone and say that he
was coming. It was Friday afternoon and no one in
Washington would miss him if he slipped away
early.

It had been a good weekend. First there had
been the bachelor dinner, an excuse for a lot of
drink, with a bunch of the guys from Jamaica
High School he hadn't heard about or thought
about in years. More of them had stayed in the old
neighborhood than he had realized. He was the
one who had moved on, had gotten out of touch.
Going away first to college, upstate in Ithaca, then
right into the Army; too much time had gone by.
He had always meant to come back for a visit, but
had never quite got around to it. He had no family
left in Jamaica; his few remaining relatives were
in Detroit. Dad had died while he was in Nam,
cancer, and his mother had followed him just a
few months later. Out of loneliness people said. It
could be true. She had been that kind of woman.
But that was all in the past. Getting back here had
turned out to be a lot of fun despite these
memories. But he had been too tired, had drunk
too much, to even consider returning to Washing-

ton on Sunday.

The first shuttle flight out of LaGuardia on a damp, chill Monday morning is a special kind of hell. Particularly with a hangover. Packed behind the chromium rails waiting for the flight to be called, cardboardy Eastern Airlines coffee spilling out of the container, poked in the eye by the New York Times, then jammed into the tiny shuttle seats. Wonderful, only twelve planes ahead of them waiting for takeoff. Longer on the ground than in the air. We're glad you chose to fly Eastern today, the outside temperature is . . .

The coffee from the QCIC machine was a lot better; Troy sipped it from a crockery mug in order to get the cardboard taste out of his mouth. There was a single item in his In tray. A phone call, please return urgent. From a lieutenant with a telephone number he didn't recognize. But there were a lot of lieutenants in the Army.

Except this wasn't the Army. This was a lieutenant in the District police.

"I'm returning your call Lieutenant . . . Anderson. This is Lieutenant Harmon."

"Yes, lieutenant. I wonder if you could get down here to talk to me. I'll give you the address . . ."

"Can you tell me what this is about?"

"Only that this is a homicide investigation and we think you might be able to help us. Can you come here this morning?"

"On my way now."

A murder of some kind? What could it have to do with him? But at least it would be a change from working on the case of the surly, gold-hoarding colonel. He had the receptionist phone for a cab. A thin pounding behind his eyeballs had reminded him that the weekend was still more than a distant memory. He had no real desire to walk around the city in the cold drizzle.

The police station was modern and clean and nothing at all like the rundown wooden dumps that you saw in the television serials. Lieutenant Anderson was no TV hero either. He was scrawny and well past fifty, his short-cropped gray hair and granny glasses making him look more like a school teacher than a cop. He was also very, very black.

"Sit down, lieutenant," Anderson said in a soft Virginia accent. "I'm getting some coffee—want some?"

"Yes, please."

"Sorry to drag you out like this, but we are having trouble running down a lead on a double homicide. Now I've come to believe that maybe you could assist us. All at once it appears that the military are in the picture."

"Glad to help. It has been a rotten Monday morning so far. If I can do anything constructive ..."

"Good." Anderson pulled over a thick file and opened it. "At first it looked like we had an ordinary break and entry, with homicide as a fringe benefit. The incident occurred in an apartment out on Connecticut past the park. Fire escape window kicked in—there's a big Fox lock on the front door but no bars on this window—they never learn. Place torn apart, valuables missing, girl name of Marianne Sobell beat to death with a steel poker on the livingroom floor. Looks like she surprised the party or parties unknown and got wasted for her interest. Had a roommate, one Tricia Broderick, who apparently walked in on all this fun and got choked for her troubles. This is the kind of thing we get too often, a couple every day."

"I don't see how this has anything to do with the military. Either girl work for the Army?"

"Nope. Just wait a minute, then I'll tell you about the Army connection. First off, a couple of things interested us, like why was the electricity turned off at the fuse box? It didn't fit the MO. Then it appears that the killer, or killers, went out through the front door, since it was slammed shut and the safety locks weren't locked. But the thing that we found most interesting was this." He took a photographic print out of the file. "We found this written on a mirror by the door."

Troy took the photograph and his eyes narrowed. OAFFEY PIGS DIE. He threw it back.

"So what. So a black did it. Some militant with his head screwed on wrong. Who doesn't even know how to spell 'ofey'. Probably doesn't even know that it is pig-latin for 'foe.' Is that special? You're a little dark for a kluxer, aren't you . . ."

"Peace, brother," Lieutenant Anderson said. "I got this assignment by routine of rota and I didn't know what you looked like until you came through that door. I'm not trying to make a racial case out of this. But someone else is. Let me show you what smells bad about this, what really stinks. Here's a photograph of the first murdered girl, Marianne."

It was bad, but he had seen a lot worse. Of course in Nam they weren't good looking girls like this. But death was death. There was too damn much of it. "And this is the other girl, Tricia." Troy took the photograph and looked at it—and froze. His eyes rose slowly to meet Anderson's.

"Goddamned son-of-a-bitch," he breathed. Anderson nodded agreement.

Tricia Broderick was a black girl. She was—or had been—a dark skinned, black haired beauty. Still lovely in death.

"It has to be a cover-up of some kind," Troy said. "This is no ordinary break-in."

"My thoughts exactly. Deliberate murder made to look like homicide during a burglary. Some gray-skinned bastard trying to disguise it as a race killing to get the pressure off him. I don't know what the killer had in mind, but I did know that I wasn't going to put this case on the spike and have it forgotten. That's when I started to dig deeper into it myself. I investigated both girls and found Tricia's boyfriend first. He drives big cross-country rigs. He's just back from a run and he and the girl had a date that night. They were going to be married next month. He's really broken up. And he's not a suspect since he was at the garage at the time of the killings. He sent Tricia home from his parents' house in a cab. His garage is just two blocks away so he walked. He called her from there, always does, to see if she got home alright. No answer. He's on a tight schedule. He took out his rig, but was worried. Called again an hour later from an all-night eatery out on Interstate 95. Still no answer, so he telephoned the police. Which is how we got onto the case so fast."

"How fast is fast?" Troy asked, staring grimly at the photographs. Anderson sighed.

"Never fast enough. I've reached a dead-end with Tricia, but we found a possible lead with the other girl, Marianne. In her typing pool. She has no real friends, but there are a couple of girls there that she talks to during coffee breaks. It appears that she has had a new but steady boy friend for the last few months, an Army officer . . ."

"The military connection?"

"Right. And it gets better. We wanted to talk to him, so we could trace her movements early that night. But she never mentioned his name or his rank, nothing at work. But the day of the killing she left early because, as she told the other girls, this was going to be a *big* date. At The Jockey Club where she had never been before. She said that she had to be there by seven. So we checked. There was only one officer who had reserved a table for two at that time, a man name of Colonel McCulloch."

Troy's hands slammed down on the desk as he half rose to his feet. "Colonel McCulloch? Do you mean Colonel Wesley McCulloch?"

"The same one. Now you know why you are here. We of course wanted to interview the colonel —but for some reason he couldn't be found. Not at home or at work. He's gone. As you can imagine our investigation lit some fires. The FBI was on to us ten minutes after we called him at the lab where he is stationed. After we told them what was happening they told us to contact you. They didn't say why, just that you were the man we should talk to. Can you tell me why?"

"I don't know if I am permitted to. Let me make a call first."

Anderson pushed over the phone and busied himself with his paperwork while Troy called Admiral Colonne and described this latest development. Then listened to his orders. He replaced the receiver and Lieutenant Anderson looked up from the papers he was working on, raising a quizzical eyebrow. Troy counted off the items on his fingers.

"One. The colonel is involved in high security work. So if I don't give you some of the details please don't ask what they are. Two—I am permitted to tell you everything that the FBI knows about the colonel, which frankly is just about all that I know. If you can whistle up a car, just like they do on TV, I'll tell you about it on the way to McCulloch's house."

"On the way. But we don't have any TV chauffeurs here. Just a five year old Ford that needs a ring job. And I drive it myself. Let's go."

At least the Ford had a siren and some flashing lights which got them through the traffic to Alexandria. The messenger from QCIC was waiting in front of the house; on his motorcycle he had managed to reach there ahead of them. He handed Troy the envelope, then roared away. Troy tore it open and took out the ring of keys.

"Is this legal?" he asked as he unlocked the front door of McCulloch's house.

"This is a murder investigation. I'd have the thing broken down if you weren't here. Just unlock it and step aside." Anderson opened his jacket and drew his police .38. Troy smiled at the middle-aged policeman.

"I think that after Nam I've been through more doors than you have, lieutenant. So just stay close behind me and keep that thing ready."

They went in fast, though it turned out to be an unnecessary precaution. The house was empty. Nothing appeared to have changed since Troy had been there on his first illicit visit. In the bedroom he kicked the rug aside, opened the panel and pointed to the safe concealed beneath it.

"What if I opened that? Does a murder investigation cover this thing as well?"

Anderson shrugged. "Depends on what we find. I imagine you can close it just as easily as you can

open it. You saw the photographs. I saw the girls.
So crack the damned thing and we'll worry about
legality later."

Troy still had the little printed slip in his wallet
that the locksmith had given him. He bent and
spun the knob in slow, careful sequence. At the
last number the door pressed up against his hand
in eager welcome. He opened it wide.

The safe was empty. The gold was gone.

No, not completely empty. There was a folded
piece of paper in the bottom. They bent together to
look in at it.

"Got your name on it," Anderson said.

"Do I get to read it?"

"Why not? Too small for a boobytrap. Just hold
it by the edge when you take it out. Push it open
with a pen. There could be some fingerprints."

Troy caught it between his fingernails and drew
it carefully out, then laid the folded slip on the
dresser. Anderson held it secure with the end of
his own pen while Troy poked it open.

The lettering inside was bold and clear, printed
with a large, red felt-tip pen.

Keep looking for me jig.
But you're not going to
find me!

NINE

"Are you the jig that he's talking about?" Lieutenant Anderson asked.

Troy nodded slowly, his face locked in an expression of cold anger. "I'm the one, all right. He got his back up the one and only time that we ever met. Angry when he first talked to me and got angrier all the time."

"He's got kind of a dirty mouth for an Army officer. Thought you had an integrated Army?"

"It was, last time I looked. Doesn't mean there aren't any rotten apples in it. Do you think this particular rotten apple is the kind who is so stupid that he can't even spell something simple like *ofey*?"

Anderson nodded. "There's something very wrong going on here. I'm certain of that. Legal or not, buying all that gold must have had some importance, or you and the FBI wouldn't have been looking into it. Let's do some guessing using the facts that we know so far. Marianne had this heavy date with McCulloch on Friday night. They had steaks, lobster, champagne—the works, and the evening was heavenly. Particularly back in his house where they mutually enjoyed some passionate sex. But she found out something, I don't know what—but something she shouldn't have known. So instead of sending her back in a cab the kind colonel drives her home, takes her up to her apartment. And kills her. Fakes it to look like a burglary. Then turns off the lights and waits in the dark to kill her roommate—who might be able to identify him as Marianne's date of the evening. It hangs together, doesn't it? In a particularly nasty way."

"How much of that is guesswork and how much do you really know?"

"I'm only guessing that she found out something here in this house—and I'm also guessing what happened back at the apartment. Everything else is fact, facts that fit together like pieces of a jigsaw puzzle. We know they went out to dinner together that evening. Coroner believes that she was not raped, but she did have intercourse. She's on the pill, traces of it were found in her blood. Semen in her vagina, recent bruises on her shoulders and breasts. Doorman states that she has been coming home from late dates in a cab the last few months. He didn't let her in that night. But every tenant in the building has a key to a rear entrance to the parking lot."

Troy read the note again, then turned away in disgust. "It's not pleasant to think about," he said. "But it does make some kind of perverted sense. If his disappearance has something to do with the gold—and it was planned well ahead—he might very well eliminate anyone who found out about it, who might interfere. He was in the Green Berets. He knows something about killing people. But just where does that leave us now?"

"It leaves me out of it," Anderson said, folding the note with his pen and pushing it into an envelope. "As far as my department is concerned this particular lead stops right here. We'll check this note out, dust the house as well, put an APB out for the colonel, do all the routine things. But I have a strong hunch that we've reached the end of our resources. Of course we'll investigate the case further, follow up any other leads, and I'll keep you informed of any developments. But it looks to me like my little case of murder is small potatoes next to your case of national security. You did tell me that McCulloch was involved with classified work?"

"He was. And his disappearing like this is really bad news. I have a feeling that a big flap is coming down. If there is anything I can tell you later, you know that I will."

"You bet. I won't call you, you'll call me."

"Sorry. But there's nothing else I can tell you."

"Don't worry, son. I've worked in the District all my life. When government steps in we step out."

"Thanks. Can I have that note?"

"We'll hold the original. Send you a photo this afternoon. Will that do you?"

"Great. Can you give me a lift on your way back?"

"Door to door."

The fine mist that had been falling all day had changed to a steady, hammering rain that reflected Troy's dark mood. He rode in silence, his thoughts turned inward, seeing again the murdered women, the empty safe, the derisory note aimed directly at him, and the even more empty house with McCulloch gone from it. He did not know how or why, but he felt just as the policeman did, that all of these inexplicable acts were somehow tied together. He intended to do everything he could to find out just how.

As soon as he came through the door of the house on Massachusetts Avenue the receptionist waved him over.

"Orders from the admiral. Wants you in his office soonest. Third floor, little green door at the end of the hall."

"Not the conference room this time?"

"Feel honored, you're among the chosen few. Just leave your raincoat here and run. I'll let him know that you are on the way."

The door was half-open when he came to it. He hesitated but the admiral's voice sounded from inside.

"Push in, Troy. And close it behind you."

Troy had not known what to expect—but certainly not this. There was none of the usual senior-executive furniture here, or even bridge-of-battleship navy. The room was windowless and bare, except for the gray metal cabinets that covered one wall. The admiral sat with his back to the other wall, facing a computer terminal. The only other object in the room was the high speed printer against the third wall. There was a telephone next to the terminal—and nothing else, not even another chair.

"This is where the work really gets done," the admiral said. "Everything I need to know comes in either through the terminal or the phone—and goes out the same way. I don't believe in paper anymore. We live in an age of high-speed electronics. Now tell me all you know about this disastrous affair with Colonel McCulloch."

There was no place to sit—other than on the floor—so Troy stood at ease, hands clasped behind his back, as he carefully outlined the facts and the conclusions that he and Anderson had reached. The admiral looked at the screen instead of at him as he talked, occasionally typing in a few words as though updating a file. He looked up, only once, when the empty safe and the note were mentioned.

"Do you remember what the note said?"

"It's a little hard to forget, admiral. It read— keep looking for me, jig, but you're not going to find me."

"Interesting. He must have realized that your visit to his office was really to investigate him— not the Army corporal. Which means he was either aware of the FBI surveillance, or was expecting it. If he did kill the two women it could indicate that he might have been on a fixed schedule of some kind and did not want it upset. If all of these suppositions are true, he was apparently only trying to buy enough time to bring these arrangements to some conclusion. His plans had obviously been made for some time, for him to get out, go somewhere with the gold and leave his life, his career behind him. It must have been something damn important. Do you have any idea what it could be?"

"No, sir. But I do have some suggestions for immediate action. I feel that it is imperative that a description of McCulloch be sent at once to all airports, border points, customs stations, any place where he might attempt to leave the country. I am certain that there are grounds for asking that he be detained."

"Damn right there are. How about desertion for openers? The last I heard that was a shooting offense."

The admiral was typing furiously at the terminal as he talked. He read the quick response, then typed in another command and leaned back. The high speed printer rattled into action and spewed out a yard of paper.

"Acknowledgement from the FBI with details of the action taken. Bless the computer networks. We'll have the country sewn up tight inside of three minutes."

"Do you think that it will do any good?"

"No. Wherever he was going, you can be sure that he is already there—or well on his way. But there is nothing wrong with the late slamming of barn doors. What is your next course of action?"

"I did some hard thinking about that on the way over here. But I would like to know first if I am still in charge of the operation?"

"Until you are told differently."

"All right. Then I'll want to spend some government money. I need help from the FBI here, the CIA overseas. I want every detail on every bit of McCulloch's life that they can turn up. I want to find out who his friends are—and when they are contacted I want them questioned so we can also find out who his enemies are as well. I want to know all of his contacts, the name of every one of his girl friends, anything and everything about the man. It will be a mass of garbage that will have to be sifted through very slowly. But somewhere in there will be an answer to all our questions about the colonel and his gold."

The admiral nodded. "A sound beginning. I'll see to it. Meanwhile, what are you yourself going to do?"

"I want to go to the colonel's place of employment and talk to everyone there who knew him. This might uncover a lead. Some of them may be involved with this. I know already that he told Corporal Mendez, the one I was supposed to be investigating, something about me that rubbed Mendez the wrong way. I want to find out what that was. I'll also have to have complete access to the Weeks Electronic Laboratory, and be able to talk to anyone there as well. Do you know what kind of research they are doing there?"

"No. Top secret high technology work, that's all I know. Do you think that the project there is relevant to the disappearance?"

"I have no idea. But I am going to have to explore every possible avenue. Did McCulloch know what sort of work they were doing?"

"I'm sure that he did."

"Then I'll have to know as well. Can you arrange it?"

"Probably. If your security clearance is good enough there should be no problem. I'll ask the right questions and we'll know soon enough."

It took less than an hour for the okay to come through, which was little short of miraculous considering the delicate security area involved. It also demonstrated the depth of concern in high places about McCulloch's disappearance. Just an hour after the permission arrived Troy was called to the conference room by the admiral. He tried not to show concern at the sight of the full colonel and the two star general who were also waiting there for him. The admiral made the introductions.

"General Stringham, Colonel Burkhardt, this is Sergeant Harmon. As you know he is operating as a lieutenant on this particular assignment."

Troy threw the sharpest salute that he could. The salute was returned in silence which stretched on and on until Admiral Colonne had left the room.

"The general will now administer the oath for your Top Secret clearance," the colonel said. "As soon as that is done and I have witnessed it you will receive your new ID and pass to the Gnomen Project. I will then escort you there. You will raise your right hand."

This was the first time that Troy had heard the name of the project that was being worked on in the laboratory. It meant nothing to him. The ceremony was a swift one, and as soon as it was over he was rushed out with the colonel to a waiting staff car. Two motorcyclists led the way as they plowed through the afternoon traffic. For the first time Troy began to realize just how deep were the waters that he was fishing in.

"Rotten weather," Colonel Burkhardt said. "Early too. Bet we have an even worse winter." He leaned forward and slid shut the glass panel behind the driver's seat. "You've got to find out where this traitorous son-of-a-bitch has gone and then nail his goddamned hide to the wall. Do you understand?"

"Yes, sir. Might I ask, are you acquainted with this Gnomen Project?"

"No. Don't know a damn about it except that the name of the director is Doctor Delcourt, whom we are on our way to see right now. It is also about the most top-top secret research project that we have going. The budget is right up there in CIA

figures. So when the security officer who is supposed to be guarding something like this, when he
ups and vanishes, why I get scared. And you better
realize now that we will undoubtedly get some
high-powered investigation team on to this assignment as soon as someone figures out just whose
backyard it is in. Meanwhile, since you are the one
who initiated this investigation, you will proceed
with it until relieved. Which means that we want
you to get us some answers, and I also mean
instantly or even sooner."

Yes, sir, was the only answer to that one. After
this one-sided conversation Burckardt slumped silently back in his seat and angrily chewed an unlit
cigar for the rest of the trip. At the laboratory
their identification swept them by the security
checks and on into the main building. A guide took
them up in the elevator, directly to the director's
office.

Dr. Roxanne Delcourt was in her middle fifties.
She was gray haired, not unattractive—though her
face was barren of makeup—and was efficiently
dressed in a gray worsted suit. The only jewelry
that she wore was a string of cultivated pearls
tucked under the collar of her white silk blouse.
There were no rings, certainly nothing on the third
finger of her left hand. She shook hands with Troy,
then showed Burckhardt to the door as he left. She
relaxed a little as soon as he was gone, and smiled
as she turned to Troy.

"Well, lieutenant, please sit down. It has been a
most traumatic day with all the comings and
goings. It appears that Wes McCulloch didn't
show up this morning and for some reason this is
being treated like the end of the world."

"You must admit, doctor, that this could be very

serious. After all he was head of security here."

"I know, but we have nothing here that any spies could possibly be interested in. Gnomen is a research project, pure and simple. An exercise in higher mathematics and nuclear physics. We are beginning to get results, but I'm afraid that applications are still years away at this stage."

"Did McCulloch know anything about the research here?"

"Everything. He had to, of course. Security."

"Well then, doctor, I'm afraid that I will have to know what is going on here as well. Could you please tell me—just what is the Gnomen Project all about?"

TEN

"Oh, dear," Roxanne Delcourt said. "You want me to explain exactly what we are doing here with the Gnomen Project?" She leaned back in her chair and twisted a yellow pencil between her fingers. "That can be difficult. It begins with a mathematical theorem . . ."

"I must tell you, doctor, that math was never my best subject."

"It is the same, I am afraid, for most people. And, please, my name is Roxanne. Doctor is not my first name, just as I am sure that Lieutenant is not yours."

"Dead right, Doctor—I mean Roxanne. It's Troy."

"All right, Troy, let me tell you *about* the mathematics without telling you exactly what the math is. My work has always been involved with the theory of particle movement, sub-atomic particles that is, and their relation to the unified field theory . . ."

"You lost me on the first fence. Which theory is this?"

"The unified field theory grew out of Einstein's theory of general relativity. Simply speaking it is an attempt to tie together and prove the inter-relationship of all of the forces in the universe. This is not an easy thing to do. Down through the years a number of people have worked very hard to either prove or disprove it, to get to grips with it in some way. As was Einstein, I am a mathematician, not a physicist. But unlike him, I have more laboratory results and experiments to build upon. And more facilities now exist to put to the test any new theories. Which is what we are doing here."

"What?" he asked, mystified.

"Tying down the relationships of space-time. If I could show you what we are doing, perhaps then you might understand more clearly."

He didn't. Troy followed her through the building and looked at particle accelerators, cloud chambers, racks and banks of equipment that apparently didn't even have names. Enthusiastic scientists pointed out to him curly white lines on black photographic prints, as proud of them as if they were photographs of their own offspring. He finished the tour thoroughly depressed, knowing that he was far out of his depth, while wondering at the same time just what he could do about it. When they were done, Roxanne took him to the executive's dining room, an alcove off the company cafeteria, where they were served first class coffee and toasted Danish.

"That's a very impressive set-up you have here," Troy said around a mouthful of Danish.

"It certainly is. Do you now see how exciting our work is?"

"No," he admitted. "But I think your security arrangements are top rate."

They both laughed at that. "No, I'm being serious," Troy said. "McCulloch seems to be involved in some kind of wickedry that we still don't know much about. But as a professional security officer he sewed this place up tight as a drum. It may look casual to an outsider, but the entire establishment is divided into guarded blocks with first-class security checks between each one. Records are automatically kept of every one going in and out of each block. This information is computerized so that the whereabouts of every person in the entire set-up is known every instant of the time. Very effmore."

"But other than that, Troy . . .?"

"Very little penetrated. Look, Ms. Delcourt . . ."

"Roxanne."

"Roxanne, sorry. During our little tour you impressed me in two ways. First off you know everything that is happening here in every detail. I don't know if you noticed it, but you answered questions when you were asked about a number of different things. Without hesitation. I haven't the slightest idea what you were saying—but the other people did and they seemed to go away satisfied. You're a pretty high-powered lady."

"Why, thank you, Troy. I don't think anyone has said anything as nice to me in years." She smiled at him across her coffee cup and, with her business expression banished for a moment, she was quite lovely.

"That's not flattery—but the honest truth."

"Which is even better. But you said that there

were two things about me that impressed you. Make my day—tell me something else!"

Once again they laughed together. "The second one is easier," Troy said. "You're a person who knows what they are talking about. Who operates without any, well—"

"Bullshit?"

"Right. And that's what I mean. You know what you're doing, you're in complete control of the situation here, while at the same time you're a walking ad for femlib. Which depresses me even more."

"How?"

"It must be me. I still don't know what is going on around here."

She shook her head. "No, Troy, it's all my fault and I apologize. Everyone I normally talk to is up to the eyebrows in technology. I'm so used to it that I am afraid that I have forgotten how to communicate in ordinary language. I don't give interviews to the press, or have a husband to talk to about every day matters, or any important interests outside of my work. Looking at it that way I suddenly realize that I must be a damn boring person."

"I didn't say that!"

"Well I did! And here is where I begin to reform. Let us leave this coffee and get back to my office and open the bar." She frowned at him with sudden concern. "You do drink?"

"Try me!"

"Good. I'll build a couple of swellegant gibsons and under the ameliorating affects of alcohol I will attempt to rejoin the human race."

Fifteen minutes later Troy was sitting back in the deep armchair as he sipped gratefully from the reviving glass of frigid gin.

"That is good, really good. I can now confide in you that I am recovering from a very alcoholic weekend, and you have found the cure that I have been looking for."

"Wonderful." Roxanne sipped hers, then delicately picked out the tiny white sphere of the onion with her fingertips, popped it into her mouth and crunched it thoughtfully. "All right, here we go. If I stray from the straight and narrow and you miss as much as one word, why then shout *whoa!* All right?"

"Shoot."

"All forms of energy in the universe are inescapably linked together. If you want an example you can see this clearly in a luminescent light bulb, where electrical energy is transformed to heat energy, that in turn being transformed to light energy. Sometimes the relationship is not quite as easy to make out. Take for example the movement of objects in a gravity field. Let us say that you lift a weight and tie it to the ceiling. It apparently just hangs there. But it still contains the muscular energy you used to lift it, only this energy is now in a different form. It is potential energy. If you cut the supporting rope it is transformed into kinetic energy and the weight drops."

"Fine so far," Troy said, and extended his glass so she could refill it from the shaker. "In fact it has a familiar ring to it, something from high school."

"Mechanics, first term physics. You knew this all the time—I'm just reminding you about it. Now let's jump over all the theory and experiments to the reality of what we are trying to do here. The thing that we are being funded for. My original theoretical calculations have been tested in a number of physical ways. The work has pretty well proven the theory to date, though there are still some holes in it that are causing trouble. But on the simple, experimental end, we are beginning to get results. Using multidimensional parameters notionally affecting temporal displacement without physical impairment . . ."

"You just did it," Troy broke in.

"What?"

"Spoke a sentence without one word in it that I could understand. Other than the first word which was *using*."

"You are absolutely correct and I apologize. I'll try again. In the laboratory, with the expenditure of a great deal of electrical energy, we have managed a minimal transformation into temporal energy causing a physical displacement—"

She heard her own words and had to stop and laugh.

"Incorrigible," Troy said. "But a message is seeping through. Are you saying that you moved something in some way for a time?"

"Yes, I mean no. It moved, but not for a time but *in* time."

Troy put his glass down most carefully onto the end table, then looked up at Roxanne.

"Please stop me if I am wrong," he said. "But are you trying to tell me that you have moved a hunk of something through time?"

"Roughly speaking, why yes."

"Then you are also telling me that down there among all that stuff—that you have built a time machine?"

"Well, I think . . ." She smiled brightly. "Why, yes, I suppose that we have."

ELEVEN

"No wonder everyone's so upset about the security here," Troy said. "A time machine—why just the idea of the thing, it's almost too big to take in! On television, sure, you see people jumping back and forth through time, but everyone watching knows that it's just actors in costumes and cardboard sets. But to have a real one, here, in this lab—" He ran out of words, looked to see if his glass was completely empty, then drained the remaining drops. Roxanne saw this and stood and hurried to the bar.

"Sorry. I'm being a rotten hostess. But you're right, the kind of time machines that zip into the past and future like temporal trolley cars, they happen only on television. Ours is not quite that impressive. When we turn it on we use enough electricity to light up all of Chicago to, well, do very little."

"Like doing what?"

"I'll show you. Let's just finish these before the ice melts."

He sipped—and was struck with sudden apprehension. "Could your machine, could it have anything to do with McCulloch's disappearance?"

Roxanne thought for a moment, then shook her head *no*.

"I think that is highly unlikely. You mean could he have sent that gold somewhere for his own nefarious purposes? That is so close to impossible that it *is* impossible. The biggest target object we have used so far only weighed a few grams. But let's get down to lab nine before they lock up for the day. I'll show you just what I mean. We'll have to hurry. Bob Kleiman comes in at the crack of dawn—but he leaves just as early as well."

Laboratory nine was right down at the bottom of the building. They hadn't been here on their earlier tour. The heavy entrance door was locked and even the security guard could not open it. He had to telephone through to security central and identify the two visitors before the lock clicked and the door slid aside. They went in and, as the heavy portal closed behind him, Troy had the strange sensation that the hair was stirring on his head. He held his hand to it and felt it writhing under his fingers. Roxanne noticed his shocked expression and smiled.

"Nothing to worry about," she said, rubbing at her own hair that was now standing straight out from her head. "Static electricity. A few million volts of it, but no amps to speak of, so there is nothing to worry about. Side effect that happens when the machine is in operation. But it gives you some idea of the kind of juice we use here."

It certainly did. The electrical fittings were most impressive. Wires thicker than his arm swung from gigantic ceramic insulators, looping down into the guts of hulking great machines. Most of the apparatus was grouped in the brightly-lit center of the room—where the floor apparently bulged upwards. It wasn't a bulge, Troy saw when they walked closer, but a ridge of gray stone that projected up through the white concrete floor. Some of the machines were bolted to it, while others hung out over the stone on shining steel arms. A man in a laboratory smock was working at one of the machines; he turned around when Roxanne called out to him.

"Bob, you've got a visitor. Lieutenant Harmon, Doctor Kleiman. Troy, Bob."

"My pleasure," Kleiman said, wiping grease from his hand onto his already stained coat before extending it. They shook hands. Doctor Kleiman looked very much like the classic image of the scientist. His graying hair was raggedly cut and long overdue for a barber's attention. And his eyesight was bad; he blinked through bottle-thick lenses at Troy.

"If you are here to recruit me for the Army you are too late. I been four-F since I was born." Troy smiled.

"You're safe," he said. "You don't look like cannon fodder to me."

"You betcha. So, since the purpose of this visit is not official—what is the purpose?"

"A demonstration," Roxanne said. "I thought Troy would understand the project better if he could see just what we are doing. Are you running any calibration set-ups?"

"Been doing them all day, and if you don't mind

some self-adulation I will humbly tell you that I have added two more zeroes to the right of the decimal point."

"How wonderful!"

Roxanne almost clapped with joy and Troy almost wished that he too could get so excited by decimal points and zeroes. But he knew better than to ask for an explanation.

"However, don't take my word for it," Bob Kleiman said, turning to a computer terminal. "Let me just feed in some info and I will show you. You, Troy, do you have a quarter with you? Admission to this show is two-bits. Good, thanks."

Bob took the coin over to a workbench, laid it flat, gave it a few rasping strokes with a file, then handed it back.

"Look close," he said. "I've put a nick right behind the cute little bow on George's pigtail. Correct?"

"Right."

"And the date on the coin is 1965. Is this coin unique enough so you will be able to recognize it again? Some people always claim they were tricked."

"They could have been," Troy said. "I didn't notice the date when I gave you the quarter. You could have substituted another one just like this, and have a prepared duplicate as well."

"You're right, this guy is a sharpy, Roxy, watch out for him. So do some additions yourself, Mister Sharpy. Take this knife and the coin and make it unique so you will be positive there is no hanky-panky."

Troy scratched a cross on Washington's noble forehead then returned the quarter. Bob backed away from it, hands raised. "No way, Sharpy," he

said. "You put it down yourself, over there on top
of the rock, on the laser spot. Otherwise you will
claim that I palmed it."

There was a flat area on top of the rock that was
marked in the center by a disc of ruby light. Troy
laid the coin on the spot of light and stepped back.

"The experiment begins," Bob said, throwing
some switches, then squinting at the VDU screen
of the computer to see the figures displayed there.
He used them to set a different set of instruments.
"Done," he said. "If you people will kindly join me
behind this insulated barrier we'll be able to avoid
some of the sparks. That's it, on the rubber carpet,
hold onto the brass rail at the same time. Troy,
does that fancy Army turnip on your wrist have a
stop-watch function?"

"Yes."

"Okay. Switch it on and start it going when I hit
the controls. Now!"

There was a sharp crackling in the air and a
vivid display of coronal sparks from a number of
metal surfaces. The effect died away very quickly
and Bob led them back to the experiment area.
The rock was bare.

"Where's your coin?" he asked.

"Gone."

"You have keen eyes."

"Thanks. But where did it go?"

"*When* did it go would be more grammatically
exact. Keep watching. It should be exactly seventeen seconds. Now!"

The coin reappeared, there on the rock, looking
as though it had never moved. Yet no one had gone
near it; the nearest piece of apparatus was a good
two feet away. Troy had pressed the button on his
watch by reflex. He looked at it now. Seventeen

point seven seconds. He reached out and picked up the coin. The nick was there, as was the cross. 1965.

"That's really great, Bob," he said, closing his fist tightly on the coin. "Now would you kindly tell me just what the hell happened?"

"My pleasure. At a cost of approximately four bucks worth of electricity, your twenty-five cents was sent ahead in time for exactly seventeen seconds. For us, in the eternal present, the coin appeared to vanish. But it wasn't gone, it was just sitting on top of the rock, seventeen seconds into our future, waiting for us to catch up with it. Seventeen seconds later we did—and from our point of view it suddenly came into being on the rock. Which was not true. It had been there all along. It just took us some time to get there. Now say that you don't believe it."

Troy opened his hand slowly and looked at the coin. "I believe it," he said, and was surprised at the hoarseness of his voice. "I don't understand it —but I believe it."

"Congratulations," Roxanne said. "The overwhelming majority of people who see this demonstration just don't want to believe what they have seen. It goes against their image of the world and they just can't accept it. That's why we do all the games to mark the coin. But despite this, most of the time they still refuse to believe what has happened and prefer to look for the gimmick that fooled them."

"One general took his pocket knife to the rock;" Kleiman said. "Swore that it was cardboard and hollow. Broke the blade, you can still see the scratch right there."

"I can accept it all right," Troy said. "Though it

does give me a strange feeling just behind the eyes when I think about it. Does this thing work both ways?"

"What do you mean?"

"It went forward in time—but can it send things back in time as well?"

"Theoretically, yes," Kleiman said, turning off a series of switches while he talked. "But we just don't know yet. Experiments have been made, with just a few particles of matter at first, then slightly larger objects. The objects vanished all right, but they never reappeared again. So we went back to the drawing board to overhaul the theory before we made any more experiments."

Troy was trying to get the possibilities of the machine straight in his head, and at the same time was worrying at the idea that the machine might have some connection with Colonel McCulloch. "Can you send anything, anything at all?"

"So far what has been sent has made the trip. Were you thinking of anything specific?"

"Gold?"

"Why not? There's some silver in that quarter of yours, probably minute traces of gold as well. No problem."

No problem? A big problem. What possible earthly connection could there be between McCulloch, the gold, this machine, and the future —since the past was ruled out? What? Absolutely nothing he could think of. And his head was beginning to hurt. "Thanks for the demonstration, Bob. I appreciate your help."

"You're welcome, I'm sure. Could I ask what your interest in all this is? Or is that classified?"

"Not classified at all. I'm in security and I'm making an investigation that involves some people here. So I just have to know more about the mechanical details of the project."

"Security? Now isn't that great." Bob bent over his console and disconnected a canon plug. "Just the man I want to see. I've been trying to get ahold of Old Snarly, your Colonel McCulloch, all day. All I get is excuses."

Troy's eyes met Roxanne's and he saw his own worried tautness mirrored there.

"What do you need the colonel for?" Roxanne asked.

"To do his job, that's what." He straightened up and shook the end of the cable at her. "Deadlines you give me, and reports to fill out, but do I complain? I do not. But I do not labor alone. Harper, my assistant, who does all the paperwork, is a paragon, never late and never out sick. But today hs is not only late he is not here. Not is he at home when I call him on the phone. Nor is Old Snarly at his post when I need him. So can you maybe find out what is going on around here and let me know?"

TWELVE

"That's just the sort of thing that I'm here to take care of," Troy said, allowing none of the sudden concern into his voice. "I'll check out what is happening and get back to you. I wouldn't worry about it if I were you."

"Me worry? I'll only get an ulcer. A little one. And then I'll work until midnight doing his job as well as my own. When you talk to Harper don't forget to mention the ulcer."

"Thanks for the demonstration," Troy said. Kleiman tipped an invisible hat in return, then turned back to his machines. Troy waited until they were out of earshot before he spoke again.

"Who is this Harper?"

"Allan Harper," Roxanne said. "An electronics engineer, a whiz on circuitry. You're worried, I can tell. Why?"

"It smells wrong. Too much of a coincidence to

be a coincidence. The same day that McCulloch disappears—so does Harper."

"Do you think that the two things are connected in some way?"

"I don't know enough yet to even guess—and I certainly hope not. But whether they are connected or not this matter is still very serious. Particularly if Harper has access to classified information. Would he know much about the Gnomen Project?"

"Everything," she said, suddenly just as worried as he was. "We'll go to my office. I have his home address there."

Troy dialed the number and let it ring. And with each unanswered ring in the distant room he felt the tension in his midriff grow. The address was in Bethesda, not too far away. He had to get over there. He hunched up his shoulder to hold the phone in place against his ear while he dug the police detective's card out of his wallet.

"No answer?" Roxanne asked.

"No. Do you have a company car I can use?"

"There's a panel truck and a station wagon . . ."

"The station wagon, if you please."

He pressed down the button and disconnected, then quickly dialed the number on the business card.

"Hello. I'd like to talk to Lieutenant Anderson. This is Lieutenant Harmon. He isn't? Can you reach him on the radio? Good. Please have him call me at this number. Urgent. It may relate to the Connecticut Avenue murders."

Anderson called back within the minute and, without asking any embarrassing questions, agreed to meet Troy at the Chevy Chase address.

It took an effort of will for Troy to hold the

wagon down to a steady 55 along the Beltway. He turned off at Exit 33 and looked at the street names. Just after the country club was the street sign for Black Thorn. When he turned the corner he saw the police car waiting up ahead. He pulled up behind it just as Lieutenant Anderson was getting out.

"What is it about?" Anderson asked.

"I was out at the lab where McCulloch headed security. One of the key employees didn't show up for work today. Doesn't answer the phone. It may have something to do with the colonel."

"Then again it may not. Can you tell me anything more?"

"Frankly—no. Except this is top security, top priority work."

"I'll take your word for it. But we can't go kicking doors down just on suspicion." He looked up at the old apartment building. "Is the man married?" Troy shook his head *no*.

"Single. And lives alone."

"Then if he doesn't answer when we ring his bell we can suspect illness or accident and we have sufficient grounds to ask the super to open up for us."

The superintendent was unshaven and surly and had obviously just woken up.

"Whatcha wanna see him for?"

"We don't want to see him," Anderson explained patiently. "We are just investigating a missing persons report. All you have to do is unlock the door, then stay with us when we go inside."

The man didn't want to cooperate, but Anderson's gold badge was a powerful persuader. Muttering under his breath the superintendent led them to the elevator. Not only hadn't he shaved, but he hadn't bothered to wash as well. They were greatly relieved when the door opened on the fifth floor. The large ring of keys rattled and jangled and the super cursed as he searched for the right one. When he finally had the door open, Anderson went in first. The curtains were drawn and all of the lights were on.

"Mr. Harper," he called out. "Are you home?" There was no answer. "Troy, stay here with the super while I look around."

They watched in silence while he went across the living room and glanced into the bedroom. Pushing the door open with his toe, touching nothing. It must have been empty because he turned away and started towards the kitchen. He stopped at the door, looked in, then turned away and came back, fishing into his pocket as he walked. He took out one of his cards and handed it to the superintendent.

"Call this number," he said. "Ask for Detective Sergeant Lindberg. Read my name off the card and tell him where we are. Tell him that I want the homicide unit."

"Listen, I got my work to do. You want me to make phone calls . . ." Then the meaning of the words penetrated. The super opened his eyes wide and stepped back, then turned and hurried away.

"Dead?" Troy asked.

"Very. Come look and see."

Allan Harper was sprawled on his back on the kitchen floor. A broken glass lay shattered on the linoleum beside him; the milk it had contained had puddled and dried under his head. His eyes were wide open and staring, his mouth gaping in a soundless cry of pain.

"What is it—what killed him?" Troy asked.

Anderson shrugged.

"No sign of wounds or a weapon. We'll find out soon enough. Is this case going rotten on you?"

"You could say that. Which makes it vitally important that I find out if this man had any connection with McCulloch. I'm getting back to the laboratory now. You have the number. Ask for security. Could you let me know as soon as you find out what happened to him?"

"No problem. But I'm going to have to ask you more about the deceased."

"All right. I'll tell you whatever I can, whatever is not classified. I'm going there to dig out his records now."

Troy went directly to the security building when he returned, without going near the laboratory. He wanted to get some facts before he answered any more questions. Inside the building there was a restrained feeling of panic. The three girls in the office carefully turned their eyes away from him when he came through the door.

"Who is in charge here?" he asked. None of them answered or even looked his way. He pointed to the nearest, a blonde with an impressive head of curls. "Miss. Yes, you. Would you come over here please? What's your name?"

"Daisy," she answered, almost in a whisper.

"All right, Daisy, would you please look at my security clearance papers . . ."

"I don't know anything about that kind of thing. I just work in the office."

"I know you do but—hell, who is in charge here?"

"Colonel McCulloch."

"I know that. But when he's not here, who is his second in command?"

"No one, sir. The colonel's always here."

"Well he's not here now and something has to be done about it. If he didn't delegate authority here, he still must have reported to someone in authority above him. Who would that be?"

"The Defense Department," she said brightly. Troy tried not to grate his teeth.

"I know that. But *who* in the . . . The hell with that. Get onto the Pentagon and contact General Stringham. If he isn't available then get hold of a Colonel Burkhardt. I'll talk to either of them."

It took fifteen minutes to locate the general, but it did the job. Daisy hung the phone up slowly and turned to Troy with widened eyes.

"You're in charge now, sir. That's what they said. You're the one in charge. Lieutenant Harmon."

"Good. Now get me the security record on one of the lab employees. Name of Allan Harper."

"Yes, sir, lieutenant. Take a minute for the printout. Everything's in the computer."

It took a lot more than a minute for the computer to produce the file. Troy was methodically going through McCulloch's desk so was only vaguely aware of the whispered voices in the other room. He looked up when Daisy hesitatingly came into the office with a single sheet of blue-lined, perforated-edge paper.

"I don't know what happened, Lieutenant Harmon, but something's gone wrong. We can't seem to locate Mr. Harper's file. Maybe the computer is broken. Because whatever we asked for, this was all that we could get."

She was trembling when she held out the sheet. He took it and read it at a single glance.

"Thank you, Daisy. Can you tell me just who has

access to the computer files?"

"Us. I mean all the girls in the office."

"I see. That means you can both enter and retrieve information in the security files?"

"Oh, no. We don't have the code to make entries
or changes. Only Colonel McCulloch has that. We
can just use the computer for making copies and
looking things up and things like that."

"Thank you, Daisy. That's all for now."

He heard the phone ring in the other office and a
moment later his own telephone buzzed. He
picked it up, still staring coldly at the sheet of
paper before him.

"Lieutenant Harmon."

*"Harmon, Lieutenant Anderson here. We've es-
tablished cause of death for Harper. He died of
poisoning. Strychnine. Very painful, very fast. The
glass of milk was filled with it, the carton on the
table as well."*

"Was it suicide?"

*"Not likely. There was also an unopened carton
in the refrigerator. This was also heavily laced with
strychnine. Further examination found a minute
puncture mark under the flap. The stuff was probably squirted in with a hypodermic. No reason for a
suicide to play around like that."*

"But it is something that a murderer might
do. I have a suspect for you. Colonel Wesley
McCulloch."

"Do you have any grounds for this suspicion?"

"I certainly do," Troy said grimly, clutching the
computer printout so hard that the paper tore in
his grasp. "What I am going to tell you is off the
record for the moment. But McCulloch was the
only one with access to security files here. He
wiped Harper's record clean. It's gone completely.

In its place he left a brief message for whoever accessed the file next."

"Can you tell me what it is?"

"Yes. It's very short. As follows.

"Jig, I said that you weren't going to find me."

THIRTEEN

"It has been over a week now since McCulloch vanished," Admiral Colonne said. "Have you come up with any answers yet?"

The meeting was taking place in the conference room again, not the admiral's communication cubby where most of his work was done. He could relax here, lean back in the deep chair and smoke his pipe. But while his body rested his mind was as alert as ever; Troy shifted under the penetrating gaze.

"Not as many as I would like," Troy said, sliding the stack of papers out of the file onto the table before him. "If anything, we seem to have come up with more questions."

"And they are . . . ?"

"First and most important—what was McCulloch's motive for killing Allan Harper, the electronics engineer from the laboratory?"

"You're sure that he is the killer?"

"The police are so certain that they have issued a warrant for his arrest. McCulloch made absolutely no attempt to cover his trail. A forged prescription, in his own name, was located in a drug store not three blocks from his home. It was for a large amount of strychnine hydrochloride, the same substance found in the containers of milk. A handwriting expert believes that McCulloch wrote the prescription—while the doctor remembers him visiting his office some months ago during the course of a security investigation."

"When he could have pocketed some prescription blanks?"

"Correct. But while we have evidence to tie McCulloch to the murder—we have no motive. But I keep coming back to the work being done in the Weeks laboratory. I am sure that there is a tie-in between the gold, McCulloch's disappearance— and the murder as well. Have you been informed yet what kind of research is being done in the lab?"

"No. But at your suggestion I put the question to the authorities. They have responded and I have been cleared to receive all classified information about what they called the Gnomen Project, on a need to know basis. So you can tell me just what they are doing there and how it affects this case."

"That will make it a lot easier to explain my thinking. Could I please see the authorization?"

The admiral took his pipe from his mouth and leaned back, with real or assumed surprise. "I'm your superior, my boy, you may take my word for it."

"I can't, admiral," Troy said grimly. "However, I will contact General Stringham . . ."

"There's no need. I have the authorization here." He took an envelope from his jacket pocket and passed it across the table. Troy opened it, having the feeling that he had just passed a test that he hadn't even known he was taking. He scanned the page, checked the signature, then handed the papers back.

"Is this room security tight, admiral?" he asked.

"Swept twice a day. We can call it secure."

"All right then. The scientists at the lab have built a working time machine—"

"You had better be serious," the admiral growled.

"Never more serious in my life. It is still being perfected—but I've seen it operate and it works. Now what use could McCulloch have wanted to put the machine to? Harper could have been in on this, he knew all about the operation of the machine. He could have been killed because he knew too much about the colonel's plans. There is even a chance that he might have known just what McCulloch planned to do with the gold."

"Given that this time machine does work, and I will accept that for the moment without thinking about the terrifying possibilities inherent in the supposition, I can instantly think of one good plan. You could send the gold back in time to yourself. A man could make a fortune that way. Invest it at ten percent, compounded, you could treble the sum in less than thirteen years. Send it back thirty years—ha!" The admiral took out a pocket calculator and punched quick figures into it. "There's your answer, Troy. In thirty years that ten-thousand would be worth—my goodness!—over one-hundred and seventy-four thousand dollars. And his gold was worth a lot more than that. That would be motive enough."

"It would be, sir. But the time machine doesn't work backwards. It just sends things into the future."

"Then forget that." The admiral cleared the calculator with a swift poke and put it back into his pocket. "What else have you found out?"

"A few things. Corporal Mendez is not involved. He gave me a hard time when I interviewed him because McCulloch told him, and I quote, that a nigger MP was looking for trouble. But the urgent investigation that I ordered done on McCulloch has brought in a mountain of reports." He tapped a thick sheaf of paper. "This is an abstract of the material. Let me tell you some of the most important parts. First, and most important, McCulloch has been lying about himself ever since he got into the Army. He tried for OCS but didn't make it, his high school marks and test results weren't good enough. So he worked his way up through the ranks. Everyone he talked to knew his background. He told anyone who would listen. Rich antebellum family fallen on bad times since the War between the States. That's what he always called the Civil War. But they still have an historical family name and are related to a lot of the great families in the South. Among his noted ancestors was the important Confederate General Ben McCulloch. It makes a great history."

"It does. So what is wrong with that?"

"Everything. It's all a lie. The colonel's kinfolk appear to be all white trash, and he has had nothing to do with them since he left home. You might say that they are all spongers and grifters, with the whole lot on welfare as far as we can find out."

"So what's wrong with that? Local boy makes good. It's an American success story."

"Not quite. McCulloch has worked very hard to conceal this background from everyone—including those same relatives. Just once, as far as we can discover, one of them found him and paid a visit. A first cousin came to see him when he was stationed at Fort Dix. McCulloch gave him such a beating that the man was in the hospital for three weeks. At first there was talk of a lawsuit, but the cousin dropped the charges and went home. Rumor at the time had it that a large sum of money changed hands to shut him up."

"I'm beginning to like your colonel less and less. What else have you found out?"

"That in the last year he has had some new interests that just don't fit his past history. You'll remember that he never read, never bought a book, never went to the movies or even looked at television. That all changed quite suddenly. He began to buy books, to go to libraries and museums. I am very curious to know why. The FBI is feeding all the details that we can uncover into a computer, to see if we can uncover trends, topics, interests of some kind that might explain what he was doing. And in about one hour I have an appointment that may help to clarify things." Troy held up a letter.

"The police have been intercepting all of McCulloch's mail. This letter arrived in the morning delivery today. A curator at the Smithsonian wants to see him at once, about matters of the utmost urgency. He obviously doesn't know that McCulloch is missing. I made an appointment in his name."

"None of this makes sense," the admiral said, looking into the bowl of his pipe as though seeking to find an answer there.

"No—not yet. But it will. It is just a matter of fitting all of the parts together and seeing the pattern that they make."

Now, sitting in the stuffy waiting room in the Smithsonian Institute, Troy wished that the answers were as obvious as he made them sound when he was talking to the admiral. But they would be, they *had* to be. The answer might be incredible—but it would be clear.

"Mr. Dryer will see you now," the secretary said. Troy stood and went in. He was not in uniform, but instead was wearing a dark suit under his raincoat.

"You're not Colonel McCulloch!" Dryer said, drawing back. He was a beanpole of a man, tall and thin, with his well-worn jacket hanging from him in loose folds. His neck was wrinkled and wattled with age, his white hair a loose cloud around his head. This picture of advanced senility was relieved only by his dark eyes, as clear and penetrating as a youth's.

"No, I'm not. My name is Harmon. My work . . ."

"I really don't care what your work is, Mr. Harmon. What I have to discuss with the colonel is confidential. Please return to him and tell him that he must come himself, in person. He will know why."

"I would like to know the reasons why myself, Mr. Dryer. Here is my identification. The colonel is under investigation at the moment. We hope that you will aid us in that investigation. If you are in any doubt I have an extension in the Pentagon for you to call . . ."

"I have no doubts, no doubts at all, young man. My work deals with military documentation and I know the real thing when I see it. Could you tell me what the investigation concerns?"

"I'm sorry, but that part is classified. But I can assure you that Colonel McCulloch will not be able to see you at the present time. All of his mail goes to the police department. They forwarded your letter to me."

Dryer pressed his hair down as he nodded; it sprang back as soon as he released it. "Well, I shan't push you any more on that. But it sounds more drastic than anything that I wanted to discuss with him. I just wanted to point out to the colonel that certain documents he borrowed were library file copies and that, strictly speaking, they should not have been removed from this building. But exceptions are made, of course, to a military man of his rank, considering the nature of our collection."

"May I ask what that is?"

"The Technological Archives of the United States Army. We have grant money from both private industry and the military. Our facilities are not open to the public, though any qualified researcher may have access. And military officers as well, of course."

"May I ask what the archives contain?"

"Books, models and documents relating to the history of American military technology—from the birth of our nation right up to today. We are rather proud of our rifled flintlocks, some rare specimens, as well as the working drawings of the research that preceeded the development of the first tanks . . ."

"I do agree, quite impressive. But could you tell me what Colonel McCulloch's interest was?"

"History of small arms. He was a serving infantry officer so that is understandable. He is really quite knowledgeable in this area, and I speak with authority when I say . . ."

"Yes, Mr. Dryer, of course." Troy had the horrible feeling that if he didn't interrupt he would be in this chair, getting lectured to, for the rest of his life. "But what exactly was it that the colonel took and did not return?"

"Blueprints. Of the Sten gun. The 9 millimetre Sten machine carbine, Mark Two to be exact."

"I've never heard of it."

"No reason that you should. It hasn't been manufactured for over forty years. But it is well known in military circles, while the blueprints do have a certain historical value. I want them returned at once. If they are returned nothing will be said about the matter. But you must understand, abduction of historical documents is no laughing matter."

"No. It certainly isn't," Troy agreed. Neither is murder. But how did this ancient gun fit in? "Do you know why the colonel was interested in this specific weapon?"

"No particular reason, I am sure. I told you he was interested in all weapons of this type. He was also enthusiastic about comparing various weapons, and has many times pointed out to me characteristics I would never have noticed, things that he saw when he actually had them in his hands. I sincerely hope this present difficulty will be . . ."

"Excuse me, I'm sorry to interrupt, but you say he held the weapons? Do you have models here?"

"Not models, sir, the real thing. The Army has donated many obsolete weapons, private collectors as well."

Perhaps looking at this old popgun might help to explain McCulloch's interest. And yes, Dryer would be happy to show it to him. "They are not intended for public display," he explained, unlocking a door and leading Troy into the darkened depths of the building. It smelled of dust and oil. "We do prepare displays for museums and the like, when we have the financing, using our duplicates of course. We have more than one example of many of our weapons, so in this way we can preserve the best specimens. Down here please."

Rows of metal bins vanished off into the darkness. There were labels on the shelves that Dryer peered at closely as he walked. He stopped in front of a shelf and pointed.

"Here we are. Now I'll just unwrap it." He seized up a bundle of stained canvas and carefully opened it. The weapon inside was thick with preserving cosmoline. He turned it over as he examined it. "No, not this one," he said, carefully rewrapping the bundle. "That is an interesting variation, the silenced version, did yeoman service during the Korean War. The one that we want is here . . ."

Dryer was suddenly silent as he picked up a length of canvas, then dropped it again. He poked into the darkness of the bin, then stepped back.

"What's wrong?" Troy asked.

"I can't understand this. I put it away myself. I know I did. But it's gone. How could that have happened?"

How indeed, Troy thought. McCulloch, of course. But why? Instead of getting any simpler, the mystery was deepening. What could this last development possibly mean?

FOURTEEN

In the fall of the year, when the leaves are turning to their autumn golds and reds and yellows, it is very pleasant to drive out of the city on the George Washington Memorial Parkway. The river lies below with the forested bluffs rising up behind it; the landscape is a most relaxing one —as long as it is not the rush hour and the parkway has not been jammed solid by the notorious District traffic. But by midafternoon the cars had thinned out and Troy could drive with little attention to the road. He had left the Smithsonian, deep in troubled thought, and driven away with no destination in mind. Without thinking he had found himself headed for the Pentagon. There were no answers there. At the next junction he had turned and driven north, in the opposite direction.

The pieces to this puzzle were all there now, he could feel it. But they still made no sense. How could he tie in the gold, the murder—and now the missing blueprints and the antique weapon? They were linked together, he was sure of that, but what did it all mean? And the time machine as well; that had to be the crux of the situation. All of McCulloch's unusual behaviour had begun after he had been assigned to the Gnomen Project. Something about the project had interested him, started him thinking, reading, going to the museum—then buying the gold. It had to be that. The answer was at the lab, and the only way he could find it would be by concentrating on McCulloch's movements since he had gone to work there. That job would have to start now.

Troy pushed down on the accelerator and moved up to the speed limit, turning off at the junction with the Beltway. When he reached the lab he checked into the security office, but there were no messages. He thought of talking to the director, then changed his mind. Roxanne had helped him as much as she could. Whatever had drawn McCulloch's attention was located in Laboratory 9. He headed there.

Bob Kleiman was seated at his desk, a cup of cold coffee in front of him, staring into space. He turned when he heard Troy come in.

"Dead? Murdered? Just like that? I can't get over it, and frankly, I find it hard to take in. I was working with him, right here on Friday night. Now . . . Poor Harper. Couldn't something have been done?"

"I'm sorry, Bob. When his body was discovered, it was far too late. He had been dead for some time when we got there."

"Perhaps earlier? If I had called the police earlier instead of hakking around here and doing nothing—"

"Please. Don't beat yourself. He died during the weekend, so there is no possible way that you can possibly assume any blame. But there is something you can do now to help."

"What do you mean?" Kleiman took a sip of the cold coffee, then made a wry face and pushed it away.

"I mean you can help me find the man who murdered him. The police are very certain about who it was."

"They are? There was nothing in the papers about it."

"That's because the facts aren't for public consumption yet. Harper's death is just part of a far more important case, one that is highly classified. I'm talking about the disappearance of Colonel McCulloch."

"A mystery that, you should pardon my saying this, you shouldn't bother to solve. Old Snarly can stay vanished and no one will miss him."

"Not even if he is the one who killed Harper?"

"He did?" Kleiman twisted around in his chair and leaned forward. "This is the truth? He's the momzer who killed Allan Harper?"

"We are almost certain that he is. And I am equally certain that the murder, his disappearance, as well as a number of other items, that they all tie in with the Gnomen Project."

"How?"

"You tell me."

Kleiman shook his head in bewilderment. "You've lost me, really lost me. What can I possibly tell you that could help the investigation?"

"You can let me know about the project. The way I see it, something here, something to do with the work in this laboratory, captured McCulloch's attention. In order to find out what that was I want to find out everything that McCulloch knew about the operation here, everything that he might have uncovered on his own or that Harper might have told him. For openers, what can you tell me about their relationship? Were they very close?"

"Not that I knew. In fact, now that I think about it, they barely talked to each other. If anything, I always had the feeling that Harper was afraid of the Iron Colonel, even hated him. I caught him a couple of times looking at McCulloch when he didn't know he was being seen, with his face all twisted like he would like to kill the man. But he never said anything at all about it."

"They must have had some sort of relationship —or the colonel wouldn't have killed him. Why? Did Harper know something about him—or perhaps Harper discovered McCulloch doing something here in the lab . . ."

"That's impossible. The colonel was a dunce. I doubt if he knew enough about technology to even change a fuse. About this highly complex and specialized electronic equipment I can guarantee you that he knew bupkas, or even less."

"That's important information. So now we know that he couldn't have operated alone in here. If he somehow did make use of the time machine, then he must have had to have help. Could it have been Harper who aided him? But you said that the man hated him. So perhaps Harper was being forced to help him—which would explain his dislike of the colonel. There would certainly have been no love lost if McCulloch were blackmailing him."

"Makes a good theory. So what's next?"

"Could the colonel and Harper have had access to the equipment when you weren't here?"

"Why not? Harper usually stayed on working

here after I left at night. McCulloch could have joined him. He did almost all of the electronic maintenance in the evenings, so I could set up the experiments during the day. That's why he never came in until after noon. It was a good schedule for both of us."

Troy rubbed at his jaw as he looked around at the roomful of unknown machinery. He had the strong sensation that the answer was right here, obvious, waiting for him to pick it up.

"So if they were here alone at night they could run the machine, even make unauthorized experiments?"

"I don't think they would do that. For one thing I wouldn't permit it."

"How would you know?"

"A good question." Kleiman stood and paced back and forth, thinking better on his feet. "There might be a record of their staying on here at night, but I'm not sure. I think the guard just logs people in and out. But so what? That just means they were on the spot, but it doesn't say anything about what they were doing. That means nothing. Did they use the machine? I have no idea. If they left any records of any experiments I've never seen them. We'll never know."

"But we *have* to know. Think. Isn't there a record book kept of what is done here? Maybe there is a dial that shows if the machine has been turned on and off?"

"Please, Troy, don't make this billion dollar hunk of highly complicated apparatus sound like an office copying machine that counts the number of copies made. It doesn't work that way. It's all new, all experimental."

"I know. But there still might be records kept of

something. Does it use things up, you know like welding rods or carbon sticks in an arc lamp?"

Kleiman drew back and pressed his hand to his chest. "My God," he gasped. "You live in the mechanical Dark Ages. Haven't you heard of the new physics? Even in Korea they get rich now knowing about that. Haven't you ever read about solid state circuitry or very large integrated circuits? We don't use radio tubes or filaments—not to mention your welding rods and carbon sticks—nor switches nor relays or anything like that any more. It's all solid state now, one big lump. The only things that move are the electrons and you can't see them. The only consumable—other than paper for the printer—is electricity."

"Well electricity then. Is there a meter? Any record kept of how much you use?"

"No way. I suppose we get a bill every month or something like that which someone in the office pays. Not my department. I know that we use a hell of a lot of it. So much so that about a year back we were popping breakers in the substation and they had to run in a new line . . ."

Kleiman stopped suddenly and stared into space. Then he blinked and shook his head, turning slowly to face Troy.

"Do you know what you are?" he said. "You are a genius. The Sherlock Holmes of Foggy Bottom. You act like a nebbish about science—when all of the time you are leading me by the hand to the answer. I'm the one who is the yold. Without your kick up the ass I never would have remembered."

"Remembered what?"

"Remembered about the time when the electric company got all excited, and we got excited too because we were losing experiments that crashed when the current pooped out. That was when we started to monitor the line to find out how much juice we were using—keep a record so they could guarantee a sufficient supply for us at all times."

Troy felt that he was close to an answer now, very close. "What kind of a monitor?"

"It wasn't really a monitor. They tried to bring in one of their usual recorders, but you should have seen the monster. Clanking and sputtering while it drew a graph on a rotating drum. No one wanted the big dirty thing leaking red ink all over the place. It really was Stone Age technology. I remember, they tried to set it up, but we tossed them out. All of the functions of the equipment here are controlled and monitored by our mainframe computer. It has, I don't know how many K, of random access memory, plus hard disk, plus a real time clock and all the extra goodies anyone might possibly want. So one of the software people wrote a program to monitor the electricity being used, and after that everyone was happy. We had the records we needed and life was beautiful."

Troy was puzzled. "But wouldn't this computer meter be disconnected after it was no longer needed?"

Kleiman shook his head. "You got it wrong. We didn't *add* any meters or junk. We just wrote a program, instructions for the computer, to remember some facts for us. All of which operated invisibly and unseen until someone asked the thing to tell us what had gone on. We even added some inputs of our own to help us in recording experiments. Very handy it was in the early days."

"But you no longer use it?"

"We no longer *access* the information. You've got to learn the jargon if you are going to be hanging around here. Once a program is started it will keep running forever unless you stop it." He waved his hand at a row of steel cabinets. "It's all in there. All you got to do is ask."

Troy gazed in wonder at the featureless doors. "Are you serious? Can we really find the record of all the experiments?"

"Every one. Just ask the right question."

"Then ask!"

"Not me," Kleiman said, reaching for the telephone. "This is the age of the specialist, young man. I'm a physicist, not a flow-chart doodler. For this you need the right person. Nina Vassella, our head programmer. She'll know what to do . . . Hello, Nina? *Come 'sta? Bene?* That's what I like to hear. Look, we got a little problem down in nine that only you can solve. When? Now of course. Be a sweety-pie. That's my girl. Thanks." He hung up. "She'll be right down."

Nina was dark, petite, lovely—and she knew her business.

"Of course I remember the program," she said. "Particularly since I wrote it."

"Is it still running?"

"Undoubtedly. Since it would probably crash the entire system if one of you ham-handed masters of cosmic theory tried to get anywhere near it. And I haven't wiped it. So it must still be ticking away. Let's see."

She pulled the chair over in front of the terminal, then spun the adjustment to raise it up high enough for her. When she sat down her legs dangled like a little girl's, her feet not reaching the floor; she twined her legs around the chair supports. But she knew very well what she was doing. Her fingers flashed over the keyboard, pulling up a menu of all the programs running, then accessed the one she wanted and checked it through. Thirty seconds later she leaned back and pointed her thumb at the rows of numbers marching down the screen.

"There it is. Ready and waiting."

"Great!" Kleiman said, patting her on the shoulder. "You are a genius, baby. Now give us a printout, if you please."

"What? There are all of two years plus of readout in there. Haven't you heard of the energy crisis and the paper shortage?"

"That's the name of the game. Type."

She pressed two keys and the highspeed printer against the far wall began to hammer away with a rapid, paper-tearing sound. The printing head tore back and forth across the endless sheet of fanfold paper which began to pile up higher and higher in the wire tray.

"Is that all you geniuses need now?" Nina asked.

"Thank you, doll. I'll remember you in my will."

When the printer had finally lapsed into silence, Kleiman tore the paper apart at the end of the last sheet and carried the book-thick pile of printout over to his desk.

"Now we see what we will see," he said, turning the pack over and pulling free the last pages. "Right up to date, yep, here's the one I did this morning. Now let us flip back a bit, to last weekend when the colonel went missing . . . mamma mia!"

"What is it?"

"There it is, right here, late last Saturday, when the joint was supposed to be closed up. Power, man, power. Whatever they were doing in here they were burning enough juice to light up Chicago. We've never pulled a ten-thousandth of that amount. I'm surprised that they didn't vaporize every one of the circuits. And what's this? No, this I do not believe! Too much!"

He pointed to the line of printout, his thumb on a set of numbers. It looked in no way different to Troy than anything else on the page. Kleiman flipped through the sheets in consternation, then back to the original page. Then he shook his head with disbelief.

"Here, see it, right there. The polarity of tau input, it's reversed. It shouldn't be like that. We never do that—look at all the others. The results were consistently negative, we abandoned that approach."

Troy held his impatience under tight control. "What does it mean? This tau thing. Why does it bother you?"

"It doesn't bother me—it's just impossible, that's what. It can't be done. But it *has* been done."

The papers slipped from Kleiman's fingers and fell to the floor. He turned to Troy, and when he spoke again his voice was hushed, his face drawn.

"Whatever was moved in time wasn't moved forward. It was sent in the opposite direction.

"Sent back in time—to the past."

FIFTEEN

Troy accepted the fact of time travel without hesitation. Why shouldn't he? He had grown up in the age of technological miracles. First there had been the atomic bomb, well before his birth, then, one after another; the hydrogen bomb, atomic energy, jet aircraft that could fly faster than sound, followed by orbiting satellites, and lastly the almost unbelievable, real-time television pictures of men walking on the Moon. There seemed no end to the cornucopia output of the laboratories and he, like many others, had stopped trying to understand how they worked. They just did. He had used electronic guided missiles in the Army. You pressed the button and they went. That's all that you had to know.

So you pressed another button and something traveled through time. There was really no difference. The only question was—what had the machine been used for? What was it that McCulloch and Harper had sent backwards in time? Was it the gold? What would that have possibly accomplished? But if it hadn't been the gold—then what had it been?

When the question was asked this way, the answer became obvious. The pieces fitted together at last. Troy spun about and called out to Kleiman, who did not hear him. The physicist was muttering to himself as he pawed his way through the sheets of printout. Troy had to raise his voice to get the man's attention.

"What?" Kleiman said, looking up and blinking distractedly. "What did you say?"

"I asked you, can you tell from the figures how big the thing was that was sent through your time machine?"

"How big? Its mass you mean? Yes, we can find out. I'll have to work out the equation though, the tau settings against the power consumed as the factorial aspects . . ."

"Can you tell me now, even roughly, how big a mass can be moved through time?"

"Though we have only used small objects up until now there is theoretically no limiting factor on size. If we had a field big enough, why I suppose that we could move the Washington Monument. There is nothing in the theory that precludes the possibility."

Troy hesitated before he said it. "If that's true, then it is within reason, it is possible—that a human being could be sent through time?"

"Yes, why not, mass is mass—" Kleiman stopped, and he tilted his head as he looked at Troy. "Are you getting at what I think you are getting at? Is it your theory that this explains the colonel's sudden disappearance?"

"Possibly. It might explain a lot of things. The way he committed those brutal murders just to buy himself some time. Then there was his apparent indifference to leaving a trail that could be followed later. Why should he care what crimes he committed—if he were no longer here to face the consequences of his acts?"

"You're right, he wouldn't care in the slightest. If his escape through time were possible. But during the research to date we never even considered using living creatures in our experiments. It might very well be lethal, we don't know. It was never tried."

"So try."

"Spoken in the true spirit of science. And I know just what we need."

Kleiman rooted around in his desk until he found the in-house telephone directory. He checked a number, then push-buttoned it into the phone. Then leaned back in his chair with his feet on the desktop as he listened to it ring.

"Is that you, Hugo? Yes, Bob Kleiman here. I know, long time no see. This is a big place, we're all overworked. Listen, I got a question for you if you've got a moment. Great. You remember about six months ago I set up a small field generator for you, so you could check out the effect of the tau field on cellular life? Any results? Well no news is good news. Did you ever move on from unicellular forms the way you said you would? Good news indeed, white mice. Maybe I can help. I want to put one through the entire field at full strength. Right —I thought you would be interested. But please send me one that you are not too fond of, because there is no guarantee how healthy it will be after it

has zipped its way through the space-time conti-
nuum. You're a bubeleh, thanks." He hung up the
phone and turned back to Troy.

"A messenger is on the way. I'll set up the
experiment now and we'll soon have the answer to
at least one of your questions."

It was a very small white mouse. It had pink
eyes and a pink nose, and sat up while it daintily
cleaned its whiskers with its front paws. It looked
on with interest while its cage was placed on the
laser marker at the experimental site.

"Blast off," Kleiman said, pressing the button
that initiated the experiment. The cage vanished.
"I'm giving it a full five minutes. The alarm will
sound ten seconds before return. Now let me
check this printout again. Because I have been
doing some thinking myself. It is obvious by hind-
sight that those jokers must have run some kind of
experiment that we never thought of. Some way of
finding if past projection works, a way of testing
the theory experimentally without getting involved in time paradoxes."

"You've lost me again."

"Sorry. But like it or not, when we begin to talk
about reverse time flow we very quickly find ourselves getting involved with the old saw about
what would happen to me if I went back in time
and killed my grandfather before my mother was
born."

"What would happen?"

"That's the question. If I killed him, why then I
could never be born, so I couldn't have gone back
and killed him, therefore—"

"A paradox."

"Correct. We never found a way to set up an
experiment that would get around this difficulty.

And of course very brief time movements were out of the question. We had proof of that before we even started."

"You wouldn't care to explain that in some detail, because once again I haven't the slightest idea of what you are talking about."

"It's obvious. We never found anything lying on the transmission site on the rock—so we never sent anything back that we could find lying on the rock. So we didn't try. If we had found something unexpected on the test site we would have known that we in the future had sent it back in time to be found, so therefore we would have to make the experiment later to send it back. It gets complicated."

"*You* think that it is complicated!" Troy burst out laughing. "Can you imagine how it looks to me? This stuff is just not in my league. After high school I went to college, graduated with a BA in history, then was instantly snapped up by the draft. For a couple of years I got shot at, so I learned how to shoot back. I stayed in the Army after the war. I've forgotten most of my history but I know a lot about modern weaponry, as well as how to stay alive when a lot of other guys are trying to kill me. But about all this equipment here, I know—what was that word you used?— bupkas."

"A good word. It's Yiddish for goat shit. And what could be of less value than that?"

"Nothing. Bupkas. For openers, I don't even know why that rock is there."

Kleiman looked at the gray mass of granite rising out of the floor and nodded. "That's an easy one. When you think of time you have to think of physical movement. Not only do people move around in physical space during any given time interval, but the Earth also revolves around the sun. While the entire solar system itself is moving through interstellar space. This is a complication that we luckily do not have to face. The tau field works in what we call world time. That means that objects are displaced in time—but not in space. An object on top of that rock will move minutes into the future and still be on the rock. Which is why we use it. If we used something like a workbench instead, there is always a chance that someone might move the bench. The object would move in time to the space where the workbench used to be —but no longer is. Crash, tinkle, the experiment hits the floor. Therefore our pet rock. This very solid object is a hundred percent metamorphic granite. It has been on this spot for a couple of million years, and hopefully will be there for as long again. The preliminary research was done before my time, but I understand that a geological survey was made of the area before this lab was built. In a sense it was built here, because that stone was here . . ."

The ping of the bell interrupted him. They turned to the rock just in time to see the cage reappear. The mouse was sitting up, looking at them. It hurried over and sniffed Troy's finger when he put it between the bars.

"Another question answered," Kleiman said cheerfully, picking up the cage and smiling at its very lively occupant. "Time travel is good for you. A tonic. This mouse never looked better. Hugo will be happy to get the results." The smile vanished. "So, to answer your earlier question. Yes, the iron colonel could have escaped through time. How or why, I have no idea."

"Then we'll just have to find out. You're doing great so far. Do those figures tell you how far into the past he went?"

"Those figures tell me little or nothing at the present moment. We must calibrate—and we can save time by finding out how McCulloch and company calibrated their own experiments. For openers we can reverse the equation that we use for future displacement. However, there is no guarantee that the terms will work precisely in reverse. But McCulloch and Harper must have done something to calibrate the time displacement or they wouldn't have dared risk the big trip. If they did it—we can follow their lead, get their results and use them ourselves. Let me see if I can find their traces. There's a coffee machine in the corner. Pour us a couple of cups while I browse through the printouts looking for their footsteps. It shouldn't take long."

It didn't. By the time they were finishing their coffee, Kleiman had found the entry he was looking for.

"Eureka! Which, in case your classical education was deficient, is Greek for I have found it. There are some smaller probing experiments here, a lot of them, but I looked for a big one. And here it is. It took place a little over a year ago. Look at the juice they used! Don't show the electricity bill to the taxpayers. Now some quick work with the math."

Kleiman checked the figures twice, and the results remained the same. He scribbled on a ruled pad, then tore off the sheet and passed it over to Troy. "December tenth, 1941," he said.

Troy looked at it. "This is the arrival date?"

"Correct. Something weighing approximately fif-

teen kilos was sent back to that date. Or at least I
think that is the date. The mass is correct, but the
date is simply an inversion of the future equation. It
may not check out exactly, but we can do the same
thing they did to find out. Check the newspapers.
Whatever they sent back had to be unusual
enough to make news. A rabid wolf, twenty-five
plucked and deep-frozen two-headed chickens, I
don't know what. But you can be sure that whatever they sent, it was something odd enough so
that they knew it would be noticed and reported in
the papers."

"Are you sure of this?"

"Nope. But it's a good enough theory to start
with. Why don't we split the work? I'll keep
analyzing the printout and put together a list of
how much they sent and when. While I'm doing
that you drive over to the Washington Post and
look through their files for that date. If there is
nothing recorded, look forward and backwards
until you do find something. It *has* to be there or
McCulloch wouldn't have gone ahead with his
nefarious plans."

"I agree. How late will you be here?"

"Until you phone." Kleiman placed his hand on
his heart and looked heavenward. "I break a long-
standing rule to be out of the shop by five and into
the first martini by five-thirty. No sacrifice is too
great for the cause. Go, and come back with your
shield or upon it. I want good news or none at all.
You can do it."

Why not, Troy thought, as he drove back into the
city. Just stick with it until he uncovered some
trace. He would do this because he had the
sure knowledge that the information was there.

McCulloch had found it—and so would he.

The files at the Post were well organized. Copies of back issues were available for consultation or purchase. But in order to save space, after some weeks had gone by, the newspapers were stored on microfilm. Troy filled out an order form for the December 1941 reel and pressed the button on the counter to call the clerk. There was a long wait. He didn't appear until Troy rang the bell again.

"Patience, brother, patience," he said. A mulatto youth with an impressive afro, the hair standing out a good eight inches from his head. He took the call slip from Troy and vanished back into the files. But returned in less than a minute and gave the slip back to Troy.

"Can't do it," he said. "No way I can oblige you with this one."

"Why not?"

"It's not there, man, that's why not. Happens once in awhile. Sometimes they get misfiled, sometimes the dudes even walk away with them. This is a hard world. It could have happened a long time ago for all I know. We hardly ever get requests for stuff this old. The reel might have been missing for months even. But whatever happened—this one is gone for sure."

SIXTEEN

The colonel had got there first.

Troy looked down at the slip and knew that their
suppositions must have been correct. McCulloch
had been here, had found what he had wanted,
then had covered his tracks.

"What about the period just before or after
this?" Troy asked. "Could I see them?"

"This is really your bad day, man, because you
are still shit out of luck. We get about four months
of newspaper on every reel of film. The date you
want is somewhere right in the middle of that
spool."

"But—this can't be the only copy you have.
Don't you have permanent records on file?"

"We got the master in the vault, for a backup.
People got no respect for property these days.
These public prints get scratched and torn and
thumb-printed to death. So we make new ones

whenever they're needed. But that takes time. I put the order in now, be at least three days before we get it back."

"I don't have the time. Would it be possible to look at the master?"

The clerk shook his head in a slow *no*. "No way. We got rules here. The masters stay in the vault. No way I can get one out. You'll just have to keep your cool and come back when the new print is ready."

They were alone in the room. Troy took out his wallet and extracted a twenty dollar bill. He placed it on the counter; the clerk's eyes followed it. "Couldn't we make an exception just this once?" Troy asked. The clerk took a step backwards and looked around.

"Man, you trying to bribe me?"

"Yes."

"It's a deal. I don't like the mothers that run this place." The bill vanished and fifteen seconds later the film appeared in its place. The clerk touched his finger to his lips. "This going to be our secret. Use the first viewer there and let me have the film back before you split."

"Thanks. This shouldn't take long."

But it did. He could find nothing on the tenth of January, no matter how he searched, that might possibly be relevant. He went through this issue of the paper three times to make sure. All right then, keep searching. Bob Kleiman had said that he couldn't be certain of the exact date. He would just have to keep looking.

An hour later he found the item.

This was it. It had to be; it fit perfectly. A small article on the second page.

INVASION SCARE IN MARYLAND
Mysterious Explosions and
Lights Cause Great Alarm

*The possibility of a German invasion alarmed
hundreds as a series of explosions and flaring
lights near Clewerwall broke the silence of the
night. Police and firemen were called out and
found the site easily since the explosions continued for over two hours on a rocky promi-
nence close to Saunders Farm. It was the
work of pranksters, reported Police Chief
O'Sullivan. A metal box was recovered that
had been filled with flare launchers of the
kind used at sea in time of distress. The
perpetrators of the hoax were not found.*

There it was. This *had* to be it. Troy returned the
roll of film and had a photoprint made of the page.
When he left he found himself in the middle of
heavy traffic as the civil service employees poured
out of the offices in their endless waves. By the
time he had returned to the project it was after
six.

"Message for you," the guard at the gate said.
"Doctor Kleiman says for you to meet him in the
director's office."

"Thanks. I'm on my way."

Roxanne Delcourt had the bar open and was
stirring a mixer full of gibsons when Troy came in.
Bob Kleiman was already sipping a large one.

"Any luck?" he asked.

"A lot," Troy said. "McCulloch stole the original

newspaper record, or at least someone did. But I got hold of a duplicate—here's a copy. With the exact date."

"A drink?" Roxanne asked, while Kleiman read the clipping. She passed it over. "Bob caught me before I left for the night, told me what you two had found out. He thinks that you're a better detective than Dick Tracy."

"I am. Thanks, just what I needed." Troy drank deep. "It was really just a matter of persistence. McCulloch left a trail—and we followed it."

"That's easy to say now. But none of this would have been discovered if you hadn't been here. Aside from the McCulloch matter, what you have found out will have the most tremendous impact on our work. I suppose we would have eventually worked out the reverse tau, but we hadn't even scheduled experiments in that direction. What we have here is a whole new ball game. Thanks to you."

"Please—I'll get a swollen head. I'm glad that this has helped you in your work, but I still have my own to do. McCulloch is a thief and a murderer and I am staying with this until I find him."

Kleiman handed the copy of the newspaper article to Roxanne. "Not much chance of that if your quarry has slipped away through time. If he's done that—forget it."

"Why?"

"Well, for one good reason, if he went back more than fifty years, why then he is surely dead by now and the case is closed."

"What if he went back only a few years, taking the gold with him? If he did that, why then he is still out there somewhere. If he is—then I intend to find him. Therefore my next question, the important one. If he did use the machine to move back in time—can you find out exactly how far he went? Do you think that the last big experiment you found in the record, that this was really him?"

"Don't know. I got sidetracked after you left and didn't work out the figures. This whole break-through became so important that the reason for the entire investigation vanished from my pointed head. Sorry. I'll get onto it."

"Finish your drink first," Roxanne said. "What's done is done. Part of history. It will wait."

"True enough," Troy said. "But I would still like to know the date. It might reveal the motive."

Kleiman said, "Shlep that gold back in time, invest it, pop back to the present, then walk around to the bank and collect it and you are an instant millionaire."

"Wrong," Roxanne said. "You're forgetting the most important thing."

"I am," Kleiman agreed. "It won't work, of course. Time travel is a one way trip. You can go— but you can't get back. Maybe you could if you took all of lab nine with you. If you didn't do that, why then you are just not going to return. But that still doesn't destroy my theory. Take that amount of gold back to 1920, during the depression when there were no liquid assets, and you would be a rich man. I bet that's what he did."

Troy shook his head. "It just doesn't ring true. The motive doesn't fit the man. As far as we can tell McCulloch had everything material that he wanted right here. So the simple explanation of going back in time to be wealthy, that doesn't fit. It doesn't explain the books that he read, or all of the research he did. And what about the stolen blueprints and the gun? He had something in mind, some sort of motive that we have yet to discover."

"I'm with you now, Sherlock," Kleiman agreed. "Find the motive and you'll find the man. Therefore I put my rusty-trusty pocket calculator to work. I've still got the readings here. It *could* have been a man who was sent back. The mass of the object was ninety-five point four five kilos."

"The colonel couldn't have weighed that much," Roxanne said.

"No," Troy agreed. "But that weight would be right if he were carrying a bag—along with a quarter of a million dollars worth of gold."

"Of course. Let's see what Bob comes up with."

"I've got to make a correction first," Kleiman muttered, working away at the keys. "The arrival date was a good deal distant from the one that I predicted. So we put the difference into seconds, good enough for a rough estimate now, divide the difference into the time . . ."

They watched him in silence, each deep in thought. Roxanne Delcourt found it hard to even consider the colonel who had started all this, because the impact of the discovery was too great. The project that she had devoted so much time and energy to was opening out in new and exciting ways.

Troy could not forget McCulloch that easily. A killer. There was a very sick man locked away inside the smooth exterior, hidden so well that no one had ever suspected him. Could he be found and brought to justice? There was no telling. This entire matter was getting too deep.

"Got it," Kleiman announced, waving the calculator over his head. "Now this is not exact, since I have rounded out the figures to simplify the equation for the moment. But there can't be more than just a few days error, say a week at the outside, either way. Of that I am pretty sure . . ."

"Robert," Roxanne broke in. "Enough of the lecture. The date, if you please."

"Yes, sorry. Allowing for the variations I just mentioned, the ninety-five kilogram plus mass was sent back in time over one-hundred and twenty-four years. So, Troy, you don't have to worry about finding Old Snarly anymore. He's been long since dead and buried. But that still leaves the very question."

"I know," Troy said. "Motivation."

"Absolutely correct. The question that lies behind everything. Why on earth did he want to leave the pleasures, pains and antibiotics of the twentieth century to go back to the year of our Lord, eighteen fifty-eight?"

SEVENTEEN

The stack of documents that made up the McCulloch pile was very impressive. Assembled together they stood at least a foot high. Troy had transferred them all from the house on Massachusetts Avenue to the office in the security building at the lab, the one that had formerly been the colonel's. Now his. It was a far better place to study them, here where McCulloch himself had worked.

Colonel Wesley McCulloch, Wes to his friends. Troy settled himself behind the desk, pulled a ruled yellow pad towards him, and wrote *Wes* at the top. He wanted to get to know the man, to get inside his skin and really understand him. The clues he was looking for were somewhere in this stack of paper. If he studied them closely enough, learned what made the man really tick—then followed his trail through the documented history of his life—the reason for everything that had happened would surely emerge.

He broke for coffee at eleven o'clock, stretched and rubbed at the small of his back. It was tiring, just sitting there and leaning over the desk. But the yellow pad was filling up and a shadowy picture of the man was beginning to emerge. He hated to leave it. Bringing the coffee back to the office he stood and looked out of the window. Just as McCulloch must have stood and looked numberless times. He must learn to see with that man's eyes. Whatever he looked at now, he wanted to see it just as Wes McCulloch had seen it. A knock at the door cut through his thoughts. He turned about just as it opened.

"My name is Van Diver," the uniformed man in the doorway said. "Major Van Diver."

He walked in and, over his shoulder, Troy could see a number of officers and noncoms in the outer office; then the door closed.

"May I ask just what the hell is going on?" Troy said.

The major nodded, his pink jowels flapping when he moved his head. He had thin blond hair and obviously artificial white teeth; his watery blue eyes blinked from behind steel-rimmed glasses. "I'm relieving you," he said. "Here are the orders. Issued this morning at the Pentagon. Lieutenant . . ."

He lingered over this last word, a tight little cold smile on his lips—which opened slightly as his teeth peeked out between them, then slipped back. He must have had a badly fitting upper plate; he kept pushing it back and forth with his tongue. Troy ignored this disconcerting sight as he read through the official papers. They seemed very much in order. The wheels of the military were finally grinding on this case and he had been squeezed out. He handed back the orders.

"All right, Major. It will take me about a half an hour to clear my desk and get all my papers together—"

"No. All of the records stay here—and you get out as of now. The troops outside don't know it but *I* know what's going on around here. I know that you are just a sergeant attached to one of the spook outfits. When I said you were relieved, *sergeant*, I meant it. In every way. I don't hold with all the goddamn undercover agencies that proliferate under the present administration. The Army can conduct its own investigations of an officer; that's what we have military intelligence for. You took over this investigation at a low level, something to do with gold. That's finished now. This is a major case. You're out. The records stay here. I hope that I've made that clear. Dismissed, sergeant."

Troy opened his mouth to speak—then slowly closed it. He had received his orders. That was it. Period. There was nothing that he could say that would change the situation. The work he had done, the work that still needed doing, the theories he had, none of this was relevant. He was out and that's all there was to it. He had no choice, no choice at all.

He snapped to attention and saluted; Major Van Diver returned it. Then he turned on his heel, went to the office door, opened it, and walked out. Through the office, not looking to the left or right, and out to the parking lot to his car. He started it up and drove slowly down the drive to the gate, watching it swing wide at his approach. The guard nodded and he waved back as he drove past. Only after he was well clear of the grounds did the knot of tension in his midrif slowly begin to ease away.

He smiled, then laughed aloud as he drove.

"I've been relieved!" He shouted as the buildings grew smaller in his rearview mirror, then vanished from sight. "New orders cut. The specialists taking over! Well go ahead, you government issue assholes. You pinheads are never going to find out a thing. You're *dumb*. You relieved me—but you never even thought to take back my security pass."

He patted the pocket where it lay. By the numbers, he knew how they would work. Knew how little they would find out. Let them. This case was his and he was still working on it. Or was he? That was really up to the admiral. He would have to see him at once; he headed for the District. On the way in he passed a barbecue drive-in and realized that he hadn't eaten for over six hours. After finishing a sandwich he telephoned the admiral's secretary from the phone booth, in the gas station next door. Yes, the admiral was in. He would see Troy in thirty minutes.

Admiral Colonne did not seem surprised in the slightest by the Army's action in relieving Troy. He sucked on his pipe and nodded as he listened to the details.

"SOP," he said. "This agency has performed its function, we have watched the watcher and have made our report. Now the watchman is gone. End of our responsibility. The regulars move in and we step aside. Standard operating procedure. The case is closed."

"I'm sorry, sir, but I don't believe that it is. You assigned me to investigate the colonel, to determine the reason why he was buying all that gold. That fact hasn't been determined yet. In the meantime McCulloch has disappeared, after committing a number of crimes which the police and G2 are investigating. All well and good. But the original case is still open and unsolved."

The admiral nodded. "I can understand your point of view. But what do you think you can possibly accomplish—that the other departments can't?"

"I can find out what really happened. I've had some good results so far, you've seen my report. And I've really only just started. There has to be a tie-in between the gold, the murders and the thefts. When I find the answer to one I'll know the answer to them all."

"You believe that you can do this?"

"I think that I can, sir. After all of the time and energy already invested in this case, I'm only asking for a bit more time. At least the chance to try. Am I still on the case?"

The admiral gazed through the cloud of smoke for a moment in silence. Then nodded. "You are. I agree with your thinking. As far as this department is concerned the investigation of Colonel McCulloch is still in the active file. What do you intend to do next?"

"Ask the admiral's permission to contact all of the agencies who submitted documents on the investigation of McCulloch. I want copies of their reports. That major booted me out so fast I couldn't even take along my notes."

"Impossible. Although you and I think differently, QCIC is officially locked out of this investigation. Even if I requested the information the other agencies involved would be sure to refuse.

"Damn!" Troy jumped to his feet and paced the length of the conference room. Slamming his fist into his palm, over and over again. "That tears it.

I'll never get the man without those records. I'm stupid. I should have made copies of the documents the instant they arrived."

The admiral nodded agreement. "You've come late to the decision that I reached decades ago. Establish a working routine. The instant a paper comes through the front door a copy is made for the files. I'm sure that after this little object lesson you will agree on the intelligence of that procedure . . ."

"Did you—were copies made of all these files?"

"Of course. I said that it was standard procedure. I'll have duplicates of them made now and sent to that cubby in the basement that you have been using for an office." He raised his hand. "No, don't thank me. QCIC is my department. I want to see this case resolved to our satisfaction just as much as you do."

Troy could not contain his enthusiasm. "It's tremendous. I have to thank you. You've saved my bacon. I'm going to crack this thing yet."

"I look forward to receiving your report."

Troy started to leave, then turned before he reached the door. "May I ask you a personal question, sir?"

"You may ask. There is no guarantee that I will answer."

"It's not really that personal, more a point of information. It's, just what did you do in the Navy? I'm not knocking the Navy, don't misunderstand me. In fact, the way you run this intelligence operation, maybe I have been wrong about Navy organization."

"Then again maybe you haven't. The Navy does have a tendency to work by the book and to show little imagination. Perhaps that is why I am here.

Then again—perhaps I never was in the Navy at all. Consider yourself, you have never been a lieutenant—but you're wearing the uniform of one right now. I suggest we leave it at that for the time being. I look forward to receiving your progress reports."

It was probably the best answer that he could expect. Troy went down to his cubby and buried himself in the work. The papers gradually spread out to cover the desk, and even slopped over onto the floor as he tried to arrange them in some sort of coherent order. It was only after he had worked his way through the entire, laboriously detailed FBI report, that he hit paydirt. A three page evaluation of McCulloch's personality that had been analyzed from his personal history and medical records by a government psychiatrist.

It was heavy going, and very Freudian. Much was made of the colonel's having left home at an early age; this opportunity to speculate about maternal rejection and sibling rivalry led to some fancy theorizing. Troy flipped through the pages until he came to the summation.

It is my conclusion therefore, tempered as I have stated earlier by the regrettable fact that I have never met the subject, that he has a strong paranoid personality, whose adjustment to life is further hampered by schizophrenic interludes. He feels that he has been passed over by others less qualified than he, that his lack of success is not his own responsibility, but rather the fault of society. His service in the structured military has enabled him to operate in a reasonably satisfactory manner despite these handicaps. But his military record, and the charges of murder during active service in Vietnam, even though the charges were later dropped, is evidence of strong homicidal tendencies. It is not that he does not know right from wrong, but rather that he believes himself right at all times and wishes to impose his will on those he knows to be wrong. Most important, in a serving officer, is his repressed but still violently held anti-Negro sentiments. His early membership in the Klan supports this conclusion. His deepest motivations are those of hatred. I firmly believe that he will not suppress these feelings much longer.

"Didn't need a shrink to tell me that," Troy said, dropping the papers onto the laden desk, then unconsciously wiping his fingers on his pants leg. "Felt that the first time I saw him. At least this proves it. But what else do I know?"

One by one he picked up what he felt were the relevant documents and stacked them to one side, away from the others. He tapped them with his fingers, speaking aloud to clarify his thoughts.

"The shrink says that McCulloch is a homicidal, violently racist nut case from way back in the Mississippi slashes. Now we have to add to that the police report that he killed three people in order to push his secret plan through. All we know about this plan is that it involves a large quantity of gold, as well as a sub machine-gun, complete with blueprints for same. Since McCulloch went to a great deal of effort to obtain these items we can be reasonably certain that they were important to him. If he traveled back in time the chances are that he brought them with him. To the year eighteen fifty-eight. Why? And why that year? What was important about it? Nothing that I can remember. A relatively quiet period in American history, with nothing much happening to make it memorable in any way. A lot of politicking and trouble between the different states, but the Civil War didn't start for two and a half more years.

"I don't *know* what he is up to!" Troy shouted, in sudden anger, slamming his fists down on the piles of paper. "All I know is that he is up to no good, no damned good at all. People are going to get killed—or why else is he carrying that weapon around? And, knowing the major, I don't need a crystal ball to tell me that a lot of these people are going to be black. I'm sure of that."

But anger wasn't the solution. Any explanations of the colonel's motivations would be found by reason and logic, not by emotion. Troy tore off his notes and put them to one side, then started a fresh sheet of paper. Question: what had the colonel taken with him? Answer: gold, the gun, the blueprints.

Question: how did these fit together?

Answer: not easily. Think. Gold is money, the kind of money that is good any time, any place. When McCulloch arrived back in 1858 he would be a rich man—and he was certainly going to be rich in the South. No chance of him going North! He would dive into Dixie, good old slave-holding Dixie. He would be right at home there. This alone would be motivation enough for a man with his prejudices to make the trip back through time. Live in the land he loved best, where integration was just a mathematical term. Great. But why did he pick the year 1858? Within three short years the Civil War would begin and the world the colonel loved would disappear forever. If he went back to 1830, or even earlier, he could live a full life cracking the whip over the darkies' backs. He would love that. But this way, 1858, he only had a couple of years to enjoy the fun.

But he had taken more than gold. The gun. The approaching war—and the deadly submachine gun. They went together. They fitted together.

Troy had a sudden, terrible and depressing feeling that he had hit on the truth. No, it couldn't be possible. But it *was* possible. It had been done. The colonel had gone back in time with his gold and his blueprints and his gun.

The psychiatrist's report had suggested that McCulloch was a paranoid with criminal schizophrenic tendencies. That was another way of saying that he was insane. And his idea was insane. Just about the most insane idea that a certified nut case had ever dreamed up.

Colonel McCulloch had traveled back in time to change the outcome of the Civil War.

He wanted to alter history so that the South would win.

EIGHTEEN

"What exactly is the question that you are asking? What things are special about the Sten gun? I am afraid that I don't take your meaning, sir," Dryer said. The curator turned the submachine gun over and over in his hands as though he were searching for an answer.

"Then I'm not expressing myself very well," Troy said. "Let me try again. We have a common ground in that neither of us look at guns in the same way that the man in the street does. You are curator of the technological archives here, a specialist in weapons of all kinds. I'm a specialist, too. I've used them in the field. As did Colonel McCulloch . . ."

"The colonel, yes. You were in about him some days ago weren't you? Have you recovered my missing items yet?"

"No, but the case is still being worked on. That's

why I need to know more about the gun the colonel walked away with. Is it a particularly accurate weapon? Does it have a high rate of fire, or low rate of stoppages?"

"No, quite the opposite in fact. It was a gun designed in a great rush at the beginning of the Second World War. The rate of fire is slow, it is not very accurate—and the clip has a tendency to jam."

"Not very attractive, indeed," Troy said. He picked the gun up himself now and ran his finger along the crude welds that held the receiver to the metal tube that formed the stock. "Were many of them manufactured?"

"Over four million in all."

"That's an awful lot of guns. But, why? If the weapon was as unsatisfactory as you say, why on earth did they make so many?"

"Young man, you must understand the situation that existed at the time. The Germans were winning the war hands down. France and the Low Countries had been lost and the British were facing this deadly foe almost single-handedly. And they were fighting with few if any modern weapons. Despite all of the clear lessons about the future of modern warfare that the Spanish Civil War had spelled out, the British began the war without a submachine gun of *any* kind. It was a time of panic, the Germans were expected to invade at any moment. So any weapon was better than no weapon. This particular gun, the Sten gun, was conceived in an atmosphere of extreme haste and emergency. Although it had all of the shortcomings I mentioned, it was nevertheless very simple to produce. Subcontractors literally made parts in converted barns and sheds. And it was cheap, each one costing in the neighborhood of around two pounds and ten shillings if my memory serves me correctly. That is less than six dollars. An unbelievable sum in this day of multi-million dollar weapons. So Sten guns were churned out by the millions. This ugly little gun proved to be one of the most outstanding weapons in the Allied armory. And that was only the Mark One, mind you. The Mark Two had an even more interesting history."

Dryer laid the gun to one side, then unwrapped the other weapon that he had brought out of the storeroom. If it were possible, this one was even uglier than the previous one. There were file marks on the receiver, rough welds on the bolt housing. Dryer patted it affectionately.

"Over two million of these were made—in less than two years. Probably the most basic weapon ever conceived, certainly the most basic sub-machine gun. The barrel is a simple steel tube held in place by a screwed-on jacket, the stock nothing but a piece of bent tubing. See, the firing mechanism could not be simpler, little more than a bolt and a spring. You pull the trigger and it blasts away. Sprays bullets like water from a hose. A deadly—yet simple—weapon."

"Simple is the word. It couldn't be cruder if it were made by hand."

Dryer smiled and patted the gun. "But it was, Mr. Harmon. Resistance fighters in many countries *did* make copies by hand. This one was manufactured in Copenhagen by the Danish resistance, right under the Germans' noses."

The pieces of McCulloch's plan were beginning to click into place. Troy remembered very little about the weapons that the Civil War had been fought with—but he was certain that no gun like this had existed at the time. The colonel might be insane—but that did not mean that he was stupid. He knew weapons, he knew tactics—and he knew war. He had fought in Nam where a primitive army, fighting with weapons not even as good as this one, had licked the most technologically advanced country in the world. McCulloch must have learned his lesson well.

"Is there anything else I can tell you?" The words cut through Troy's dark thoughts, and he shook his head.

"No, no thank you, Mr. Dryer. You've been of immense help. We'll let you know if there are any developments in this case. But just between the two of us, I think you had better write the gun and the blueprints off as shrinkage. You'll not get them back."

"Oh, dear, that is bad news. The blueprints can of course be replaced, but the weapon itself was unique."

"Sorry. Good day, Mr. Dryer, and thank you again for the help."

The drive out to the laboratory was a quick one, and Troy had only a single moment's worry as he drove up to the outer gate and the guard waved him down. Had Major Van Diver remembered his security pass—and had it canceled?

"Message for you, Lieutenant. From Doctor Delcourt. She says for you to come to her office when you get in."

"Thanks, Charley, I'll go there now."

He drove the opposite way around the buildings to avoid the security office. If they had forgotten about his pass he wasn't going to remind them about it by letting them see him now. He used the back stairs that emerged close to the director's office.

The secretary sent him right in. Bob Kleiman was there, sprawled back in a chair and sipping from a mug of coffee; he waved hello with his free hand. Roxanne looked up from the papers spread across her desk and smiled.

"Troy, come in," she said. "You got my message then. Your office said that you weren't in, but they would let you know."

"I was on my way here in any case; the guard at the gate told me you wanted to see me."

"Yes. To let you know that we have pinned down exactly the temporal displacement your Colonel McCulloch used." She picked a sheet of paper off her desk. "He returned to this date, to the Fourth of July, 1858. It appears that our friend the colonel must be quite a patriot."

"I doubt that very much. He must have other reasons altogether. Probably wanted to be sure that he could arrive there without being seen. On the glorious Fourth everyone might be watching the parades and that kind of thing."

"I'm sure that you are right. I never thought about it that way."

"I have," Troy said, grimly. "For some time now I have been trying to get inside the colonel's head, to reason like him—react like him. I think that I have succeeded to some degree. But it's not very nice in there. The colonel is a sickie. I won't go into every step of the logic involved, but I am pretty certain now that I know what plan he had in mind. It may sound a little far-fetched, so try not to laugh when I tell you."

"Nothing is laughable about that man," Kleiman said. "Allan Harper was my friend. That poisoning, that was an awful way to die."

They listened, patiently, with disbelief at first—then with growing understanding. "You make a strong case," Roxanne said, "and what you say could be true. It is an insane idea—but McCulloch is no longer sane, is he?"

"Nutty as a fruit cake," Kleiman said. "And let me tell you, I hope that Troy is right and that this is what he has done. Because it means that he has gone forever and, from our point of view, he is long since dead. He may have lived for a time in the past, but at least he never brought this particular insane plan to fruition."

"How do you know?" Troy asked.

"Because history hasn't changed, has it? The South lost the war and that is that."

"They lost the war here—but perhaps they didn't in a parallel of time," Roxanne said.

Troy lifted his eyebrows. "I don't follow you."

"One of the many theories of the nature of time. It rejects the most accepted theory which holds that time is like a river, sweeping from the past, through the focal point of the present, and on into the future. Unchangeable. We can watch it, but we can't affect it. A modern version of the ancient argument of predestination. But this comes into instant conflict with the argument for free will. If the future cannot be changed, why then we are all just puppets of time, predestined to live out our lives with no more freedom of choice than actors in a movie film. But if we have free will, and can alter our future, then from the point of view of the future—we will have altered the past."

"Deep stuff," Kleiman said. "Physics shading off into philosophy. But we really have to think about these problems now, since we know that travel through time is possible. Which brings us to this other theory about the nature of time, the multi-branching time of parallel possibilities. For instance, let us say that the British killed George Washington as a traitor before he could win the revolution. If that had happened, the US today would still be a British colony. So perhaps there exists another universe where this did happen, a parallel world to our own. There may be an infinity of such universes, each one brought about by a probability in time, a choice, a selection made that launched a different possible world."

"Some theory," Troy said.

"Indeed it is," Kleiman agreed. "Which returns us to our starting point. If the theory of parallel probabilities exists, then it doesn't matter to us what McCulloch did back in the past. It can't affect us. If he accomplished nothing, then our world remains the way it is. If he got away with his fiendish plans, then he started another branch in time and we are still not affected. But if time can be changed for us—and it hasn't changed, why then his plans have failed."

"You have forgotten another possibility," Troy said. "Perhaps his plans failed because someone stopped him. Someone from the present time who knew what he was up to, who went back and prevented him from carrying those plans through."

"An interesting speculation," Roxanne agreed, "but one which we will never be able to answer. It's another time paradox. Either the colonel failed because he was doomed to fail, therefore there is no need for someone to stop him, or he was stopped by someone from the present. But since we know he has been stopped there is no reason to stop him. What's done is done, and it is certainly not our problem."

"I still think that it is," Troy said grimly. "The colonel, I can't forget him. Nor can I forget what he has done—and what he might do. Whatever you say, I still feel that he has to be stopped."

"If he could be stopped, fine, but how can that be done?" Kleiman asked. "I think you will find that is not an easy question to answer. He has escaped justice here by fleeing through time. Perhaps the best thing for all of us to do is just to forget him. We can do that if we concentrate on the fact that as far as this world is concerned, he has long since been dead and buried in the past."

"That's all right for us here, today," Troy agreed. "But what about the people whose lives he might affect? We know that he is there, in the past, with some murderous plan. Isn't there a way that he could be apprehended?"

"I doubt it," Kleiman said. "What do we do? Send a message back through time to the police? Warn them to be on the lookout for one Wesley McCulloch wanted for murder in the next century?"

"No, that's impossible, I realize that. But you have the time machine. There must be some way it can be utilized to stop him. If only there were some way to send a posse after him, to bring him in. It wouldn't even need a posse. One man could do it. One determined man. McCulloch wouldn't be expecting it, not to be tracked down through time."

"Agreed. But what you are talking about is too much to ask any man to do. To leave the world where he has been born, to go back in time to the past, to a more dangerous existence. And to know that this was forever, a one-way trip. No, Troy, forget it. The colonel's gone—and good riddance I say."

"Yes. I know that he's gone from here—but I can't forget that he is still causing trouble somewhere, or somewhere else."

"But we have analyzed that situation in great detail," Kleiman said. "There are no options open, no way that it can be done. I think you will find that you have posed a question that is impossible to answer. He has escaped justice in the present by fleeing through time. The best thing that you can do now is just to forget him. As far as the world is concerned he is dead and buried in the past."

"No," Troy said. "I won't forget him."

He said it firmly, without emotion. He had reached a decision, something he knew that he had been thinking about for days now at a subconscious level. The realization had finally surfaced, and with it the knowledge that the decision had already been made.

"McCulloch is not going to escape. Because I'm going after him."

NINETEEN

Silence greeted Troy's words. Kleiman started to say something, then changed his mind. It was Roxanne Delcourt who finally spoke.

"That's quite a decision to make. Have you thought it through clearly?"

"No, not really. It's more of an emotional decision than a logical one. I've been on this case since the beginning. I've met the colonel, just once, and I didn't like him, not at all. Since then I've seen what he has done—and I'm certain that he plans worse. I have grown to loathe the man. He must be stopped. And right now, from where I stand, it looks like I'm the only one who can do it."

"But—it's irreversible," Kleiman said. "You can go—but you can't come back."

Troy nodded slowly. "I know that. But I'm not going that far. It will still be the US of A. Only it will be a few years ago. And it will certainly be a

new kind of experience! Added to this is the un-
arguable fact that there really isn't that much here
that I am going to miss. Maybe I'm being too
morbid or depressed, but, personally, things
haven't been quite the same since my wife died.
Going on two years now. She had been ill a long
time. It wasn't very nice for her. And it hit me
hard. I was ready for a section eight there for a
while. But the work has helped, keeps my mind off
how I feel. Helps me sleep when I'm tired. Helps
with the depression. I felt suicidal for awhile, but
basically I'm not the suicide type. Sorry. I don't
know why I'm telling you this."

"Because we're your friends," Roxanne said.

"Yes, I suppose you're right. It's not easy to
make friends in the military. You move around a
lot, particularly in the kind of work I'm involved
in. With Lily, I suppose I didn't need any other
friends. I have no family to speak of. I might as
well follow the colonel." He had been staring
down at his clasped hands while he talked; now he
looked up and smiled. "It's no big deal. But I'm
going to do it."

"You can't!" Kleiman exploded. "Look at what
you're leaving behind. The technology, the
advances in science, the things that are happening
in research . . ."

"Bob. None of that means anything to me. I
don't live your kind of life. The kind of work I do—
I can do just as well in 1858 or 1958. And what I
really want to do is nail that son-of-a-bitch. Are
you going to help me?"

"No! It's suicide. I won't be a part of it!" His
anger slowly wilted before Troy's calm gaze; he
lowered his eyes. "All right. You talked me into it.
But I still don't like it." He smiled suddenly and

clapped his hands together. "But, by God, what an experiment into the nature of time! What we can learn! I'll do it, but you have to promise to help. We must think of a way for you to send a message to us. What do you think, Roxanne?"

"I think that we should help Troy, if he feels that this is what he must do. Out of gratitude, if nothing else, after what he did to force us to discover the true nature of our machine. But, Troy, shouldn't you take this up with your superiors?"

"No. They'll only think that I'm insane. The Army will, at least. I think I'll tell Admiral Colonne, the man I'm working for now. I have a feeling that he will understand. There's another thing, and I'm sorry to have to ask, but won't you have to make a report about this? That could get you into trouble?"

"Not really," Roxanne said. "I file reports, but I don't include records of every experiment. If we do this, do what you ask, don't worry about us. Though I can't help wishing that you would change your mind."

"Thank you for the consideration. But I still feel that it has to be done."

Now that the decision had been made, Troy wanted to be alone, to think it out. And there was really little else to be said. As soon as he could he made his excuses and left. Before returning to his apartment he drove back to Massachusetts Avenue; he wanted to get McCulloch's file. The night man admitted him and he was just putting the papers into an envelope when the admiral looked in.

"You've had over twenty-four hours to work on those records. Any conclusions yet?"

"Yes, sir. The evidence seems quite conclusive

to me, but I'm not sure that you will agree with my theory."

"I will—as long as you believe that Colonel McCulloch has traveled back in time in an attempt to change the outcome of the Civil War. Don't gape like that, man. Sit down and be comfortable. And I'll sit over here and light my pipe while you detail the steps by which you reached that conclusion."

"But, admiral, you . . . well—"

"Surprised you? Why? I've seen the same reports that you have and kept my own copies of all these files. I like to keep abreast of all the operations around here. Particularly one as fascinatingly exotic as this one. At first I couldn't believe that the homicidal colonel would have had the imagination for a thing like this. But then it became obvious. His obsession with race and class, coupled with his love of the old and vanished South. The moment he discovered what the Gnomen Project was about this idea must have struck him. And it helps to be mad if you have a plan like this. Insane or not, he went about putting the idea into practice in the most logical way. Buying gold, the most practical way of transporting wealth to a different era. And the Sten gun, that was the giveaway to me. A simple and deadly weapon that can be made by anyone with a little metalworking experience. At this point we can't know what he plans to do with the guns, but we can be sure that it is nothing good. Have you reached any decision about what the next step should be?"

"Yes. I'm going after him."

"Good. I am in full agreement. You have reached the only possible decision. Someone must run him to earth."

"But some people might think that following him is just as insane as his decision to escape into the past."

"Yes, but I am not some people. I am in charge of this singularly important organization. Here in QCIC we have the ultimate responsibility for the nation's security. It is obvious that we must protect that security in the present and in the future. What is not quite as obvious is that our responsibility extends into the past as well. Colonel McCulloch shall not be permitted to threaten the existence of this nation. I can now tell you, quite frankly, how pleased I am with your decision. If you had given me any other answer I would have been forced to take you off the case and have you reassigned. Now I don't have to. I must congratulate you. Even though we have worked together for but a short time I can say, truthfully, that you are the best operative I have ever had. Probably because you think just the way I do. A very left-handed compliment."

Troy smiled. "Perhaps it is, but I understand it —and appreciate it. I thank you. But, let me ask you, what would you have done if I hadn't told you that I was going after McCulloch?"

"I would have gone after him myself. I couldn't assign anyone to a one-way trip of this kind. You might as well know that the powers that be are after me to retire. I don't want to. But I would jump at a chance to do what you are doing. If I were forced to leave this department, why then a voyage like this would be far superior to retirement. You are very lucky, my boy."

"In a way, I think I am."

"You are. This is a great adventure you are embarking on. I envy you. Now, to details. Have you discussed this with your contacts on the project?"

"I have. They agreed to help."

"They couldn't say no. Your trip will tie in with everything they are trying to do. Next stop. Finances. How much do you have in the bank and how much can you raise?"

"Nothing like the colonel's nest egg. I'm not rich."

"Neither was he. Just crooked. He borrowed money, a large building loan, and he used his house as security—a fact that he forgot to mention when he sold the house. In addition he has a number of personal loans outstanding, as well as large cash advances on all of his credit cards. No more than a quarter of that money was his own— the rest he embezzled. How much can you raise?"

"About five thousand dollars."

"I thought so. Not enough. Here's a check for twenty thousand dollars from our special fund. Deposit it in your bank tomorrow. Then get over to this shop, De Vrou's, one of the largest coin dealers in the country. Get as many coins as you can easily carry. McCulloch had long range plans so he could take the time to sell his gold. You won't have to bother doing that if you take the coinage with you. I'm also arranging for a weapon, but I'll get back to you later on that. And I'm preparing a list of items that you will need to take with you. You must make one up as well and we will compare them. Take your time, make the list a complete one since you will not be able to return for anything you might have forgotten. We will also have to think of a way for you to prepare some kind of report for us that we will be able to find. And there is one thing more. It has to do with your race. Slavery was still legal in 1858. So I suggest that documents division should draw up papers for you proving that you are a free man. Is that satisfactory?"

"I hadn't thought about that but, yes, it should be done."

"Good. That seems to be everything. Unless you have any questions?"

"Just one, admiral." Troy looked at the check, then folded it and put it away. "The important one. I can't very well convince the authorities to arrest McCulloch after I find him. So what should I do?"

"You know the answer to that as well as I do. But if you wish me to put it into the form of an order I will be happy to. What must be done has been obvious since you reached your decision to follow Colonel McCulloch. You are to search for him and you are to find him.

"And when you do—kill him."

TWENTY

"American coins only?" the clerk asked.

"That's right," Troy said.

"Any particular denomination that you are interested in?"

"Not really. Just as long as they are not later than 1859. What do you have?"

The young man stepped back and raised his eyebrows. "If you wait a moment, I'll have Mr. De Vrou himself come to help you. He's very much a specialist in early American coinage."

The clerk hurried away; Troy looked around the store. He had never been a collector as a boy, neither coins nor stamps—nor anything else for that matter. But he could see the appeal of a hobby like this. The multicolored bank notes, from all over the world, were immensely attractive. The coins came in unexpected sizes and shapes. He was bent over a glass case looking at a Roman denarius when the owner came up.

"May I be of help, sir? You are interested in the purchase of American coins?"

"That's right. The condition isn't too important, but the date is. I want nothing later than 1859."

"You do!" De Vrou leaned forward confidentially. "Would it be asking too much, sir, for you to tell me why? I can be of great aid to you in obtaining exactly what you need."

"No particular reason. I'm just interested in that period."

"Please, understand, I can be most discreet. There is something I should know."

"Like what?"

"Like—*why!* I know coins, sir, know all about them. But there is something here now that I don't know and I wish you would let me in on it. One hand washes the other, as they say. I will give you a very fair price on your purchases. But would you please tell me what is so important about this period? I ask because another gentleman was in here some months ago making the same kind of purchase."

"Tall man, sharp nose, gray hair?"

"The very man!"

"He's the one who told me I should buy these coins. I don't know why. I'll tell him you asked."

"Then you know him? Know his name?"

"No, not really. We just meet by chance once in awhile. Now—the coins if you please."

The coin dealer sighed. The secret would remain a secret, at least for the time. "Yes, I would appreciate your letting him know." He placed a velvet lined tray on the counter. "Please inform him that I have a new shipment of coins that will interest him. See, here is one, a fine twenty-dollar gold-piece . . ."

"I'll take it. What other denominations do you have?"

"In gold, here. A ten dollar, a five and a three. I'm sorry, but I have no two-and-a-half dollar gold-pieces right now. But here is an almost mint gold dollar."

Troy picked up the tiny coin, the size of his fingernail. "I'll take this as well. Are there any coins of a smaller denomination?"

"Over here. Most interesting. Half dollar, quarter dollar, a one cent and a three cent coin."

"No nickels?"

"Of course not, sir. You will have your little joke. We both know there were no five cent pieces at this time. The half dime instead. And of course the dime itself. Here is a beauty that dates to just after the revolution. The disme, as it was called then, a middle English variation of the old French *disme* from Latin *decima*, or a tenth part. Later corrupted to dime."

Troy packed his purchases into his case, then looked at his watch and hurried out. He had only twenty minutes to get to the stable for his riding lesson. The colonel had the advantage on him there since he had served in the cavalry. Troy wasn't happy with the lessons, he was still aching from the last one, but if he was going to do anything besides walk he had better learn to handle a horse.

He was very glad of the admiral's help. Their lists of necessities matched in many ways, but the admiral had thought of a number of items that he hadn't even considered. Things that he had always taken for granted. Like antibiotics, which he discovered had only been in existence for less than forty years. Those sealed metal tins might very well save his life one day. And halazone tablets.

Water purification was unheard of in the middle of the nineteenth century; plague and disease were a constant menace. His arms still hurt from all the preventative injections that he had taken. There had also been a hurried trip to the dentist where two gold crowns on his teeth were replaced with porcelain caps.

After the riding lesson he went straight to the house on Massachusetts Avenue. Just sitting down hurt now. The admiral was waiting for him. He pushed over a long-barreled steel pistol.

"This is a Colt revolver made in 1857. A precision instrument, even if the cartridges are pin fire. They are slower to load than center-fire cartridges, which weren't introduced until the 1860's, but they work just as well. The pistol resembles the original exactly, but the barrel and chambers, all of the important parts of the firing mechanism, are of modern steel. I've had a thousand rounds made up and can get more if you need them. We have a small shooting gallery in the basement. Get down there and fire the thing and get used to it. Your life may depend upon it."

In two weeks the preparatory work was finished. The lease on his apartment had been canceled and all of his personal possessions were in storage. He was certain that he would never see them again, but could not bear the thought of simply disposing of them. The admiral had understood and had promised to pay all the storage costs. Neither of them mentioned just how long this might be for.

The arrangements were done, the lists complete, everything ready. They came out of the Massachusetts Avenue building into the rain-filled night.

With the admiral at the wheel the big Cadillac steamed like a barge through the darkness. When they turned onto the Beltway he glanced at Troy sitting silently beside him. "You've checked the list carefully?" he asked.

"At least two dozen times. All my clothing is in the suitcase on the back seat. The equipment that we put together, it's in the saddlebags. All I need now is a horse."

"The Colt—and the money?"

"In the bottom of the bags. It's all in order."

"Yes. I suppose it is. I imagine that you are as prepared now as you'll ever be. You know you'll be strung up in a second if they find the gun?"

"I know that. But I'll have little chance of getting one after I arrive. Blacks—I mean nigras—don't get near that kind of thing in the old South."

"And that is what really concerns me . . ."

"Don't let it. The odds would be exactly the same if I were white. At least I have what might be called protective coloration!"

"Don't joke about it . . . all right, joke. Damn, but I wish I were going in your stead. How I envy you! My job is looking more and more boring every day."

"It's an important one, sir. And you are the one person who can do it best."

"I know that—or I would have been taking the riding lessons instead of you. This exit?"

"That's right. Look for the small road."

It was half-past eleven. It had been agreed that basic precautions must be taken to prevent any investigation of Troy's disappearance. None of the laboratory staff, or the military security people, would be on duty at this time of night, so they did not have to be considered. Their arrival was carefully timed; just before the guards changed shift at midnight. Their visit would of course be logged in the security computer, but the fact that Troy had not logged out might not be noticed at once, since it normally would be in the next day's file. In any case, since no trace of him would be found in the buildings, and the admiral would state that they had gone out together, it might very well be chalked up to computer error.

Bob Kleiman was waiting for them inside the front door. Troy introduced them. "I've heard a good deal about you, Admiral Colonne," Kleiman said.

"And the same, Dr. Kleiman. I'm looking forward with great anticipation to seeing this machine of yours. May I congratulate you on a truly miraculous achievement."

"Save your thanks for Dr. Delcourt, Roxanne. It's her equations that got the whole thing rolling. She's waiting for us in lab nine. Here, let me help with the bags."

The guard at the laboratory entrance scrutinized their passes closely, then let them through. As soon as the door had closed behind them, Troy pointed to the washroom. "I'm going to change. See you in a few minutes."

It wasn't any sense of false modesty that made him wish to be alone; years in the barracks had eliminated that. It was just the desire to be by himself for a few minutes. Up until this instant everything had been talk and planning. But the moment of truth had finally arrived. He wasn't afraid, he knew more than enough about fear to recognize it in any guise, but he was possessed of a different sensation altogether. It was a little like a night parachute drop; a fall into the unknown. He undressed slowly, right down to the skin, and laid his clothes to one side.

One by one he donned his new clothes. Ankle-length cotton drawers, then rough trousers. A cotton shirt and a shapeless jacket which had been torn at the shoulder, then repaired. Patches made of a different kind of cloth covered the elbows. His high boots were handmade from thick leather, with hobnailed leather soles, well-worn and dusty. He laid aside the hat that completed the outfit. It was wide-brimmed, made of straw and drooping around the edge. Before he put his uniform into the suitcase he emptied the pockets onto the glass ledge over the sink.

Keys, coins, pocketknife, handkerchief, dogtags, pen and pencil, notebook, then his wallet with some money, ID, membership cards, some photographs. It was all staying behind. He took out the picture of Lily, smiling happily, with Disneyland in the background. Life had always been a pleasure for her, right up until those last bad months, something to be savored and shared with others. But he couldn't bring this modern photograph with him. He put it back into the wallet, then dumped the lot into the empty suitcase on top of his uniform and started to close it. And stopped. Opening it again to retrieve her picture. There was nothing else he wanted from the twentieth century, nothing at all. He would put it in with the gun and ammunition. If those were discovered, a little, crumple-edged picture of the smiling black girl wouldn't make any difference. This time he closed the suitcase all the way and snapped it shut.

Troy patted the side pocket of his jacket; feeling the bulge of the leather wallet that held all of his papers. There was a large clasp knife alongside it, as well as a square of unbleached muslin. And a few small coins. Everything else was in the saddlebags. When he turned back he caught sight of himself in the mirror and stopped short.

A stranger looked back at him. This wasn't dressing up for a party—this was for real. He stared at the solidly built black man dressed in well worn rough clothing. People wore clothes like this where he was going. There were no nylon fabrics or zippers, no cars or planes as well. A different age. What would it be like? Well, that was one thing that he would be finding out soon enough.

Then he put the hat under his arm, took up the suitcase and went out. The journey was about to begin.

TWENTY-ONE

They had been talking, explaining the apparatus to the admiral, but they grew silent when Troy came up. Seeing him dressed like this drove home the realization that this was not just another experiment, that he would be gone soon. Though they had planned this together *he* was the one who was leaving, who would travel through time. Who would leave this world forever. From the instant he was gone he would be dead as far as they were concerned, would have been dead for a century or more. Now that the moment had come, there was also the understanding that this something was more than time travel. It was also execution.

"I have never seen so many long faces in my entire life," Troy said. "Cheer up—it's not the end of the world. In fact, I am going to make sure that it won't be."

"You can still change your mind," Kleiman said.

"We would understand . . ."

"Well I wouldn't. Here I am about to go to a more healthy world, to escape from all the smog and pollution, the threat of the atomic bomb, television commercials, all that—and you want to stop me."

"We don't want to stop you, Troy," Roxanne said, stepping forward and taking him by the arms. "I think that you are the bravest man that I have ever met and I want to wish you all the luck in the world." She leaned forward and kissed him, then turned quickly away before she did something stupid like crying.

"Ready to go when you say," Kleiman said, pointing at the controls. "Everything set for your arrival on the first of August in the year 1859. At around three in the morning and, if we can believe the newspaper files, it is raining like bejeezus. Are you sure that this is the date you want?"

"Positive. The admiral and I worked it out very carefully. McCulloch will have been there for over a year now, so whatever his plans are, they should be well under way. It is those activities that should enable me to find him. The war won't start for a year and a half yet, so not only do I have time to track him down, but there is still time enough to put a monkey-wrench into whatever bit of nastiness he is up to."

"Sounds good," Kleiman agreed. "Now the other thing. You remember, you promised to let us know tonight how you would go about getting a message to us. Something that would tell us how the affair finished, what McCulloch was trying to do. Have you worked it out?"

"I have. A very simple idea. I am going to write

up a report and seal it into a bottle. Really seal it, even try to get a glass blower to melt the neck of the bottle shut. I'll put that in a solid box and bury it about six feet deep in a spot where you will be easily able to find it."

"Where?"

"Right there." Troy pointed to the granite rock before them. "Down on the north side. All you have to do is dig."

"Great!" Kleiman said. "Of course it will also mean moving all of the equipment out of the lab, then tearing up the concrete floor. I can hardly wait. We'll get onto it right away."

"Well, at least wait until I have gone!"

They were silent then, all of them, staring at the gray rock where it projected up from the scuffed laboratory floor. Down there, under the foundation, under the ground, was the message. If Troy had indeed left that message in the past, then it must be buried there right now. It had been lying in that spot for well over a century. Buried safely beside the rock, when this had been only farmland, before they had been born, before this laboratory was even built. It was an unnerving thought.

"We'll wait," Roxanne said. "This is important enough—and new enough—for us not to get involved with time paradoxes at this stage. We will have to think about them some time. But not just now."

"Amen," said the admiral.

"Seconded," Kleiman said. "Time paradoxes have to be avoided at *any* stage. You must beware of doing or saying anything that might affect events. We have no way of visualizing the consequences."

Troy nodded and seized up the well-worn saddlebags. "It's time to go," he said.

"A good idea," Kleiman agreed, pointing to the metal brackets fixed to the stone surface. "I'm putting a wooden platform there. It will raise you about an inch above the surface of the stone. So you should drop that amount when you arrive—better bend your knees. I would rather have you above the stone than, well, inside it by a fraction of an inch. That is another matter that needs investigating. So here we go."

Troy helped him fix the platform into place, then clambered up onto it. The admiral handed him the saddlebags and they were ready. There didn't seem to be much to say. The admiral looked grim; Kleiman and Roxanne were busy at the controls.

"All ready," Kleiman said, his hand poised over the red actuator button. "Count of three, okay?"

"Okay. Let's go. Geronimo."

"One."

Troy flexed his knees.

"Two."

There was a frozen silence. Troy saw that Kleiman's hand was shaking, his lips working in silence.

"Do it, man, do it *now*," Troy said.

"Three."

Darkness.

Emptiness.

A sensation of nothing. Or a sensation of lack of sensation? It lasted an instant—or perhaps an eternity. Troy couldn't tell, it was too different. It could have been over even as it began, or it could have continued for an unmeasurable time. As he tried to think about it, even as he began, it ended.

Heavy, warm rain beat down upon his shoulders and something hard smacked against the soles of his boots, rough stone, tripping him. He tried to regain his balance in the rain-filled darkness but couldn't. Slipped and fell, slithering down the rock face into the mud, the breath half-knocked out of him. He had a moment of panic as he groped in the darkness for the saddle-bags. They were there, it was all right.

Sudden lightning cut through the night, the bolt striking so close by that the rumble of thunder arrived right on top of the flash. The lightning flared and was gone, but for an instant there he had been able to see through the thick rain.

The black form of the projecting rock was clear, as well as the outline of trees against the sky. But the laboratory was gone as though it had never existed. Of course, it didn't exist, not here, not at this time. It still had to be built, its existence was still a probability in the distant future.

He had arrived. Fairfax County, Virginia. A few miles north of the nation's capitol.

The summer of the year 1859.

Clutching the saddle-bags he climbed to his feet and stood with his back against the rock, rubbing the rain from his eyes. He had done it. 1859. But it meant nothing to him. He felt numb; the truth of the situation just couldn't penetrate. Only the rain had any reality.

What should the next step be? Sitting put, that was obvious. When it was daylight he had to chart the location of this particular ridge of stone, the exact spot where he had arrived so he could be

sure of finding it again. When the time came he
would bury the message here. It was important,
not only to those yet-unborn who would someday
dig for it in the distant future, but was vitally
important to him as well. It was a link, no matter
how tenuous, with the world that he had left forever. He settled down against the rock to wait.

The rain slackened and Troy was surprised to
see that the eastern horizon was already growing
light. He had to remember to make a note of that
for the others. Calibration was important, that's
what Kleiman always said. Still, a few hours difference over the immense span of the years, that
wasn't too bad. He would have to check the date
too, just in case.

The rain died down to a steady drizzle, then
stopped. The air was close and heavy; it was going
to be a hot day. As the sky brightened the mist
lifted and a grassy field began to emerge from the
darkness, running down from the ridge of granite
to the woods beyond. A track, a cowpath really,
cut close by. He heard a distant mooing and the
clanking of a cowbell; there was a farm not too distant. Nor should this spot be hard to find again.
The ridge of rock, shaped somewhat like a ship,
rose from the summit of a small hill, and it was the
only bit of rock in sight. The cowbells sounded
closer now, and the sound of heavy, slow footsteps.

They came out of the woods one behind the
other, a file of small brown cattle. The leader
rolled her eyes at him as she approached, then
moved out around him. Troy watched her pass,
then turned back.

The boy was standing at the edge of the trees,
looking at him.

Troy did not move when the boy started forward again. He was about twelve years old, dressed in patched trousers and shirt. He carried a length of green willow to use on the cows. His hair was blond and thick, his skin spattered with freckles. His bare toes squelched through the mud as he walked up and stopped before Troy. He just looked up at him, saying nothing.

"The rain stopped," Troy said. The boy tilted his head.

"You talk funny for a nigger," he said. He had a rural Virginia accent himself, no different from the ones Troy had heard countless times before.

"I'm from New York."

"Never met a Yankee nigger before. You lost?"

"No, just traveling south. Got caught out in the rain, got lost. Going to Washington. Can you tell me the way?"

"Of course I know the way," the boy said contemptuously, swinging the willow at a clump of grass. "Right ahead to the cart track then you gonna turn left into Tysons Corners and then you reach the pike. You're not very smart if you don't know that."

"I told you, I'm not from around these parts."

"Goldy, dang your thick hide, get out of that!" The boy called out suddenly, then ran after the cows.

Troy looked after him, aware of the tension draining away. It had worked all right. His first meeting. But just with a boy. What would happen when he met other people? For one thing, he wasn't going to talk Yankee any more. Could he fake a thick handkerchief-head accent? Sho' nuff. He had better do it—his life might very well depend on it. He had heard enough of that kind of

talk in the Army, big thick kids from the South, no
education. Army even had to teach some of them
to read. Yassuh, yassuh. It sounded pretty fake.
But he would just have to learn to do it. Listen to
how the other blacks talked. Do the same. But he
must remember that until he felt secure he must
talk as little as possible.

The boy and the cattle were vanishing down the
path. Troy turned his back on them, threw the
saddle-bags over his shoulder, then started in the
opposite direction. He patted his pockets as he
went; everything was there.

Washington, District of Columbia, was ahead.

Also, somewhere out there as well, was Colonel
McCulloch. They had an appointment that the
colonel didn't know anything about.

TWENTY-TWO

By the time that Troy had reached the dirt track the sun was well over the horizon and burning hard on his back. Just a little after dawn and he was already running with sweat; the day would be a scorcher. He peeled off his steaming jacket before going on. The road was nothing more than two ruts filled with mud and deep puddles; he walked on the grass to one side. Topping a rise he saw smoke in the valley beyond, and had a quick view of wood-shingled roofs between the trees. Tysons Corners. It was surrounded by the fields of outlying farms, while just ahead, beside the road, was a ramshackle building.

No, not a building, that was too grand a word for it. A shack. He had seen miserable dwellings like this before, when he had been driving through the backwoods of Mississippi. Rude constructions of unseasoned wood, bare of paint, warped and

dried by the sun. This one was the same. The gaps
between some of the boards were wide enough to
fit your hand through. The front door opened directly onto the hardpacked dirt of the front yard.
An oak tree shaded the front of the house, and
under the tree, on a broken and backless chair, the
old man sat. Watching, staring in silence, as Troy
walked by. His skin was black and wrinkled and
only a few patches of gray hair tufted his head. His
clothes were ancient and patched. Troy nodded as
he came up, but the old man didn't move.

"Morning," Troy said. The old man shook his
head from side to side.

"Good-bye. I says that because you is gonna be
dead by nightfall."

Troy stopped and smiled, trying to make light of
the words. "You shouldn't say that, old man,
brings bad luck."

"You *is* bad luck. Where you steal those bags
from?"

"They're mine."

"That such a bad lie even I don't believe it!
Those white man bags, not nigger bags. First
white man see you gonna shoot you first then ask
after where you stole dem. You from de North?"

"Yes."

"Sound like it. But you South now."

"Can I come in? Seems I got a thing or two to
learn."

"Seems to me you do have!" The old man
cackled with high-pitched laughter. "Jus' couldn't
trust my eyes seeing you sashay down the road
like that. Mistuh Yankee-man, you got a real lot to
learn. You not back North now. When you here
you just one mo' slave."

The quiet description cut Troy to the heart,

penetrated deeper than any insult or threat—the realization that Black people were slaves here, that slavery was still legal. This man had spent his life in slavery. The lesson was quite clear. If Troy couldn't learn, and learn quickly, to act like him, think like him, why then he was as good as dead.

He almost didn't get the chance. There was the sound of men's voices down the road, in the direction he had come, and the thud of horses' hooves.

"Inside!" the old man hissed. "Hide—or you is dead this minute!"

Troy did not stop to argue. He dived through the open door, falling and rolling against the wall. The sound of hoofbeats beat louder and nearer. A man's voice called out.

"How long you been there, uncle?"

"Since it was light, captain, suh. Jus' sittin' right here."

"Then you tell me what you saw, tell me the truth or I'll lay this whip across that black hide."

"What I see? I see nothin', suh. Crows, jus' crows."

"You see a real black crow, boy? A buck nigger in fancy boots carrying stolen goods?"

"See dat? I know if I see dat! Nothin', no one pass here, I swear dat!"

"I told you, Luther, he wouldn't come this way," another voice said.

"You calling my boy a liar?"

"If I thought he was lying I wouldn't be here now, would I? I'm just saying that this buck lied to the boy, to put us off his trail. He probably went the other way directly the boy was out of sight. You back-track the way we came, I'll go into the Corners, pass the word. He won't get far, not with everyone looking for him. Bet there's a reward out for him too."

The sound of the galloping horses died away,
but still Troy did not move. He lay pressed against
the rough wood, unaware of the line of ants
moving past his face and out through a chink in
the walls, filled with a kind of fear that he had
only felt once before in his life. The time when he
had been cut off from his company. Behind enemy
lines.

He was behind enemy lines again. In his own
country—but still not his country. Not yet. History, as he knew it, had just come alive for him in a
way he had never understood from books. For the
first time he could understand at least one of the
reasons why the Civil War had been fought—and
just what the victory was that had been so
painfully won. He looked down at his shaking
fingers, then angrily clamped them into a fist and
slammed hard against the splintered floor. It was
a little early to give up.

The old man shuffled up arthritically and
settled down on the doorstep with a weary sigh.
His back was to Troy, his face hidden.

"You saved my life," Troy said. "And I don't
even know your name."

"You ain't ever gonna get my name. When they
catch you you ain't gonna tell where you been."

"How am I going to get away from them? Where
can I go?"

"Back where you come from, and good riddance. You git out in back now, hide in the scrub
behind the privvy, they ain't never going dere.
After dark, you move out of here."

"Where to? You heard them, they're all on the
lookout. How can I get away?"

The old man grunted contemptuously. "With

your dumb ways I guesses you don't. Get cotched, whupped, tel dem 'bout me fore they string you up. You is trouble, hear dat? Trouble."

He muttered to himself, rocking back and forth in the doorway, reaching a decision. "Git out where I tol' you. Come night I get in touch wif the Railroad. Let dem worry bout you. Now git."

It was hot under the bushes, the air didn't move, the flies were torture. Troy managed to finally doze off, but woke, spluttering, with the flies crawling into his nose and mouth. He spat them out, waving ineffectually at the droning clouds. The flies were a torture, but the thirst even more so. Worse than he had ever experienced before. And there was nothing that he could do about it. People passed from time to time on the road, he could hear their voices, the creak of cartwheels. By dusk his head was thudding painfully. He still dared not move. Slow footsteps sounded, and he pressed himself back into the bushes. The privvy door banged, and a moment later he heard the old man's whisper.

"Dey's a gourd wif water. Wait until I gone before you grabs it."

The water was warm and gritty—but lifesaving. Troy made it last as long as he could. After a while the air cooled down slightly as darkness fell, but even more important it brought relief from the flies. The pleasure was short lived, however, because the flies were soon replaced by humming, voracious mosquitoes. It seemed that hours had gone by before he heard the sound of the door slamming, followed by the drag of the old man's footsteps moving off down a path through the trees. He returned, an endless time later, and called out to Troy.

"Come forward now. Behin' the house. Got a boy chere gonna see after you."

A gibbous moon was drifting in and out between the clouds, spreading enough watery light for him to pick out the two figures. The old man waved him forward.

"Dis boy, he frightened but he gonna help you. You gotta help him back. His momma sick, need medicine. You got a dollar? You must have, with all dem rich clothes."

"Yes. I'll be happy to pay him for the help. If there is anything I can do for you, you're more than welcome . . ."

"Just shut yo mouth. Don' need for nothin'. You hide in th' barn where he takes you. An' don't come back."

Troy whispered his thanks after the retreating back, but the man didn't answer. He had nothing, was just as poor as it was possible to be, but he still had his pride; Troy was sorry that he had mentioned the money. He felt a small, warm hand in his, and looked down and smiled at the tiny child.

"I'm going to help your momma with her medicine," he said. "And more. Let's go."

The child's bare feet were unerring in the darkness; Troy stumbled after him, well aware of the crashing he was making. But they seemed to be taking a circuitous route, away from the road, cutting through a sweet-smelling pine forest. After they had come a good distance the boy stopped, then led them slowly and silently to a gap in the hedge. A rutted road lay beyond, clearly visible, the puddles gleaming in the moonlight. The clouds were gone, the night sky rich with stars. The road was a trap. The boy reached up and tugged at his arm, pulling him down so he could whisper in Troy's ear.

"Stay down and don' stir none."

He slipped away before Troy could say anything, moving silently as a shadow across the road. He was gone a long time. Troy thought about extracting the pistol from the bottom of the bag, then decided not to. One shot in this quiet night would alert the entire countryside. There was no way that he could kill everyone who turned a hand against him. All he could do was wait.

He jumped, startled, as the boy touched him out of the darkness.

"Men dere, gone now," he whispered, then tugged Troy forward.

They crossed the road as quickly as they could and hurried on into the shelter of the bushes on the other side. There was the outline of a house against the sky, a glint of light visible around one of the windows. They angled away from it, between rows of high corn that rustled to their passage. A darker bulk appeared out of the darkness, a barn. The door squealed slightly when the boy pushed it open.

"Hide," he whispered. "Momma's money."

Troy dug out a handful of coins, far more than a dollar, and pressed the money into the boy's hand. The tiny fingers closed on it, then he was gone. The door squeaked again as the boy pulled it closed behind him. Troy turned and felt his way through the darkness, stumbling over unseen objects, the saddlebags catching on some obstruction. He freed the bags, then found what felt like bales of hay and lay down behind them.

He was safe for the moment—but what would happen next? The old man had been angry at him

and less than clear. Something about a railroad.
He didn't know what it meant.

Loud footsteps sounded in the barnyard outside
and the door squealed shrilly as it was pulled
open. Light flared. The door banged shut and a
man called out.

"Step forward. Where I can see you."

Troy had no choice. He let the bags drop and
stood up, walked out around the bales of hay
blinking in the light from the kerosene lantern,
staring at the man who was holding the gun.

A white man.

TWENTY-THREE

"You're the one, all right," the man said. "Just keep those hands up high the way they are. I've been out since late afternoon with the others, looking for you. Couldn't find a trace, no trace at all. People starting now to think the boy made the whole thing up. But standing here and looking at you now, why I would say that he gave a fair description."

He was a big and solid man with bright red hair, his large belly swollen out over his trousers and stretching the supporting red suspenders.

"What are you going to do with me?" Troy said, looking at the long-barreled pistol aimed at his midriff. "Going to shoot me?"

"The man holding the pistol, he's the one asks the questions. So just keep your hands way up like that and tell me who brought you here."

"I don't know."

"Who told you about me?"

"I don't know that either."

"Amazing. If I had my eyes closed I would truly believe that I was listening to a Yankee."

"That's because I am one. From New York City."

"Well I can believe that—you sure are something different. Don't know what to do about you."

"While you're making your mind up—my arms are getting tired. Can I put them down now?"

Without waiting for an answer Troy lowered his hands, shifting his weight forward as he did so. If he dived, knocked the gun aside, he stood some chance.

"Yes, leave them down," the man said. He shoved the gun into the waistband of his trousers and Troy relaxed his tense muscles. "You'll be here for a bit. I'll show you where to hide. It's just a dark hole in the ground under the molasses butt, keep you alive though. In about a day or two you'll be moving out, when the other two arrive."

"Moving where?"

"North, of course."

"Sorry. My business is going to take me south. Thanks anyway."

"Thanks . . .!" The man held up his lantern and leaned forward to look more closely at Troy. "Let me tell you, you are indeed something different. Half the slaves in the South trying to get north to Canada, and you want to go in the other direction."

"I do. And I'm not a slave. The man who sent me here, he mentioned the word railroad. This wouldn't be a station on the Underground Railroad, would it?"

"You ask too many questions. Got your bags

back there?" Troy nodded. "Get them. I don't want anyone stumbling over them. Come in the house. I was just fixing dinner—I guess you could use some."

"I could, thanks. The last time I ate—I just don't remember."

"Stay next to me. I'm putting out the light. No one's close, my dogs make sure of that. But you might be seen from a distance." Darkness engulfed them. Troy retrieved the saddlebags and followed the man out of the barn. Something large pressed against him and he heard a deep growl.

"Easy, boy, easy, this is a friend. Walk slowly, stranger. If you don't make any sudden moves they won't bother you. Here, get inside before I light the lantern."

The kitchen was sparsely furnished but clean, the wooden table freshly scrubbed. The man hung the lantern from a hook over the table then pumped a pitcher of fresh water at the sink. He put it on the table along with two stone mugs.

"I didn't light the fire today. But I got the butt end of a ham and some cornbread."

"Anything. I appreciate it. My name is Troy Harmon."

"What business could you possibly have in the South, Troy?"

"Private business, Mister—I'm sorry, I didn't get your name."

The man chewed on a mouthful of cornbread dipped in molasses and shook his head in wonder. "You are indeed something. The name is Milo Doyle, since you know everything else about this place. And I come from Boston, which explains why I'm not shooting you on the spot."

"It explains a great deal, Mr. Doyle." The ham

was gristly and badly cured, but Troy was ravenous. He washed it down with the sweet-tasting water. "It explains why you're helping me, and the others you mentioned as well."

"I've been here so long, people forget. Come down working on the railroad—funny, different kind of railroad now. Married a local girl, took up farming. She died, going on three years now, been on my own since then. Not doing much other than feel sorry for myself. Actually thought of selling out and going back home. Never quite got around to it. Then one day a friend came by, he's a lawyer now but I knew him since he was that high, from back home. Asked me to do a little favor for him. Favors been getting bigger and bigger ever since. Now you know all about me, Troy, so you can tell me about yourself."

"Be glad to. Born and bred in New York, on Long Island. Went into the Army when I was young . . ."

"Watch it, son. That's the first I heard they took anyone of your race into the United States Army."

"Did I say that? I've done a lot of fighting out of the country. A lot of armies aren't too particular about skin. I can take care of myself. Right now I'm working on, well, a project. I have to find someone. And I'm beginning to realize that I can't do it alone. I'd like to ask your advice. And maybe I can help you in return. From what I have heard about the Underground Railroad it's an important work, helping runaway slaves get North."

"It's important all right, getting the freight North, but some of us are more important than others. This is kind of a small station, nothing like the one that poor Tom Garrett ran. Over two-thousand and seven-hundred passengers he carried through Wilmington before they caught him."

"I had no idea of the scope of the operation. But something this big, it can't be cheap to run. Your expenses for food and transportation, they must be pretty high. Which means we can help each other. I can pay well for any assistance. So our relationship can be a mutually profitable one."

Doyle's jaw was gaping open, a rivulet of molasses running down his chin.

"You ever think of selling snake oil? Man talks like you, he's got a great future selling things. Mutually profitable relationship indeed! Why you talk better than most preachers I know."

Troy smiled. "The advantage of a good education." Public School 117 and Jamaica High School —they should only know!

"Advantage of something. But you want me to help you, you better tell me more about this man you are looking for. A friend of yours?"

"The direct opposite. His real name is Wesley McCulloch, though he may have changed it. But frankly I doubt that. He has killed three people that I know of. I want to find out where he is now, then let the authorities know."

"A white man?"

"Yes."

"That's a tall order, Troy. Particularly in the South. You'll never be able to do it alone."

"I know that now. I was perhaps a little naive to think that I could. I'll need a cover . . ." Doyle looked puzzled, not understanding. "No, not a real cover, I mean a different role. I've been thinking about it all day. Let me know what you think. Would it be possible for me to go South as a personal servant? That would mean locating

someone white to front the operation. Do you
think that it would work?"

"I think I need a drink while I think about all
that. Can't say right off if it can be done, but I can
say that I truly believe it is the strangest idea I
heard in all my life." He dumped a heavy stone jug
onto the table, pulled the corncob plug from it and
poured their mugs full. "Try this. Farmer down by
the river makes it. Charged me a dime for this
crock. What do you think of it?"

Troy sipped, then instantly regretted it. "I think
you got cheated," he said hoarsely. Doyle nodded
gloomily.

"Overcharged. I knew it." He smacked his lips
over the corn likker, then refilled his mug. "But I
think I know the very man who might be able to
help you. He's a Scotchman, writes for the newspapers or something, in Washington. He's helped
us a lot, carries messages when he goes South. He
might be just your man."

"If he'll help it sounds ideal. Can you contact
him?"

Doyle rasped his fingers over his jaw and
nodded. "I need me some iron nails. Hogg in the
Corners is out, I already asked. So I got a good
reason to go into the city. If I leave early I can do
my errands, be back here by dusk. I can leave a
message for him, if he's not there, with our people
who'll know how to contact him. But you'll have to
stay buried in the hole until I get back."

"I can use the rest, don't worry about me."

"I'm worrying about *me* and how they would
string me up if they found you here. I'll need some
money to convince the newspaper man."

Troy dug into his pocket. "Will ten dollars do?"

"Do? I said convince him, not buy him. Now

grab your bags and let me show you the hole so I can get me some sleep."

The hideaway had been skillfully constructed. The big molasses barrel swung aside on concealed pivots to reveal an opening. Beneath it a cave-like chamber had been dug into the sandy soil, supported by lengths of tree trunk, the walls reinforced with split logs. A platform of split logs on the floor lifted above the damp earth. There was a chamber pot, a bucket of water and bit of candle end set into a notch in a beam. Nothing else.

"I'll bring you some vittles in the morning before I go," was Doyle's last words as he swung the barrel back into place. Troy found a match and lit the candle, then dug out his revolver before he lay down. The saddlebags made a satisfactory pillow and he was asleep seconds after he blew the candle out.

Troy dozed on and off during the day after Doyle had left. There was nothing else to do in the blackness of the pit. With no way to measure the time, the day stretched on and on until he was sure that something had gone wrong. He followed the slight draft until he found the open end of the clay pipe that admitted fresh air, undoubtedly angled since no trace of light was visible through it. He pressed his ear to it. Occasionally distant sounds were carried to him; he heard a cart once, then another time some children shouting one to the other.

He was dozing again when he heard the loud barking of dogs. Intruders—or was it their master coming home? In either case he was ready. When the trapdoor finally creaked open Troy was standing against the back wall, his pistol aimed.

"Come out," Doyle said. "It's all right."

Troy went warily, blinking in the light of the lantern. A slim man, well dressed in a dark suit and high riding boots, stood behind Doyle.

"Who is that?" Troy asked.

"He's the one that I told you about—so you can just put that hogsleg away. This is Mr. Shaw, Mr. Robbie Shaw. I mentioned a bit about your plans and he is interested. You can tell him what you told me. You two stay put here. The dogs are restless and I'm going to look around the grounds."

He went out, taking the lamp with him; they could hear the dogs growling.

"Foxes, perhaps," Shaw said in a quiet voice. "I believe that there are a number of them in the vicinity."

"I wouldn't know. I'm not from these parts."

"Indeed you are not. Dare I say your accent is as alien as mine."

"Yes, your accent." Troy peered through the darkness but the other man was only the vaguest blur. "You know, you sound more like an Englishman than a Scotsman. No insult intended."

"None taken, I'm sure. Benefit of a Sassenach education. Winchester. My parents wanted me to get on in the world. You strike me as being quite a well-traveled man and I'm getting more intrigued with every passing moment. Two names were mentioned by our host. You are Troy Harmon?"

"That's right."

"My pleasure, Mr. Harmon. The other name was something of a surprise, the man you are seeking. Wesley McCulloch, did I get that right?"

"You did."

"That couldn't be Colonel Wesley McCulloch by any chance, could it?"

Troy eased the Colt out of his belt and pointed it in the darkness. "He has used the title of colonel.

Why do you mention his name? Have you heard of him?"

"You might very well ask, dear boy. Because I know the colonel so well, I just wondered what your interest in him could possibly be."

TWENTY-FOUR

Troy's thoughts were as black as the darkness that surrounded them. Was this a trap? Had McCulloch set people to watch the spot where he had arrived—to see if he had been followed? Was Doyle also McCulloch's man, waiting to draw him into a trap?

There was a single metallic click as his thumb pulled down slowly on the hammer of the revolver.

"I say, is something wrong?" Robbie Shaw called out. "Is that a gun you are cocking?"

"Yes. A six shot Colt. If I miss with the first shot, I'll see you in the blast and get you with the second. So stand right where you are."

"I wouldn't think of moving, my dear chap. There is no need for this, you know. Mr. Doyle can vouch for me, my credentials as regards the Underground Railroad are impeccable . . ."

"Do you work for McCulloch?"

"No, of course not. But I must assure you that my acquaintance with the colonel has been of great assistance in the labors that your friends carry out. Through him I have been accepted in social circles that I might never have otherwise penetrated."

Sudden light flared as Doyle entered the store-room with the lantern.

"Dogs caught a fox," he said, then saw Troy's gun. "What's all this now?"

"Life insurance. Were you aware that your journalist here is well acquainted with Colonel McCulloch?"

"No, but I'm not surprised. He knows a lot of people, both North and South. Put that damn pistol away and come into the kitchen. I told you that he's one of us and you ought to be taking my word."

Troy hesitated, then pushed the pistol into his belt. "If I am mistaken—well, I apologize. But I think you can understand my apprehension."

"No apologies needed, my dear fellow," Shaw said, waving the entire matter aside. Yet at the same time he breathed an inadvertent sigh of relief. "I am really not very fond of deadly weapons. Ah, some of the local *uisge beatha*, thank you." He seized the cup of moonshine that Doyle handed to him and drained half of it in a gulp.

Troy took one too, but just sipped at his as they sat down around the table. "The interesting part," Shaw said, staring into the depths of the mug, "is that I knew Colonel McCulloch before I came to this country. Met him in Glasgow, in my father's club. They were doing some business together."

Troy leaned forward, trying not to let his eagerness show. "What sort of trade is your father in, Mr. Shaw?"

"Not trade! Dear no, nothing so crude. Heavy manufacturing, engineering plant."

"Does he make machines to work steel?"

Shaw lifted one quizzical eyebrow. "In fact, yes, he does. And brass as well. Do you know something that I don't?"

"Perhaps. Please go on."

"Yes, well, it seems that the colonel is going into engineering in a most enterprising manner over here. He's a great bore with all his talk of freeing the South from the shackles of Yankee industry and that sort of thing. Anything the pallid factory workers of the North can make the free men of the South can do better. Or something like that. I never paid much attention. But I do know that he made large purchases, paid cash, then shipped everything back here. He has a going plant in Richmond, and is always carrying on about his hinges and plowshares and googaws of that sort. But this is made bearable by the fact that he is also rich and has plenty of influential friends. So I make sure that I drop by and drink some of his whiskey whenever I pass through. And that is the whole of it." He drained his mug, then smiled as the refill gurgled into it. "Now I think that some explanation of your overwhelming interest is in order."

Troy had been thinking about it, knowing that he would have to answer this question sooner or later. It would be impossible to tell them the truth. But whatever story he told had better sound authentic. He had decided that the wisest thing would be to provide some realistic variation of the actual facts.

"Colonel McCulloch, if he is indeed the same

man, is a murderer and an embezzler. A wanted
man with a price on his head. What I must do is
seek him out in order to identify him. After I have
done that, and if he is indeed the same man, we
will let the law take its course. I assure you, it is a
matter of great importance."

"It sounds that way," Doyle said. "And you also
sound very much involved in it yourself. Are you?"

"Yes. I am determined to run this killer to the
ground. But my personal motives aren't really
important to this case. The law has been broken
and a criminal is at large. I have ample funds for
the investigation and will pay well for assistance.
As I have discovered—I can't do it alone. Will you
help me, Mr. Shaw?"

"Be delighted to, Mr. Harmon. For altruistic
reasons too, of course. But also for the money. I'm
not ashamed to admit that journalism is a damn
poorly paid profession, and my father, rich as he
is, has kept the key firmly turned in the family
strongbox ever since I was sent down from Ox-
ford. You must count me in by all means. Exactly
what sort of operation did you have in mind?"

"I shall be your servant. That will enable you to
make all the arrangements, pay for everything,
while I should be relatively invisible, just following along and carrying the bags. All right?"

"Capital! But could you possibly ameliorate
your accent and grammar slightly? I would hate to
have to explain why my servant sounds more like
my college tutor."

"Yassuh. Ah shore will try."

"Adequate—and I am sure that practice will
make perfect. Now to the details." He turned to
Doyle. "How do you suggest that we go about
doing this?"

"I suggest you start by getting out of here tonight. There has been too much coming and going for my peace of mind. I'll sell you my old mule for five dollars. He's one-eyed and swayback but still sound. Troy can ride him. I also got a pair of old split shoes for him to wear, leave those fancy boots here. Troy can put that big pistol and whatever else he fancies in a flour bag. You take his saddlebags behind you, Robbie, much too grand for the likes of him. That should do it—as long as you, Troy, keep your mouth shut until you learn to talk right."

"Yassuh."

"*Still* don't sound right. Keep practicing."

"Does your mule have a saddle?" Troy asked.

"Nope. Niggers ride bareback in case you haven't noticed. You got a lot to learn. I'm going to outfit you two so you can stay away from the towns until Troy can face them without giving himself away. I have some rubberized ponchos, blankets, pots and pans. Tie them all onto the mule. This is good weather for camping out. You two just mosey south and take your time. Now, we'll have a little bit more of this corn, I'll give you some dinner, and then you'll be on your way. I'll rest a lot easier when you're safely down the road."

They entered the outskirts of Washington City a little after dawn. Troy was hobbling along, leading the scrawny mule which he had discovered had a spine like a sawblade. Even sitting on the old wadded up blanket didn't seem to help. But his discomfort was forgotten as the city emerged from the morning mist.

At this precise moment the physical reality of

his voyage back to the nineteenth century struck home for the first time. He had been too busy just staying alive since he had arrived to really take much notice of his surroundings. The rough clothes, the simple fittings of the farmhouse, they weren't that different from things he had seen on summer vacations upstate. Even the shacks were a lot better than the hooches in Nam. But this was the nation's capitol, a real city, and even the name was different from the one he knew it by.

The city was smaller, of course, much smaller than the sprawling metropolis it would become over a century later. And it looked very different without the great bulks of the neo-Greek and Roman stone piles of the federal buildings. The buildings now were smaller, of wood and brick, the streets narrower and mostly unpaved. What struck him most was the complete absence of motorized traffic, though the streets were filled with horses, carts and pedestrians. Horses! The sharp reek of horse manure dominated all of the other smells, wiping out the odor of burning wood and even tempering the clouds of coalsmoke that blew over them when they passed a train station. Troy would have lingered here if Shaw hadn't cursed at him to keep moving on. The shining black engine with its diamond stack, gleaming brass and leaking steam, it was just imposible to pass. This was not history, this was the living present, and he was half-paralyzed with the solidity of it all. Only when he felt Shaw's boot-toe in his ribs did he remember where he was.

"Boy, stop hanging back and rolling your eyes like that. Mount your mule. We don't have all day."

"Yassah, but ah got to fix this rope first, else all

dese things gonna fall off."

"Don't touch that cinch; I'll take care of it."

Shaw swung down from his horse and bent to look at the buckle. "You're going too slow, gawking about, someone will notice," he whispered.

"Sorry. But I don't think I can ride any more. This beast's backbone has sawed me in two."

"Lead it then, but we must keep moving."

There was so much to see—but Shaw was right, they dare not stop and sightsee. But the glimpses were tantalizing. The Capitol Building, looking from the distance very much as it did in his day. But there were no suburbs when they crossed into Virginia. And there were only swamps and nodding cattails on the spot where the Washington National Airport would one day stand. The site of the Pentagon was a green meadow with grazing cows.

"This is a good time to stop for lunch," Shaw said, turning off into a field. Troy stumbled wearily after him.

"Just about time," he said. "These broken-down shoes are raising blisters on both my feet. Walking is as bad, or worse, than riding this miserable candidate for the glue factory."

"I must remember that expression, glue factory indeed! You Yankees do have an odd turn of phrase. Now, while I stretch out, I suggest that you take this bucket down to that stream so you can water these beasts."

"Yes, massah, I jus' do dat."

"Better. You're learning."

The stream had cut away a bank at least six feet high. Troy went along it until he found a path leading down to the stream's edge. The water looked clear and fresh. He cupped some in his hands and drank deep, then splashed more on his face to wash away some of the dust of the Washington streets. After filling the bucket he climbed up the path, stopping instantly when he heard voices. Carefully, an inch at a time, he raised his head behind the thick grass until he could see over it.

Two riders had reined up by their mounts and were talking to Robbie Shaw. One of them said something and the other laughed loudly and swung down from his horse, at the same time drawing a dragoon pistol from the holster attached to his saddle. Shaw took a step backward, but the man followed him, poking him in the stomach with his gun. The second man dismounted and walked towards Shaw's horse, which skittered away from him. He grabbed the reins, pulling the creature's head down, then reached out to open the saddle bags.

Where all of Troy's goods lay hidden. His money, the pistol, everything.

TWENTY-FIVE

Troy hesitated for one long moment, taking it all in, seeing the way the men were placed, before he started forward. As he came into sight he called out loudly.

"Massa, I done got de water like you say."

He shuffled slowly forward as he spoke, head down, shoulders rounded, holding the handle of the pail with both hands as though it were a great weight. Under the lowered brim of his hat he could see the dismounted man spin about and point his gun at him. His mounted companion had also produced a pistol. Troy ignored this, still shuffling forward, humming and talking to himself under his breath as though he were unaware of their presence.

It worked fine. The two men were smiling, waiting for him to notice them. Good. He would provide some good theatre, vintage Stepenfechit,

or perhaps a quaking imitation of Jack Benny's
Rochester in a haunted house.

"Lawdy!" he screeched when he got close, looking up and seeing them. He clutched the bucket to
him, trembling so much that the water slopped
and spilled over. He tried to roll his eyes, but
wasn't very good at it.

Bad as the performance was, it had a receptive
audience. The two men laughed and whooped, the
one on the ground opening his mouth wide, reveal-
ing a mouthful of blackened teeth. So great was
his merriment that his pistol barrel dropped by
degrees until it pointed at the ground. Troy
shuffled and looked around, as though searching
for a place to hide, watching the other man dis-
mount, waiting until the horse blocked his vision
for an instant.

At that precise moment he threw the bucket into
the laughing man's face.

As he staggered backwards Troy was on top of
him, driving his knee hard up into the man's
crotch as he twisted the gun from his hand. The
man screamed shrilly as they fell together. Troy
rolled as they struck the ground, swinging the
pistol up. The other man was still half-hidden by
his horse, coming into view, his own pistol aimed.
Troy extended his weapon at arm's length, sighted
along it and pulled the trigger.

It banged like a cannon and kicked like a mule,
throwing his arm high. But his shot had been
good. The other twisted, folded, tried to point his
own gun, squeezed the trigger, then fell.

As the shot was fired Robbie Shaw cried out
hoarsely and dropped to the ground. The stray
bullet had caught him. Troy started towards him,
then saw that the first man had stumbled to his

feet, groaning with pain, but still ready to fight. He reached for the scabbard in the small of his back and pulled out a bowie knife with a foot-long blade. Holding it straight out he staggered forward.

Troy aimed the gun and clicked the trigger—then saw that it was a single shot pistol. He threw it into the man's face, but the other merely brushed it aside, moaning in agony and cursing horribly at the same time. And came on. Troy stepped backwards, his eye on the knife point, stumbled and fell. The other roared and dropped on him.

It was a tiny cracking sound, like two boards being smacked together. Troy saw the black hole appear in the man's forehead, then fill instantly with blood as he fell face downwards into the grass, unmoving.

Stunned, Troy looked over at Shaw sprawled on the ground. He had levered himself up on one elbow; there was a tiny smoking gun in his hand.

"Pepperbox," Shaw said, smiling grimly as he tucked the gun back into his vest pocket. "Two barrels, over and under, two shots. I never go anywheres without it. Road agents are . . . quite common . . . these days."

He grimaced with pain and Troy saw the blood soaking through his trousers, running down his leg. Troy moved fast, turning over the dead man next to him and tearing off the man's wide leather belt, then wrapping it twice around Shaw's thigh before drawing it tight. The flow of blood slowed, stopped. Troy rose slowly to his feet and looked around.

"Bit of a butcher shop," Robbie Shaw said. "Two dead, one injured. That's quite a job you did, unarmed. Taking on those two like that, pistols and all."

"You're not too shabby yourself with that little popgun. I thought that you were a journalist, a man of peace."

"I am. But this is a hard world. My first assignment in this country was as military correspondent during the Indian wars. Worse than the Gorbals on hogmanay eve. That's where I learned how to shoot. But now, dare I ask, what do we do next?"

"Take care of your wound. We're out of sight of the road so we don't have to worry about somebody stumbling onto us. Anyone who might have heard the shots would have been here by now. The way the attack happened, I imagine that this pair of thugs must have followed us from the city. They wouldn't have started this unless they were sure that they were unobserved. We'll worry about them later. Getting you fixed takes top priority."

Troy dug into the saddlebags and pulled out the flat box that held his medical supplies. He took out one of the morphine styrettes and palmed it, then went to look at Shaw's wound. Using his clasp knife he slit the trousers open.

"Looks rather nasty," Shaw said, sitting up and leaning forward to examine the wound. "Like I'd been shot with a cannon."

"Just about," Troy said, kicking the fallen pistol with his toe. "Single shot, muzzle loader, must have a half-inch bore. Now lie back and let me look at this. Lots of blood, but not as drastic as it seems. The ball took out a chunk of your thigh muscle but it kept on going."

Under cover of his body, Troy cracked open the styrette and discarded the protective cover. One of

the newest ones, double shot. It would not only kill
the pain but would put Shaw to sleep as well. He
jabbed it into the leg and pressed down on the
plunger.

"I felt that! What are you doing?" Shaw asked.

"Playing doctor. I told you to take it easy."

He kicked a hole into the turf, stamped the
crushed remains of the styrette into it, then
covered it up again. By the time Troy had
unpacked and returned with the rest of the
medical kit Shaw was lying back with his eyes
closed, snoring hoarsely. Troy went to work.

He had plenty of experience in field treatment,
but this time he would have to be the medic as
well. At least whatever he did to treat the wound
would be better than anything else that might be
done in this primitive age. First he dusted the
wound well with antibiotic powder, then eased up
on the tourniquet. There was only a little bleeding
now. He tightened it again, put on more powder,
then applied a pressure bandage. That would do.
That *had* to do. No one could do any better. Here,
in this field, he had used medicines of a different
era. When had antisepsis started? With Lister, yes,
1865, he remembered the date from school exams.
He had always had a memory for dates.

Troy slipped a bottle of penicillin tablets into
his pocket, then put the rest of the kit away. Crows
cawed hoarsely in a nearby grove of trees. The midday sun was hot; the horses, reins hanging, grazed
the rich grass. The two corpses lay where they had
fallen. Something would have to be done about
them. Troy grabbed the nearest one by the boots,
then dragged it across the field to the shelter of
the trees. The crows, calling loudly, rose in a black
cloud and flew away.

It was afternoon before Shaw woke up. He opened his eyes and looked around. Troy kneeled next to him and held out a tin cup of water. "Thanks," Shaw said, draining it. Troy refilled it, then handed over one of the penicillin tablets.

"Wash this down. It will be good for the leg."

Shaw hesitated a second, then shrugged and swallowed the capsule. "Was I dreaming—or was there a brace of tobymen here a short while ago? Complete with mounts."

"The best thing that you can do is forget about them. If we report what happened we will only get involved with the authorities. The fewer questions we have to answer, the less publicity we get, the happier I'll be. If someone had seen what happened at the time, that would have been different. But no one seems to have noticed. So I got things out of sight. The two men are in the woods over there, along with their saddles and bridles, weapons, the lot. The horses are down by the stream."

"They'll be found."

"Of course. But we'll be gone by then. As long as we are not seen in the vicinity we won't be suspected. And I'm willing to bet that pair are known to the police. I doubt if they will be missed. So let's move on. Can you ride with that leg?"

"I think so. Truth is it doesn't hurt very much."

"It will. But by the time it does we should have some miles under our belt. We'll find a quiet spot and lay up for the night. Then tomorrow we'll see if we can buy some kind of wagon for you to ride in. That is—if you feel well enough to keep going on. We can call this whole thing off now if you're not up to it."

"Excelsior!" Shaw said, sitting up and grimacing. "Help me, there's a good chap, and we'll press on. You are a mysterious man, Mr. Harmon, and I intend to learn more about you and your mysterious ways. The more I know, the more I have the feeling that you are only telling me the smallest part of what is happening. I mean to continue until I discover some of the verities."

"You do that. Meanwhile let's get you onto this horse."

They rode until dark, then found a campsite well away from the road. Troy kept the Colt tucked into his belt and resolved that he would never be caught far away from it again. They did not want to draw attention to themselves by building a fire, so they finished off the last of the cold food that Doyle had provided. They regretted not having the fire; it might have driven off some of the mosquitoes. The only way to escape the insects' attentions was to wrap themselves in their blankets, despite the heat. But the air soon cooled down a bit and they managed to get some sleep.

Shortly after noon on the next day, they reached a small town named Woodbridge. There were some brick buildings around the square, but the rest of the houses were made of wood. Shaw pointed to a sign hanging on the side of a barn.

"Livery stable. I may survive yet."

Troy passed over a small bag of gold coins. "Get a good one. I'm going to be riding in it, too. No price is too great if it means I can get off the back of this mule."

They had prepared a story to explain their circumstance. Shaw claimed to have hurt his ankle in a fall. His second pair of trousers covered the bandage and his realistic limp gave plausibility to the story. Troy kept carefully in the background

while the purchase was completed, coming
forward only when the stable owner waved him
over to hitch Shaw's horse to their new buggy.
Troy made a mess of it; he had absolutely no idea
of where all the lines and traces went, and was
boxed on the ear and cursed out by the man for his
efforts. After that he stood to one side, hand over
his sore ear, while the man did it himself, glaring
at his back and thinking about which way would
be the most satisfactory to kill the son-of-a-bitch.

With their goods dumped into the buggy, the old
mule tied on behind, the trip became a good deal
easier. They couldn't hurry because Shaw's leg
was stiff and painful, and too much traveling
fatigued him greatly. Troy tried not to show his
concern when the wounded man developed a fever
—but it was gone the next morning. Shaw took his
penicillin every day, and there were no signs of in-
fection around the wound. It should be all right.

They proceeded at a leisurely pace, taking a
week to get to Richmond, reaching the city late
one afternoon when the shadows were already
slanting lengthwise through the trees.

"Lovely city," Shaw said, "one of my favorites."

"Are we going to this hotel of yours, the Blue
House?"

"Yes, they know me there. Inexpensive, and
the food is filling. Frequented by commercial
travelers who believe in getting their money's
worth. But we'll make a little detour on the way
there. Down this street. Pleasant homes."

"Really great. Does the leg hurt?"

"It really feels much better. Throbs a good deal
and protests if I put too much weight on it. Otherwise, doctor, the operation was a success. What
are those little pills you make me take every day?"

"I told you. An old secret family recipe against the fever. Seems to have worked, too."

"Indeed. There, see ahead? The large white house surrounded by the castiron fence."

"I see it. What about it?"

"The thing about it is that it is owned by the man I know as Colonel Wesley McCulloch. What must be determined next, I imagine, is to discover if he is the same man whom you are looking for."

Troy pulled hard on the reins and the horse whinnied in protest as it stopped. Troy looked at the house, his face tight, staring as though he could see right through the walls if he tried hard enough.

Had he found him?

Was this the end of the hunt—or just the beginning?

TWENTY-SIX

He was certainly a strange man, my new American friend, and I really wasn't quite sure what to make of him. By that I don't mean that I had doubts about his courage—or his resourcefulness. The little contretemps with the highwaymen had certainly proven his abilities on that score. It was a number of small things, as well as his overall manner, that I found so disturbing. His determination was rocklike and steadfast. It was in every ligament of his body as he sat now, his jaw clamped, staring at McCulloch's house as though wishing to destroy it on the instant. I am driven to admit that I felt a small shiver at the sight; I would not wish to be this man's enemy.

"Okay, that's enough, where to now?" he said, giving the reins a snap to wake the nag up.

"Three streets ahead, then turn right."

That was part of it, his use of language. What on

earth did *okay* mean? I had vague memories of
having heard the term used before, though I could
not remember the circumstance. Troy used other
expressions like this from time to time, spoke
them most naturally, though usually when
relaxed. I had ceased to question him because he
only put me off with vague explanations, then
changed the subject. But where had he learned to
speak in this manner? I am fairly well acquainted
with the city of New York, so that I can verify that
he certainly did speak in the New York style. But
it was more than this. At times I felt that he must
belong to some secret organization, some mysterious order that had long been locked away from the
world on a hidden island, like some mad creation
of the author Edgar Allan Poe. I longed to see what
he had hidden in those saddle-bags—but knew
better than to even attempt to open them. And his
knowledge of medicine was simply astonishing,
far superior to that of any surgeon I have ever
met. My bullet wound was healing without suppu-
ration, and I had avoided the fever perhaps because of the strange and bitter tablets he made me
swallow.

But it was his manner that I found so disconcerting. As though he were a white man turned
black. When we discussed things at night, when he
was invisible to me, there was nothing in his voice
to indicate that he was other than an educated
Yankee. I have met many men of his race and have
found them universally untutored, thick of speech
and bereft of any grasp of grammar, savages but
lately drawn from their jungle homes. But not
this man. He was a mystery.

As always I was greeted with much enthusiasm
at the Blue House Hotel, undoubtedly since the

owner, Mrs. Henley, entertains the baseless hope that some day I shall smile with favor upon her not unattractive daughter Arabella, marry her and take her away to a far superior life. I encourage this ambition just enough to assure that the service and the accommodation are of the finest, but not enough to entrap me in the treakly mire of matrimony. Mrs. Henley herself admitted me and I quickly distracted her attention so she would not see the look of quick anger on Troy's countenance when she peremptorily sent him to the stable to bed with the horses. I do feel sorry for him; he is so unable to accept the social circumstance that his color forces upon him. But I was not sorry enough to regret my sleeping on a featherbed while he shared the equine hay. For I am greatly in need of the respite, my wound having made me restive when trying to sleep on the hard ground night after night. This night I fell instantly into the embrace of Morpheus and stirred not a jot until I awoke in the morning feeling truly refreshed for the first time since my injury. I breakfasted heartily on ham, cornbread, fried corn fritters, eggs, kidneys, rashers of bacon, and sweet preserves. I was whistling when I joined Troy in the stable, but ceased instantly I caught his eye. He was scowling mightily and trying to brush bits of hay from his clothing.

"Good morning. Have you broken your fast?" I said.

"I have—if you consider cold grits and sour buttermilk a breakfast," he growled.

"The food here isn't too good, is it?" I said, trying to put from my mind memory of the breakfast I had just eaten. "Have you considered our plan of operation for the day?"

"A great deal—and I've decided to risk it. Letting McCulloch take a look at me, that is. If I go sneaking around it's only going to look more suspicious. I'm counting on the fact that the last time he saw me was a long way from here, and under very different circumstances. I don't think he'll recognize me. If he does, or asks you about me, do you know what to say?"

"I do. I have the cover story memorized." He nodded, accepting my use of the term 'cover story,' not realizing I had only recently learned this unusual phrase from him. "You are a servant of my friend in New York, Dick Van Zandt, loaned to me for a time to assist me until my leg injuries are mended. Satisfactory?"

"Great. And don't forget, my name is Tom." For some reason he smiled at that. "Now let's get moving. I want to get this over with."

Troy was silent during the drive, and I was aware of the tension that gripped him as we approached the house and halted before the front doorway. He helped me down and held the horse while I addressed myself to the bellpull. A servant answered, one familiar to me.

"Is your master at home?" I asked.

Before he could answer there was the drumming of a horse's galloping hooves and the colonel himself rode up the drive.

"I'll be damned—is that you Robbie?"

"It is indeed," I said, turning and taking a hobbling step towards him as he dismounted. He took no notice of my servant, but over his shoulder I saw Troy's face frozen rigid as a rock. I think he had found his man. McCulloch shook my hand, then indicated my leg.

"Fall off your horse?" he asked.

"Just about, an equally boring accident. Which forces me to travel about in this infernal buggy."

"Well, come inside and I'll give you some whiskey that will make you forget your troubles. Your darky can take the trap around to the rear."

He looked behind him as he said this, waving Troy off in a peremptory manner. Then he lowered his hand, but remained half-turned for an instant looking at Troy as he nodded then shuffled off leading the horse. The colonel took my arm as I made my slow way up the steps.

"Your servant," he said. "A new purchase on your part?"

"Tom? No, he's just a nigger I borrowed from a friend in New York, to drive me around. Why do you ask?"

"No reason. Just thought I had seen him before —but I couldn't, could I? All these apes look alike, don't they?"

He laughed, and I pretended equal merriment. When in Rome. We went in—and the whiskey was as good as promised.

"Dammit, Wes," I said, smacking my lips over it. "As much as I love the distillate of the western isles, I must say that your Virginia product has a great deal to recommend it."

"Coming from a Scotchman—high praise indeed. And your arrival is a fortunate one. I have a question about some of the machinery that I am sure you can help me with. I must write to your father and you can tell me what to say."

"I'm no engineer, my father saw to it that I escaped the reek of the works and had a proper gentleman's education."

"Damn the gentleman! You grew up around those machines and you know as much about them as any man."

"True—but don't tell father—or he'll resent every farthing spent on my school fees."

"Finish that drink and we'll go over to the factory and I'll show you the problem. Okay?"

"Yes, agreed, as long as we can return to the rest of this bottle."

Okay. That's where I had heard that strange term before. Right here, from the colonel's own lips. The same word that Troy had used. What was the bond between this man of such high station and the black man who had sought him out? I itched to know—yet dare not ask either of them.

The colonel was quite proud of his manufactury, for in a year's time he had built it up into quite a going concern. The problem he wished to discuss concerned one of his drill presses. He pointed it out to me, shouting above the roar of the leather belts whining about their pulleys above our heads.

"Broken in half, see it, the large supporting arm. Dumb nigger let it drop when we were moving it. I took a yard of hide off his back, but that won't fix the damage. Can I get a replacement—or must I return the entire drill press?"

I bent stiffly and ran my fingers over the frame. "See here, this number, cast right into the metal? That's the identification of the wooden mold that this was made from. All you have to do is write father, describe what happened, and give this number. They'll make a new sand mold, cast the part and ship it to you. One of your fitters can tap out the old sleeve here, then drill the new arm out to receive it. There will be no trouble putting it right again."

I kept my eyes open as we finished the tour, but the only thing at all out of the ordinary that I could discover was a locked and barred store-room. Since the colonel had been boring me with exact details of everything else we had seen I felt that it was not out of order to question him about this. His manner was so offhand that I was sure he was lying.

"Secrets, Robbie, industrial secrets. I am working on an improvement upon Whitney's cotton gin that will make my fortune one day. But none shall see it until it is perfected. Now let's get back to that whiskey."

I made my apologies as soon as I could after lunch, pleading an aching leg, which was certainly the truth. Troy brought the buggy around and helped me up into it, biting his lips shut, forcing himself to remain quiet until we were well out of sight of the house before speaking.

"He's the one, the Colonel Wesley McCulloch that I'm looking for!"

"He appeared to recognize you too, or at least he was interested in your identity. He accepted my explanation, never mentioned it again. Just said something about all of your race each resembling the other."

"He would, wouldn't he, the son-of-a-bitch. Another thing that I can tell you, he's not very loved by his servants. They were almost too frightened to talk to *me* about him. One old man finally did. Seems that McCulloch beat one of his slaves to death a few months ago. I believe it. He must be in hog heaven, Massah McCulloch." As he said this, Troy spat with hatred into the dusty street. "Servants also said that you went to his factory with him. What did you see there?"

He was too casual with the question; there was something else about McCulloch that he wanted badly to know. I pretended innocence.

"Just one more dreary plant. I've been standing up too much. I'm looking forward with great anticipation to stretching out and putting this leg up on a cushion."

"Were they making anything in particular? I mean anything unusual?"

"Unusual in what way?" When he failed to answer at once I decided that the time had come to put the question to him. "I have a feeling that there are a number of items that you have neglected to tell me about. Isn't it time that you took me into your confidence? Or do you mistrust me?"

He shook his head solemnly. "No, Robbie, I have all the trust in the world in you. But there are some things that I just can't explain. You'll just have to take my word for that. But I can tell you that our friend the colonel is up to no good. It has something to do with weapons. Were they manufacturing anything like that in his factory?"

"Emphatically no. Of that I can be certain. Mr. Remington's rifle barrel drill is an object I would recognize at once. And they certainly weren't casting cannon."

"There are different kinds of weapons. I have reason to suspect that McCulloch might be involved in the manufacture of a new kind of gun. One that might be assembled out of very commonplace steel parts. Was there anything like that?"

"Steel parts galore, but I don't think any of them resembled gun parts. Of course if it were a new invention, why then I couldn't tell. But there was one portion of the plant that we didn't enter. Locked and sealed. An improved cotton gin was what he said. I remember thinking at the time that he must be lying, though I didn't know why."

"That's it!" he said, striking me a stunning and enthusiastic blow on the shoulder. "Do you think that your game leg can stand up to a little more riding? I want you to show me where this factory is, then give me some idea of the location of the sealed area. I'll come back tonight by myself and see just what that bastard is trying to hide!"

TWENTY-SEVEN

The time must have been close to three o'clock in the morning; the night still and hushed. When the moon had set soon after two-thirty the sleeping city had sunk into an even deeper slumber in the warm darkness.

Troy slept in the hayloft, close to the outside wall of the stable, where the night sky was clearly visible through the wide gap between the boards. He had woken twice, looked out and squinted at the moon, then gone back to sleep. Now he was awake, dipping water out of the bucket and rubbing it over his face. One of the horses stirred in its stall when it heard the small sound, then blew restlessly through its lips. It quieted when the barn door opened and shut noiselessly and silence descended once again.

Damp, hot, dark, the enemy on all sides; it was so much like Viet Nam that Troy's hands felt strangely empty, missing the M16 that had been so much a part of him. At first he had intended to bring the revolver, but then had changed his mind. If he had to use a weapon it would mean that the mission had been a failure. He wanted intelligence —not a fire fight. The steel lockpick was the weapon of choice this night. He also had his clasp knife, as well as a candle stub and some matches. There was nothing else that he needed.

Moving through the darkness of the unlit streets he felt secure, knowing that he would see or hear anyone long before they could be aware of him. He was on familiar ground now, a night reconaissance, a straightforward mission.

Once a dog barked, catching his smell on the warm breeze, but Troy was well past before it had detected his presence. Later on he became aware of approaching footsteps. He stood silently in the darkness as the two men passed just a few yards away, talking quietly to each other.

Less than half an hour later he stood with his back to a picket fence, looking at the outline of the wooden building against the stars. McCulloch's factory.

Troy remained there, motionless, for a long time, the constellations of stars above dipping and vanishing in the west, patiently waiting. Nothing disturbed the quiet of the night. There appeared to be no watchman, and no dogs. A horse whinnied in the distance, then grew silent. This small noise did not disturb the stillness of the night, deep and profound.

He was in the clear. Troy moved away from the fence and drifted silently across the road. The front door of the building was before him and he pressed against it, his fingers feeling for the out-

line of the lock. Getting through this was almost
too easy, the lock too simple. And there were certainly no electronic alarms or detectors to worry
about. The lock snicked open and he pushed into
the office beyond.

All of the interior doors were unlocked. He felt
his way into the larger, open space of the workshop, filled with forms barely visible in the star-
light that filtered through the high windows. To
the rear, Robbie had said, a door in the back wall
to the right of the forge. He moved forward, step
by careful step.

Though he could not see the forge he felt the
radiant heat of its presence. Soundlessly he crept
by it, running his fingertips along the wooden wall
until he found the outline of a door frame. A hasp
held it shut and it was sealed with a padlock. Troy
ran his fingers over its face, finding the keyhole,
touching the pivoted shackle where it went
through the eye of the hasp, feeling it move under
his fingers.

It was unlocked.

He stopped, motionless, not breathing, not
making a sound. This was an unexpected bit of
luck.

But was it just luck?

While his conscious mind considered this
logical problem he found his body growing tense.
He became aware of a growing sensation of un-
ease. It appeared to have no physical source; he
had heard nothing, seen nothing. Yet there was
this expanding fear whose existence could not be
denied. It was a sensation that he had experienced
only once previously in his life, on a night patrol.
Just before they had been ambushed. It was a
reaction at an instinctual level, far removed from

any rational thought processes.

It was completely irrational and emotional. Yet he had the sensation that something fearsome and deadly lay just beyond the wall. Waited there, scant inches away from him. It did not make any kind of logical sense—but he *knew* that something was there in the darkness. He tried to dismiss the sensation, but he could not. The danger was unmistakably present.

He did not want to face it nor discover what it was. But he had to respect it—more than respect—he was terrified of it. His heart was thudding with this irrational fear and he wanted to get out of this dark trap, to leave at once, to run and keep on running. But that was the one thing he was not going to do. Instead of opening the door and facing whatever evil lay hidden on the other side, he would use other means to exorcise it. The traditional one. Still in absolute silence he withdrew the clasp knife from his pocket and opened it. Slowly and carefully, in order not to make the slightest sound, he pulled his shirt tail out of his trousers and used the razor-sharp blade to cut off a piece of cloth. He crumpled this, bent and placed it against the wall, then took out a match, cupping it in both hands. It made a small crack and ignited as he snapped the head with his thumbnail.

As soon as it was burning well he dropped the match onto the crumpled cloth, watched for a moment as the cloth flared and caught fire. The flame, small as it was, gave off enough light for him to move quickly across the workshop and out of the building the way he had come, finding shelter in a small grove on the far side of the road.

Where he waited with unmoving patience.

Inside the building the fire would be slowly

spreading, eating into the wooden wall, moving along the floor. Some minutes passed before he saw a flicker of light through one of the front windows of the building. Only seconds after that there was the sound of a door crashing open in the back of the building, a horse neighing with excitement, then the quick hammer of hooves as horse and rider burst out into the street.

"Fire! Sound the alarm! Fire, fire!"

Troy smiled to himself in the darkness. He knew that voice.

McCulloch.

His was the presence of evil sensed on the other side of the wall. He had been laying in wait, ready to spring the trap. It had been well-baited, Troy suddenly realized, a plan undoubtedly galvanized by his own presence. McCulloch had not been sure of his identity or he would have been seized on the spot. But the colonel must have started to worry about the resemblance. Being a thorough man, once he had started on this train of thought he would have followed it through to the end. He would have considered the possibility of his being followed back through time. And the colonel was a careful man as well. There was always the possibility that the resemblance might have been a chance one, but the trap had still been laid to take care of this possibility that it had not. Therefore the guided tour, the implied secret of the locked room. McCulloch was a master tactician and his plan should have worked.

But it hadn't. It had come within a hair's breadth of succeeding. Yet it had failed. But it had been a very close run thing. If Troy had so much as opened that door a fraction of an inch he would have been dead on the spot, shot down instantly.

He was sure of that now and felt the cool touch of perspiration at the realization of how close he had come.

But would there be anyone else lying in ambush here. No, McCulloch must surely have done this alone, trusting no one else with his secret, baiting the trap, then lying in wait. But he had gone for the firemen. Was there a chance now to get into the room? There had to be a back door.

No, too late. Lights were coming on in the houses; voices called out one to the other. Fire! A constant danger in this city of wooden buildings. Everyone was aware of the communal threat and hurried to help. More and more people appeared and Troy drew deeper into the shadows.

Within minutes the first of the fire apparatus appeared, horse-drawn and primitive. But effective. Shouting men threw their weight onto the pump handles and the first streams of water jetted from the hose.

It was organized bedlam—but it was getting the job done. A bucket brigade formed, reaching to the well of the nearest house, then bucket after bucket of water began to splash onto the soaring flames. Another piece of fire apparatus arrived and McCulloch was there as well now to lead them through the front of the building to fight the fire from that side. This was Troy's chance! Fire was no respecter of race. Black and white were mixed together in the battle so there was little chance that he would even be noticed.

Troy ran to join the fire-fighters who were laboring at the back of the building.

Through the open rear door he saw that the interior was now a mass of flames. The stream of water from the hose was being played onto the roof above to stop the fire from spreading, while two rows of sweating, shouting men hurled pails of water on the fire below. Troy seized up a bucket and joined them.

It was hot and desperate work. For a while the fire would appear to be under control—then it would break out again, flaring up in the dry wood. Everyone was smeared and filthy with ashes, running with sweat. Troy worked as hard as any of the others, moving in to fight the fire in the depths of the smoking building. Pushing through the smoking embers. Kicking his foot against something made of metal.

He glanced around; for the moment no one seemed to be looking his way. He bent swiftly, grabbed up the metal, and dropped it into the bucket, plunging his hand into the water after it as the hot metal seared his flesh, then turning, bumping into others, making his way out into the night.

The first casualties of the fire were on the far side of the road, coughing with the agony of their smoke-filled lungs. Troy joined them, his coughing realistic enough since he had breathed in a good deal of the same smoke. He dropped to the ground, sat there, coughing, his head between his legs, his hidden fingers slipping the metal out of the bucket and concealing it inside his shirt.

The night grew darker as the flames were brought under control. He found that there was no difficulty at all in slipping away then and vanishing in the blackness.

Troy controlled his impatience until he was far from the scene of the fire, in a silent street among dark trees. He sheltered behind a row of sweet-smelling shrubs, placed the piece of metal on the ground and bent over it. The match flared and the stub of candle caught and flickered. He let it burn for just a moment, then blew it out.

But he had seen enough. He knew what he had. Carefully he took up the blackened piece of metal, held it tightly in his hands.

He had held a piece of steel like this once before, in a different time and place. That had been in the Smithsonian Institute, in Washington.

The two pieces of metal were identical.

What he was holding now was the trigger plate of a Sten gun.

TWENTY-EIGHT

It was dawn before the fire was completely out. Streamers of smoke still drifted up from the blackened ruins, while soot-smeared and weary men stood about in small groups, or sat sprawled on the ground. Wes McCulloch kicked at a burned timber in the workshop and cursed savagely under his breath. Bad, but it could have been worse; the fire had been stopped in time and none of the machinery had been seriously damaged. It would all be working again as soon as the place was cleaned up and the leather drive belts replaced. The storeroom had had the worst of it, but even there nothing irreplaceable had been destroyed.

"This is terrible, colonel, terrible," the fat man said, picking his way delicately through the rubble. His spotless clothing and polished boots were sure indications that he had had no part in fighting the fire, no matter how great his concern now. "Do you know how it started?"

"No, senator, I don't," McCulloch said. "But you can see over there, on the wall, where the center of the fire was. It appears to have been located near the forge. Perhaps a stray spark from that, smoldering, you know how these things are." He turned as he heard the horses gallop up outside. "Excuse me, senator. We had better both get outside, it's not too comfortable in here."

McCulloch waited until the senator had started talking to some of his friends before he waved the two hard-looking men over to him.

"Hicks, I want you and Yancy to get over to the Blue House Hotel. Do you know the Scotchman, Shaw, the man who was with me yesterday?"

"Shore do, colonel. Little fancy feller."

"Get him. Wake him up, tell him I have to see him at once. If he argues with you, why take him anyway. I want you to get him back to the house—then lock him up. Use that cell in the slave quarters. He's involved in this fire. But don't let on about that until you get him away from the hotel. I want to keep this a private matter, because after we talk to him I think that he is going to vanish, quiet like."

"You think *he* set it!"

"No—but his nigger did. So look around for the black bastard before you stir up Shaw. I don't think that he'll still be there, but look anyway. If you don't find him, why this Shaw will tell us where he *can* be found. I'll see to that myself. You just keep him locked away until I get back. That won't be until later today. Now get him."

McCulloch watched as they kicked their mounts around and galloped away. *Troy Harmon.* He breathed the name under his breath like a curse. It

was a curse. The jig had followed him after all! He
never would have believed that a creature like that
would have had the guts. Not guts, just stupidity,
animal reflex like a snapping turtle hanging on
after it was dead. Well, that didn't matter now. He
was here, causing trouble. And that newsman had
brought him right to his door. Shaw was going to
pay for that. If only his mind hadn't been so occu-
pied with the pressing matters at hand, if he
had only recognized the jig when he had first
appeared. Only later had the resemblance begun
to worry him; the possibility had always been
there that he might be followed. That was why he
had taken precautions. The trap he had set had
been a good one, had almost worked. But the
jigaboo must have suspected something, found out
some way. Well, that didn't matter now. Everything else was progressing on schedule. All the
plans had been made and things were going forward without a hitch. Except for this little setback. So be it. You had to take your losses in war.
A few lost battles didn't count. The final victory
did. And that was the one that he was going to win.

As soon as the factory manager showed up,
McCulloch put him in charge of the salvage, then
rode home. It was almost seven o'clock. Plenty of
time to wash and change, even have some breakfast. The food would have to make up for the sleep
that he had missed. Coffee, and some of the bour-
bon. He must remember to take a flask with him
as well. The meeting was set for ten. If he rode out
by nine he would be there with plenty of time to
spare.

A fresh horse, saddled and bridled, was waiting
outside by the time McCulloch had finished breakfast, then gone up to the safe in his bedroom. It

had been specially made for him in London; the locks had been fitted in his presence. There were three of them, situated one above the other, and only a single set of keys for them in the entire world. He inserted the keys, one by one, turning them and unlocking the solid steel door, then dragging it open. Inside were fitted drawers containing a little gold, a good deal of currency, as well as all of his papers. And the large wooden chest. He pulled the chest to him, smiling. The future of the South lay within.

After closing and locking the safe again, he wrapped the chest in a waterproof sheet and tucked it under his arm. The slave who was holding the horse tried to help him with it, but he slapped him away with his riding crop. No black hands on this! He secured the chest in place behind the saddle, patted his pocket to see if the flask was secure, then swung up into the saddle.

He turned the horse away from the city and cantered slowly down the road.

Ten o'clock found him at a country crossroads in the hills. There were farms nearby, though none of them were visible from this spot. Which is why he had picked it. The road behind him twisted off uphill before vanishing into the thick forest. McCulloch looked at his watch, then put it away and took out the large silver flask. He took a deep swallow, then a second, and was just lowering it when he heard the other horse approaching. He spurred his own horse forward and was waiting when the other man rode up.

"You are Colonel McCulloch?" the newcomer said. He was an Army officer, a lieutenant of cavalry, and sat his spirited black horse with practiced ease. His long dark hair swept down almost to his collar. He had a full beard and long mustachios, his forehead high and fair, the eyes beneath penetrating and sharp.

"I am McCulloch. I must thank you for coming all this way, sir, with scant reason given for your mission."

"We have mutual friends, colonel, who assured me that the trip would be more than worthwhile. The most important thing that will ever happen to you, one said. I'll admit that I am most intrigued. Now, colonel, will you divulge this secret that has everyone so enthused?"

"I will, lieutenant. But I won't tell you—I will show you. But not here. If you will be patient for a short while longer, we will move farther back into this forest."

Since neither of them was given to small talk they rode in silence. McCulloch was obviously familiar with the track for he turned off onto a small path that wound up through the trees. The path ended in a small open glade that faced towards the sharp rise of the hill. The colonel dismounted and the other man swung down beside him; they secured their horses under the trees. The lieutenant looked on with unconcealed curiosity as McCulloch unslung the chest and carried it out into the sunlight.

"This is what you have come to see, sir," McCulloch said, carefully unwrapping it. "I ask your patience for a moment more while I point out some things that I believe are obvious to us both. We are Southern patriots and I know that we both have faith in our just cause. I also have reason to believe that when war comes—and come it shall just as certain as destiny—you will cast your lot unhesitatingly with the South."

The officer nodded slowly. "What you say is true, though I have only lately determined that course. And I spoke of it to no one. How could you possibly know?"

"Because I feel that I know you, lieutenant. I know your pride in your ability as a cavalryman—and your unique dedication to that craft. I am now going to show you a weapon that I am sure you will appreciate. But first, might I ask you a question? Are your troops equipped with the new Sharps breechloading rifle?"

"No—but I wish they were. In spite of all the fancy talk the Army has scarcely any of them."

"A good weapon?"

"The best. Too cumbersome to be used from horseback by cavalry, but still a fine infantry weapon. A trained soldier can get off six, maybe seven shots a minute."

"Indeed," McCulloch said, obviously not too impressed. He opened the box and reached inside. "In that case, lieutenant, what would you say to a weapon that wasn't much larger than a horse pistol—and could fire more than ten shots every *second?*"

The lieutenant's voice was hushed as he looked into the box. "I would say, sir, that if such a weapon did exist, why then that warfare would be a very different thing indeed."

McCulloch placed the steel form of the submachine gun into his hands.

"Compact, ugly, deadly," McCulloch said. "With the metal stock folded it is just twenty inches long. It weighs only six and a half pounds. This metal box contains thirty-two rounds of ammunition. It clips into place underneath the receiver, here. Now I will demonstrate how to fire the weapon.

This small knob is drawn back fully, until it clicks
into place. That is all that must be done—because
the gun will do all the rest. When the trigger is depressed it will fire. When the trigger is released it
will stop. It will do this until the ammunition in
the box is exhausted. Then it will take you only a
moment to insert a new box—the soldiers will
carry bandoliers of these boxes fully loaded. Now
watch."

McCulloch swung about, the gun at his waist,
and depressed the trigger. It roared out, again and
again, sending a hail of bullets through the trees
and into the grassy bank beyond. Leaves and twigs
floated down in the sunlight; a branch broke and
dropped to the ground. Then the firing stopped
and their heads rang with the echo of the sound. A
click and the empty cartridge box dropped to the
ground; click, a new one was inserted. He turned
and handed the weapon to the cavalryman.

"Hold it firmly. The recoil is slight, but it will
climb up and to the right. Therefore you should
fire short bursts letting the muzzle drop back on
your target again after each burst."

The lieutenant reached out and took the gun,
feeling the cool metal of the stock, the warmth of
the short barrel. He raised it slowly to his shoulder, looked over the fixed sights, then pulled the
trigger. It hammered loudly, again and again,
brass shells raining to the ground, lead bullets
screaming out. When the last shot had been fired
he looked down at the gun—then up at McCulloch
—his eyes wide with excitement.

"This—this is incredible! I never imagined anything like it. A single soldier, a mounted trooper,
can have the firing power of an entire squad."

"And he can also fire while mounted, while

riding at the enemy. The sights are fixed at a hundred yards, but they aren't really needed. The gun sprays bullets like water from a hose. Just sweep it back and forth and the enemy is destroyed. This gun is called . . . the Victory."

"And it will bring victory," the lieutenant said, laughing aloud with enthusiasm. "This will change the entire role of cavalry, turn it into the supreme striking force of a new army. It will make lightning war, hitting hard, suddenly, destructively. With this the cavalry could strike the enemy a mortal blow. They could hit and destroy —and even keep moving on while leaving the infantry to mop up. But how does it operate? How is it made? I have heard nothing of its existence before, not even a whisper of rumor."

"That is because it is a secret known to but a few, true friends of the South. I make the guns myself, openly in my Richmond plant. The parts, when separate, do not even resemble those of a gun. They are assembled at a secret site where the cartridges are also manufactured. Without these new cartridges the Victory is just a collection of dead metal. With them—why, it is the Victory!"

McCulloch pushed his thumb against the open end of one of the loaded clips and extracted a squat cartridge, passed it over. "Short and solid. The bullet weighs one-hundred and fifteen grains, the charge of powder six. The casing is made of brass drawn to shape on a special machine that is manufactured in the British Isles. The priming cap contains fulminating powder, the same sort that you will find in the pin fire cartridge. But the resemblance ends there. This is a center fire cartridge and does not have to be inserted and removed by hand. The firing pin always impacts in the correct place. The recoil of the gun is harnessed to extract the spent cartridge, then insert a new one in its place."

"So simple—and so obvious when you point it out."

McCulloch nodded agreement. "It needed but the design. The metal working and brass drawing tools were readily available. There is no mystery to this weapon. It is just better, cheaper, faster—and deadlier. I ask you now to imagine its use in battle. Soon the Union will be sundered, our South will be a country in its own right at last. The war that will surely follow could be a short, efficient war. Or a drawn out and deadly one. To be absolutely sure that the war will end at once—what must be done?"

"Why—march on Washington City, of course. It is poorly defended, the troops there raw and untrained. They would probably fight, probably make a stand at Bull Run, that's the obvious place to draw the lines."

"It is indeed," McCulloch agreed, smiling to himself. "So what would happen to these troops if you were to attack them with five thousand horsemen—each armed with a Victory?"

"What indeed! It would indeed be a victory. We would be unstoppable. We would take Washington and destroy any troops foolish enough to attempt to take it back. The war would be won and the South would be free. To take its rightful place among the nations of the world." He spun about and seized McCulloch by the hand.

"I am your man, sir. I will get the troopers if you will supply the guns. It will be done just as you have described it! Thank you, Colonel McCulloch."

"No, Lieutenant Stuard, I am but the instrument. All the thanks should go to you."

J. E. B. Stuart was only half-listening; his eyes had a distant look, as though he were gazing into the future and seeing the attacking troopers, the battles and the victories that his horsemen and this Victory weapon would surely provide.

TWENTY-NINE

It was just after six-thirty in the morning when Hicks and Yancy knocked on the front door of the Blue House Hotel. They had to knock again, louder, before it was opened by Mrs. Henley herself, arms bare, face flushed from the kitchen fire.

"Do you know what the hour is? What do you mean bothering honest people with all that hammering at this time of day?"

"Sorry, m'am, but we came to find a Mr. Shaw who's staying here. Got an urgent message from Colonel McCulloch for him."

"It's too early for messages. Mr. Shaw's asleep and I haven't even made the coffee yet."

"Well, we don't want to bother him, not when he's still abed. I hear tell he's got a nigger with him. Where he at? I can go and get him and he can stir his master up."

"Out back in the stable. And I don't have any

more time for jawing."

The door slammed in their faces. "You stay here," Hicks said. "Make sure he don't try to sashay out the front door while we hanging around the back. I'll see to that fire-raising buck."

Yancey settled down on the steps while Hicks got the big pistol from the holster on his saddle, then went quietly down the alleyway towards the rear of the house. Yancey pulled a piece of grass and chewed on it slowly until Hicks returned.

"Gone," Hicks said, pushing the pistol into his belt and pulling his coat down to hide it. "Didn't think he'd hang around, not after what he done. That Shaw, he's gonna tell us something about that . . ."

He spun about quickly as the front door opened, then smiled as he saw the young girl standing there.

"You shouldn't mind mama," Arabella said. "She's always kind of short in the morning." She reached behind her and took a tray off the table there and brought it outside; there were two steaming mugs of coffee on it. "Any friends of Mr. Shaw's are friends of mine. Thought you might like this."

"We're friends of his, all right," Hicks said, winking broadly at Yancey over Arabella's head. "This is sure fine coffee. I know he wants to see us. Do you think he's up yet?"

"He is. I brought him a basin of water some time ago. Just finish your coffee and I'll show you to his room."

It took the two men only a minute to drink the coffee, then they followed Arabella up the stairs, waiting until she had turned away before they knocked.

"It's open," Robbie Shaw called out when he heard the knock on the door. He was just finishing shaving and he looked at the newcomers in the mirror as they came in. "Can I help you?"

"The name is Hicks, Mr. Shaw. I work for Colonel McCulloch."

"Yes, Hicks, I recognized you. I've seen you there. Is there any reason for this early call?" He rinsed the straight-edged razor in the basin and wiped it on the towel.

"Big fire last night at the colonel's factory—"

"The fire alarm—it woke me up. Is it very bad?"

"Not for me to say, sir. But the colonel, he wants to see you at once. Sent us to bring you."

"That's very agreeable of the colonel. Please return and tell him I'll be over later this evening, after I have taken care of some pressing matters."

"I think he would like to see you now."

"I'm sure he would, but it is impossible. Now if you will kindly leave . . ."

"Now," Hicks said, pulling the pistol and jamming it hard into Shaw's midriff. "I want you to pack your traveling bag and don't say another word, hear? We three going to walk out that door sweet as pie and you going to look like you really enjoying it. Show him your Arkansas toothpick, Yancey."

With a surprisingly quick movement the big man produced a long-bladed knife and thrust it forward towards Shaw.

"Old Yancey here not too bright, but he knows how to use that thing. Wouldn't want no accidents when we walk out of here. Now where is your bag at?"

"The closet. I'll get it—"

"No, you won't. Yancey will. There might be a

gun in there as well as the bag and you might make a mistake and get yourself hurt. Yancey, drag it out."

Yancey shifted the knife to his left hand, grabbed the doorknob with his right hand and pulled.

Troy stepped out of the closet, bringing his raised hand down in an angled chop, the hard edge catching the man on the side of his neck. He grunted and folded, the knife dropping from his suddenly limp fingers.

Hicks heard the meaty thud of the blow. He spun about and raised the pistol—and screamed as Shaw's razor slashed the back of his hand. He groaned terribly and clutched hard at his wrist, the blood dripping through his fingers.

"Too much noise," Troy said, balling his fist and leaping forward. The single blow collapsed the man into silence.

Troy bound the wounded man's hand with the towel while Shaw rinsed his razor in the bowl, then dumped the pink-frothed water out the window. "Do you think anyone heard?" he asked.

Troy listened, then shook his head. "Doesn't seem like it. All quiet. You're pretty fast with that blade, you know?"

"I had to be. I kept it handy since there was always the chance someone would pull a gun. You were right about McCulloch sending a war party."

"He had to. That fire only confirmed any suspicions he already had. Now he is out to get me before I can get him. But he has too much strength in this town. It's no place to make a stand against him. We have to withdraw and regroup. But intelligently. That's why I wanted to wait until these roughnecks showed up. If we had just tried to run he would have had a posse on our tail. Now we have bought some time. Let's make the most of it."

He pulled the rope out from under the bed where he had thrown it and cut off a length. While Shaw finished packing his bag Troy skillfully bound and gagged the two men. "You got the story straight?" he asked.

"It's not too complicated. I grab a quick breakfast, tell them I'll be writing in my room all day and not to disturb me. Then back here and out the window and onto the barn roof, just the way you came in. Join you out back where you will have the buggy."

"Hang on. Can you make it with that leg?"

"No trouble. I might not be able to climb up very easily, but this is just a matter of hanging and dropping."

"Do it then. By the time they discover these two I want to be far away from here."

The city was just stirring to life as they went through it. "Have you made any kind of a plan?" Shaw asked.

"Good question. If you want to know, I have been thinking about the answer to that one ever since we decided to get out of here. I don't see any easy answers. Everything I come up with, I right away start worrying about McCulloch second guessing me. At first I had the strong temptation to head north to safety. But that's the obvious way and those roads are sure to be watched. The colonel has powerful friends—and they are all part of a conspiracy. I know that he is not doing this thing alone. It's too big."

"Can you tell me about it?"

"I'll tell you what I can—only later. Let's save

our necks first. If going north is out, it would be equally stupid to go south, too much like marching into the lion's den. Of course we could head east for Norfolk, but we would surely be spotted if we tried to get a ship out of the port."

"Why not a train?"

"Worst of all. The stations will be watched, and if they miss us here they can wire ahead for a reception committee."

"Turn left at the next corner," Shaw said.

Troy looked at him questioningly. "Any reason why?"

"Yes, of course. Since you have run out of suggestions I thought I would make one of my own. I suggest a ride on the Underground Railroad."

"Of course! I was dumb not to think of it. You've worked with these people, haven't you?"

"I have. And I can take you to a station that is only a half-day's ride from here, just this side of Montpelier. But we're going to have to muddy the waters a bit first. We don't want to leave a trail that points right to where we're going. The way it stands now we are pretty easy to identify."

"You can say that again! A black man driving with a white man in a green buggy towing a one-eyed mule! We might as well advertise."

"My feelings exactly. So we go and sell the mule to this livery stable just outside of the city. When we leave he sees us head north on the turnpike. Only once we are out of sight we use the side road west, me driving and you suffocating under the rug, on the floor in back. By the time they pick up our trail we will be gone without a trace."

"Sounds good except for the head under the sack bit. Though maybe I can get some sleep."

By late afternoon the buggy had left the low-lying farming country and was moving slowly along the dusty road that wound up into the foothills of the Piedmont Plateau. The day was hot, but the air was so clear that they could see the outline of the Blue Ridge Mountains far ahead. The horse was going slower and slower, almost winded, and Troy walked beside it, holding onto the reins.

"Much farther?" Troy asked. "I'm beginning to feel like this horse looks."

"A few miles more, as I remember it. Want to rest?"

"No. Keep going. The longer that we're on the road the more chance there is that someone will see us."

The road twisted through a bit of piney forest, then around a sharp bend. Directly in front of them were two grim looking men standing in the center of the road. With rifles leveled in their direction.

Troy's first spasm of fear ebbed a bit when he saw that one of the men was black. If there was one thing that he could be certain of—all of McCulloch's circle of accomplices would be lily-white.

"Keep your hands where we can see them," the white man said, wiggling the gun in their direction. "Now just who are you and where are you going?"

"It's none of your business," Shaw said quietly. "If you just stand to one side we can deliver ourselves."

Those are fancy words," the man said, but he lowered his gun. "People could talk, hear something like Stand And Deliver. But more important is, who do you know? Know Russell?"

"Of course I know Otis—because we're heading

for his farm. And he knows me."

"Does he? Almost time to tell me your name, then."

After the cryptic exchange Shaw agreed that it was, too. "My name is Robbie Shaw. I've been along this bit of track before."

"Why, you sure have!" the man said eagerly, holding the gun aside and stepping forward, hand extended. "Last time through Harriet Tubman told how you and she worked together."

"She's well—still!"

"Can't stop her. Reward on her head in every state, sent five thousand people at least down the line, still keeps going. All I can say it's a good thing you know her and Otis because strangers aren't welcome here right now. Got too many visitors up to the house, too much happening here. But some of us, we're going to march out tonight and you're just in time to see us off."

"March where? I've heard nothing."

"Of course not. Secret's meant to be kept—but the world will know soon. We're off to the Kennedy Farm, on the Maryland side of the Potomac."

Shaw shook his head, puzzled. "I'm afraid that I don't know it. Is it a house on the Railroad?"

"No, just a dilapidated old farm that we been using. It's just a few miles outside of Harper's Ferry. It has been rented by Mr. Isaac Smith himself. But that's just a name he used so they wouldn't know who he was. But you know him.

"This Isaac Smith is none other than John Brown himself. Yes he is!"

John Brown, Troy thought to himself, suddenly cold. *John Brown at Harper's Ferry. And today is the fourteenth of October.*

Clearly then, as clear as though he were reading it from the printed page of a history book he saw the date.

John Brown. The raid on Harper's Ferry.

October 16, 1859.

THIRTY

Troy sat quietly in the corner by the fireplace, sipping at a cup of coffee. The wind had come up after dark and there was a cold draft blowing through the chinks around the door. All of the abolitionists in the house were excited, talking animatedly. Only Troy did not join in. He was feeling the weight of history, feeling that these men were both alive and dead at the same time. Harper's Ferry. The attack was two days away. The details of the raid and what followed tried to push up out of his memory—but he would not let them. He did not want to know. He was here to stop McCulloch, prevent him carrying through whatever mad scheme he had to use the sub-machine guns that he was manufacturing. Therefore Troy's duty was to ignore what was going on around him, to hear nothing about the planned raid. If he said one word—he would say too many.

It had nothing to do with him, nothing at all. But he still could not prevent himself from listening to what was being said.

Everyone present was hanging on the words of a frail young man who had just arrived that afternoon. He was strange, excitable, odd to look at with his single staring eye, a cloth patch over the other one. His name was Francis Meriam and he was from the city of Boston.

"That was it," he said, "that was really it. When I talked to this Negro man, why right away I knew that this was my chance to work for this holy crusade. My uncle, he's a big name in the abolition movement, but he's not the only one in the family knows what is what. So when this man told me all about the Shepherd down here, and what this business operation was that the Shepherd was involved in, then right away I knew I had to come. I talked to Sanborn and he asked Higginson and they told me to come here. That's what they did."

There seemed to be something wrong with the man, but none of the spectators took heed of it. He tended to repeat himself and to nod a lot. Then every once in a while he would wipe his mouth on the back of his sleeve, particularly when he got excited. Now he reached behind him, drew a carpetbag close and opened it.

"I knew old John Brown, he needed my help to go stealing slaves down South, and I knew there was something else he could use." He extracted a leather wallet from the bag and shook a stream of gold pieces out into his palm. "Weapons and ammunition cost money—and that's just what I got here. Six hundred dollars in gold, you can count it if you want. And it's all for him, for the cause."

"Bless you, Mr. Meriam," the old woman said, rocking in her chair by the fire. "Bless you, because with God's help the slaves will be freed."

At that moment the outer door opened, in dramatic punctuation of her words. Some of those present reached for their guns as a man pushed in, drenched with rain, leaning hard against the door to close it against the wind. He turned to face them, a young man in his early twenties, looking about the room as though searching for someone.

"Francis Jackson Meriam—is that you?" he called out.

Meriam climbed to his feet and hurried across to greet his friend, clutching his rain-wet hand. "John, they said that you would come to meet me. Am I still in time?" He turned to the others without waiting for an answer. "Everyone, this is John Copeland whom you will remember took part in the Oberlin raid that was in all the papers."

They made the newcomer welcome. Someone handed him a steaming mug of coffee. He sipped at it gratefully while the others tried not to show their impatience to hear the news. It was Meriam who finally burst out.

"How are they? How does it go?"

"Very well indeed. We got the message that you were coming; they sent me out to get you, show you the way back. The farm is sort of crowded though, a lot of us there. Some of the men are like penned animals, been locked in that house since August. But we are going to strike soon. The pikes have arrived, and the guns. Everything is in readiness, at least that's what Mr. Cook says. He's been in Harper's Ferry a year now, working in the federal armory. He knows everything about it. He's so close to it that he even married one of the local girls. He knows a thing or two, does John E. Cook. He's a friend of mine, he was up the house and we talked, told me all about the armory and everything. We're going to the right place. Do you know how many stands of arms they turn out there? They can make ten thousand a year, that's what they can. They make everything there, got a big forge and a machine shop. Make percussion caps, barrels and secret things too, secret kind of bullet, that's what Mr. Cook said."

Bullet! The word penetrated Troy like a bullet itself. Of course! The Sten guns would be useless without a large supply of first class ammunition. He had been so intent on the gun itself that he had never considered the thousands, hundreds of thousands, of cartridges they would need. Cartridges of a kind he had yet to see here. The clues had been under his nose ever since he had arrived, but he had been too stupid to notice them. He had seen many different kinds of guns, smoothbore, rifled, muzzle loading, pin fire and percussion cap —a great variety—but none of them were capable of easy loading or of automatic fire. Ammunition. There had been no sign of cartridges or gunpowder in McCulloch's factory. An operation like that could not be easily hidden. Which meant that although the guns were manufactured in Richmond, the ammunition wasn't. Where could the necessary bullets be made?

In a government armory, of course.

The newcomer was still talking, answering questions. Troy waited, kneading his knuckles impatiently, then finally broke in.

"Mr. Copeland, I'm sorry to interrupt, but you said something a moment ago about a new kind of bullet being manufactured in Harper's Ferry?"

"That's right, that's what Mr. Cook told me, and he's not the kind of man who would lie about a thing like that. They're making these bullets in Hall's Rifle Works, out there in that island in the Shenandoah. Secret, guards all around. You can't get near the place at all."

"Did Mr. Cook describe the bullet to you, tell you anything about it?"

"Did more than that. Said that this was so secret it had to be important. He told me to tell John Brown about it, and I did that. Something else he did, he got hold of some empty shell casings when they was sweeping out, ones that had broke. For me to show to John Brown."

"Could you describe them?" Troy asked, forcing his voice to remain calm.

"Do better than that. Let you look at one. Kept one for myself."

He rooted around in his trouser's pocket, frowned, then put his hand in the other pocket.

"Don't think I lost it. Got it here some place. Yes, I knew it, here."

Troy looked at the split shell casing resting on the palm of his hand, cracked in the drawing it looked like. A 9mm Parabellum, it could be nothing else; he had fired enough of them to know. Ringed at the base and punctured for the insertion of the percussion cap.

"That's very interesting," he said, passing it back. "And you'll be guiding Mr. Meriam back to join the others?"

"Sure will. First thing in the morning."

"I would like to volunteer to go with you. May I?"

"John Brown can use every man he can get."

"I'm glad to hear that," Robbie Shaw broke in,

speaking for the first time—though he had been listening intently. "If he can use one volunteer he can use another. I'm going along as well."

He was looking straight at Troy as he said it, and permitted a quick touch of a smile to move his lips. There was much talk and excitement after that, and only later did Troy have a chance to draw the Scotsman aside.

"What did you do that for?" Troy asked. "This is no game now. People are going to get killed."

"It never was a game—but it has been a puzzle. You know a lot of things that you haven't told me, though tonight you did tell me that this new ammunition has a good deal to do with you or the colonel—or both. The way you jumped when Copeland mentioned it. Are you going to let me know now what this thing is all about?"

"No. But I will tell you to get out while the going is good. I have to go to Harper's Ferry, but you don't. Please, Robbie, take my word for it. No good will come out of this."

"I'll take your word only when you let me know what this entire matter is all about. Can't you tell me what you were looking for in McCulloch's factory? You must have found something there if you tried to burn it down."

Troy considered it. He had proof now that McCulloch was making the guns, and was also somehow involved in a conspiracy to manufacture the ammunition in a government armory. This meant that a number of people knew what was happening and it was no longer necessary to keep the Sten gun a secret. All he had to leave out was the fact that he had followed McCulloch here from the future.

"All right. It's only fair that you know now. I'm a

government agent following McCulloch. Not only did he commit those murders I told you about, but he stole the drawings for a highly secret and deadly weapon. He believes firmly that war will soon come between the states, and he must have obtained the aid of other, like-minded Southerners. He is making the gun at his factory—I found a piece from it. But he has no ammunition works there, and this gun uses a special type of bullet. With a casing just like the one I was holding. And that is the puzzle. These cartridges are being made in a government armory. Yet I can guarantee you—the government knows nothing about this."

"The answer to that one is tragically easy. The officers in command of the rifle works must be all Southern sympathizers. That would be easy enough to arrange, so many of the Army officers are from Virginia. And what better place to hide the works than under everyone's noses? It's like Edgar Allan Poe's story of the purloined letter. I'm sorry, Troy, but after this you can't possibly stop me from joining you. What a story this will make! Remember, I'm a journalist first and an abolitionist second. Whatever happens at Harper's Ferry, why it will be the news story of the decade. We're both off to join John Brown!"

THIRTY-ONE

The storm blew itself out during the night and Saturday, October 15, dawned fresh and fair. All of the volunteers were up before dawn, ate a breakfast of hoecakes, and were on the road by first light. Copeland and Meriam rode ahead, while Troy and Shaw followed in the buggy. They made steady progress, and it was early in the afternoon when Copeland reined up his horse and pointed down the hillside.

"There it is, Harper's Ferry," he said. "Other side of the Potomac there, that's Maryland. After that the farmhouse is about seven miles farther on. You can see the bridge across the river, right over there."

"Will we have to go through the town?" Shaw asked.

"Only way, unless you want to swim."

"Then you ought to know that the slaveholders

are looking for me and Troy. They could have tele-
graphed a description ahead to warn their people
here to watch out for us. A black man and a white
man in a buggy."

"Easy enough to take care of that," Copeland
said. "One of you changes places, goes through
town on horseback."

"Better be me," Troy said. "His leg is bandaged,
that's why we're using the buggy."

They rode into Harper's Ferry this way, Francis
Meriam sitting next to Shaw while Troy rode
Meriam's horse. The town was situated on a neck
of land where the Shenandoah river joined the
Potomac. This gave it a cramped appearance as
the clustered homes, saloons, hotels and shops extended along the banks of both rivers and climbed
up the slopes of Bolivar Heights behind. Copeland
pointed out the sights as they rode along Potomac
Street, busy with its traffic of horses, buggies and
carts.

"See those buildings along the street here, the
ones that look like factories? Well, they're not.
That's the federal armory, all stretched out, starting right after the fire-engine house. Forging here,
then machine and stocking shop. The big one next
is the arsenal where all the arms are stored."

"Where is the rifle factory you were telling us
about?"

"That would be Hall's Rifle Works, about a half
mile further on, along that street, Shenandoah
Street. See it? It's on that little island right out
there in the river. Always got two sentries out in
front, night and day. No one gets in or out lest
they're known."

It's in there, Troy thought, everything that I am
looking for. It all has to be in there. The machines

to manufacture the cartridges, the store of cartridges, maybe even the guns themselves. Assembled in there and stored there. Two men,
that's not much of a guard to stand against a
sudden raid.

Which raised the biggest question of all. Why
had McCulloch chosen this place, of all the federal
armories, to site his illegal weapons factory? He
must know enough about history to know that
John Brown was going to raid here. That was a
fact in all the books. It was impossible to believe
that he hadn't read about it. So, knowing that the
raid was coming—why then he must have taken
precautions to prevent it. Possibly have prepared
an ambush. But if it were an ambush, why then
John Brown would certainly have been told about
it. At least one of his spies, John Cook, worked
here. There could be others. It was all very un-
clear.

No one appeared to take any notice of them as
they passed through Harper's Ferry and onto the
covered bridge across the Potomac. It was a rail
bridge as well and a B&O train from Washington
passed them halfway across, shaking the struc-
ture beneath them and puffing out clouds of
smoke. Soon after crossing the bridge they turned
off the turnpike and onto a country lane. Being
careful that they were not followed, Copeland led
them up into the foothills of the mountains, to the
secret hideout. A ramshackle, two-story farmhouse, with a kitchen garden in front. Two young
girls were working there, and they waved to the
men as they came up. While they were tying up
their horses the front door opened and a thin man
with a full white beard stepped out. His face was
lined, craggy, his mouth wide and sealed into a
hard slit.

"Mr. Brown," Copeland said. "I have brought some volunteers to join you."

"You are welcome, all of you, come into the house and meet the others."

He nodded grimly at each of them as they went by, no touch of a smile loosening that tight-clamped mouth. As Troy entered John Brown took him by the shoulder and said softly, "You are joining in a holy crusade to liberate your people." Troy nodded and went on—there was little he could answer to that.

The small rooms were crowded with men, twenty-four in all counting the newcomers. After introductions had been made, Francis Meriam dived into his carpetbag and produced his wallet.

"This is for you, Mr. Brown, for the cause you so nobly lead."

He poured out the stream of gold and John Brown clasped his hands and lowered his head.

"We must thank the Lord," he said. "For bringing these men—and for bringing this gold. This is a sign, an unmistakable sign that it is His will that we move now." He looked around at the silent men, the gaze from his glaring eyes that of an avenging angel. "The time has come to act, and we shall. On the sabbath, the Lord's day, we will fall on the ungodly. We strike. Tomorrow! God has honored but a comparatively very small part of mankind with any possible chance for such mighty and soul satisfying rewards as shall be ours. We will capture the armory and our Negro brethren will rise in their mighty wrath and strike down their captors. So shall it be."

So shall it be, Troy thought. *But how will it really be?* If the soldiers were waiting in ambush this little handful of foolhardy men would be massacred. Could he stop them? More important

—should he stop them? Was it possible to change history, and if he did, what would the repercussions be? McCulloch was trying to change history, to bring about the world that he wanted, to perpetuate slavery into the distant future. No!

Perhaps John Brown's inspirational sermon was affecting him as well as the others. He could now understand their emotional hatred of the institution of slavery, how they would do anything to see it destroyed. They wanted to bring about the America that he knew, that he had grown up in. It wasn't perfect, he knew that, knew also that no society or institution was. But, by God, it was infinitely better than this slave state, part of a country that was half slave and half free. Being here, living here, he could understand, not only understand but *feel* the causes of the dreadful war to come. No country could possibly exist like this, divided against itself. Nor would it. The terrible conflict to come would decide that. And unless he intervened the slaveholders might win. The world that he had known might never exist.

That could not be—*would* not be! He had to make absolutely sure that never happened.

Yet, at the same time, he felt that he could not stand idly by while these good men committed suicide. He owed it to them, to the cause they all believed in, to give them some warning. It might change a footnote of history, but they deserved something better than being butchered outright.

At the earliest opportunity he sought John Brown out and drew him aside.

"Mr. Brown, could I possibly talk to you for a few moments?"

"Of course, I am at your service. We can go into the kitchen, it will be quieter in there."

They sat by the fire. John Brown looked into its depths, raised his hands to warm them there, seeing the future perhaps. Seeing his rebellion triumphant. Troy looked too, seeking a way to give his warning that did not betray the source of his knowledge.

"Do you know a Colonel McCulloch, from Richmond?"

"I know of him, though I have never met him. An evil man. I have been told that he killed one of his slaves. May the good Lord in his wrath strike him down."

"Amen to that. But I have positive information, through an organization I work for, that McCulloch has discovered what you are planning to do. He may have laid a trap for you to fall into."

"You are good to tell me this, but do not fear, for we walk in the protection of our Lord. Others have tried to betray us, for the best of reasons as well as the worst, but have not succeeded. I know for a fact that my good friend from Iowa, David J. Gue, has decided that we will all be killed if our plans go through. Though he has now repented his act he did indeed send a letter of warning to the Secretary of War. But this letter has been completely ignored. Now why should that be? Only one reason, my son. We stand in the palm of the Lord and he does protect us. I thank you for this attempt to warn us of the machinations of this man of evil. But he shall not prevail. The plans have been made, the troops assembled, the arms ready. We march tomorrow. And will you march with us?"

Troy hesitated, then nodded. He had no choice, none at all.

"Yes, I will march with you."

Perhaps this moment had been ordained since

he had followed McCulloch to this time and place. Perhaps history was already written and unchangeable.

Well, either way, they would find out tomorrow. It was impossible to decide now. He stayed awake half the night, searching for an answer, but fell asleep with the problem still unresolved.

They were up at dawn—then John Brown summoned them into the living room for a final service of worship. First he read them passages from the bible that offered hope to all slaves, then he asked them all to join him in a prayer to God to assist them in the liberation of the bondmen of this slaveholding land.

After that he explained his battle plans and Troy wished that there had been less praying and more reconnaissance. It did not need any knowledge of history to tell that the raid was doomed to failure. They planned to attack and hold the federal armory—and that was all. No escape routes had been worked out in case they were counterattacked by militia or federal troops. Everything relied on a slave uprising to save them—but no warning had been sent out to the slaves, nor had any effort been made to organize them. All attempts to convince John Brown to take precautions or to make alternate plans were turned away with a reiteration of "God will guard and shield us."

When the battle assignments were given out, Troy had no difficulty in volunteering to lead the attack on Hall's Rifle Works. The only federal troops in the city were stationed here and none of the volunteers were eager to face up to them. Shaw joined him, while some others were assigned to aid them in the attack.

That was it. The plans made, the die cast. The tension mounted through the day, until eight o'clock that night when John Brown called them together again.

"Men, it is almost time. I beg of you, when we attack, not to spill blood needlessly, but still you must not hesitate to defend yourselves. Some of you may be killed, indeed all of us may die in this attempt to strike a blow for freedom and justice in this slave-cursed land. We have here only one life to live, and once only to die. But you must remember that if we do lose our lives it will perhaps do more for the cause than our lives would be worth in any other way."

They bowed their hands in one last prayer. Then John Brown rose from his knees and stood before them, arms uplifted, with his glaring eyes and white beard looking very much like the avenging angel of the Lord that he believed himself to be.

"Men," he called out. "Take up your arms. We will proceed to the Ferry!"

THIRTY-TWO

John Brown led the way, riding on the wagon loaded with pikes that were meant to arm the freed slaves. The others followed, solemnly as though it were a funeral procession, along the country road towards the Potomac. It was a bitter, dark night and before they had gone very far it began to rain, a fine drizzle that chilled them even further. The steep road wound down from the hills, past an occasional farmhouse, then out into the valley. Ahead of them were the lights of Harper's Ferry. Robbie could see them clearly from the back of the wagon where he rode because of his bad leg. He clutched the saddlebags across his lap and shivered with cold.

Each man knew what part he had to play in the attack. They marched in silence along the canal that ran beside the Potomac, then paused when they came to the bridge. Two of the men, the ones who had been assigned to cut the telegraph lines, vanished into the darkness. As soon as they were gone, Brown waved his hand and two others moved quickly out across the bridge and captured the night watchman at the other end.

The way was now open. They crossed the bridge in silence and deployed through the streets, moving with caution past the lights of the Galt House Saloon and the Wager House Hotel. Guards were left on the Shenandoah bridge while the main force moved on the arsenal and armory buildings—which were guarded by a single, elderly watchman. They captured him, then swarmed through the buildings. They found no other guards or watchmen. When the buildings had been secured, Brown turned and leveled his finger at their terrified prisoner.

"This is a slave State—and I shall free all of the Negroes in this State. I have possession now of the United States Armory, and if any of the citizens interfere with me I must only burn the town and have blood."

With these words he waved Troy and the other attackers on to Hall's Rifle Works, the only one of the federal buildings still not secured. As they went quickly down Shenandoah Street, Troy looked carefully along the water's edge. He raised his pistol and halted the attackers when he saw what he wanted.

"There are guards at the front gate and we may not be able to take them by surprise. I want you men to approach them. If they shoot and repell you, retire and keep up a covering fire. I'm going to use this boat to get behind the works and take them from the flank. Now move out."

"I'll come with you," Shaw said. Troy shook his

head.

"No, Robbie, you'll be far more valuable to the attack if you remain here. You can take care of the saddlebags as well. I know nothing about these men—but I do know you, and can count upon you to stay and draw their fire. If the soldiers are distracted like that I should be able to penetrate from the rear. Will you do it?"

"Of course. How much time do you need?"

"Just a few minutes to get into position." As the others moved away he lowered his voice so only Shaw could hear. "McCulloch may know about this raid—so there might be a very good chance that there is a trap laid in there. Watch yourself."

"And the same. Good luck."

Troy opened his knife and sawed at the rope holding the boat to the bank, then pushed it free and jumped inside. He groped through the cold water in the bottom until he found an oar. Just one. It would have to do. He sculled out into the river and felt the current carry the boat towards the island. There was a barely visible dark patch, mud bank or sand flat, behind the building and he headed for it, feeling the boat grind to a stop. As he jumped onto the bank he heard the rattle of gunfire. The attack had begun. His groping fingers found some bushes growing at the river's edge and he tied the rope to one of them, hearing distant shouts and the increasing sound of the guns. There must be strong resistance. But on this side the building was silent and dark. There were windows, but they were small and high above the ground. No good. There just had to be another way in. He ran along the wall, pistol ready in his hand. Nothing.

Only when he turned the corner did he see the

small door let into the wall. As he ran towards it
the sound of firing increased suddenly, then died
away. Had the attackers forced their way in? No,
they must have been repulsed for the firing began
again, just occasional shots. He had to get through
the door.

It was locked, made of solid wood, and did not
budge when he threw his weight against it. There
was only one way then to get through it. A noisy
way—he would have to move fast.

He fired two shots at point blank range into the
lock, then rammed his shoulder against the door
again. It shuddered, there was the rattle of broken
metal, then gave way. Troy pushed it wide, dived
through and rolled behind a pile of crates. There
was no return fire. For the moment.

He was in a large room, filled with stacked
boxes; a small lantern on the opposite wall shed a
fitful yellow glow. It was silent. There was a good
chance that he was alone in the room. He must
keep moving. He was accomplishing nothing just
lying there.

Standing, slowly, gun ready, he ran towards the
door in the far wall. Just as it burst open and a
dark figure appeared in the opening.

There was no conscious thought involved, just
reflex action that hurled him to one side. He hit
hard and rolled over in the dust, the pistol extended before him.

The rapid hammer of gunfire sounded from the
doorway, the bullets tearing into the wooden floor
beside his body, chewing their way towards him.
He could only level his revolver at the flaring
muzzleblast and pull the trigger over and over
again until the weapon was empty. Waiting for the
return fire.

It never came. In the silence that followed he could clearly hear the slither of cloth on wood, followed by a heavy thud as the body hit the floor. The lantern was just above the dead man, the light glinting from his open, motionless eyes.

Shining as well on the steel of the sub-machine gun still clasped across his chest.

Troy acted without thinking, shoving his empty pistol into his belt and diving forward to seize the Sten gun from the dead man's grasp. Swinging it up. Facing an empty hallway lined with closed doors. A moment's respite. Keeping the gun trained ahead, his finger over the trigger, he ran his left hand over the body. Seized the two magazines stuck under the man's belt; felt with his fingertip to make sure that they were full. Pushed them under his own belt—then ran forward and kicked open the door at the far end of the hall.

It was simple slaughter. The men at the windows were armed with rifles and pistols, facing away from him, turning only when he started to fire.

The bullets sprayed out, cut them down, the clip emptied. He jammed in a fresh one and turned the gun on a wounded man who was trying to raise his rifle. Dropped him. Saw the impact of the bullets on his body. Bullets that cut through his Army uniform and into his flesh.

They were all soldiers, every man that he had killed, murdered. Soldiers in the United States Army. But as he dragged in a gasping breath he forced himself to remember that they were traitors as well to the government they had taken an oath to serve. All of them were Southern sympathizers, all were taking part in the conspiracy to bring down the Union. He dropped the emptied clip and clicked a full one into place.

The night was suddenly silent. The firing outside the building had ceased. He backed slowly to the entrance door, the questing muzzle of his gun looking on all sides. There were no survivors. He still kept it pointed while he struggled the wooden bar off the door and pulled it open with one hand.

"Is that you?" a voice called from the darkness outside. It was Shaw's.

"Right. Come ahead. I'm pretty certain that all resistance here has been knocked out."

There were two dead guards outside. Shaw stepped over the bodies and pushed the door wide, then handed in the saddlebags. "How did it go?" Troy asked.

"Not good. The guards saw us, opened fire. We returned it, got them both, but it alerted the others inside. You know what happened after that."

"I certainly do. I came in the back way. I was lucky."

"We have two men dead. One wounded. And another man who's not hurt."

"Go to him. Tell him to get the wounded man to John Brown. He is to report that we have secured the rifle works and all is well."

"Right."

Troy stood in silence, gun pointed and ready, until Shaw returned. "Bolt the door," he ordered. Shaw did so, looking around at the huddled bodies as he pushed the bar into place, then at Troy. He pointed.

"Is that the gun you told me about?"

"It is. You've seen what it can do. What do you think an army of rebels could do with guns like this?"

"Sweet Jesus," Shaw breathed. "Are we in time?"

"I think so. The weapon's existence is still being kept secret. The chances are that they might still be stored here. Let's look. You take this. Here."

He handed over the sub-machine gun and Shaw took it reluctantly. "I don't know anything about it," he said.

Troy nodded grimly. "You don't have to know, not with a gun like this. It's cocked now. Just point it and pull the trigger. It sprays death. Now cover me."

Troy carefully reloaded his pistol before they began to search. Shaw stood ready with the Sten as they went through the building, room by room. There was no one else there. They were almost certain of this when they found the guard room; Troy pointed to the beds.

"Eight of them. And eight dead soldiers. I think we have them all. But I still don't want to take any chances."

Half of the rifle works was made up of the machine shop. There were long-bedded drills for manufacturing the rifled barrels, as well as iron-framed presses for drawing the cartridges. To the rear were storerooms for bar metal and other supplies, as well as a sealed room that proved to be filled with barrels of gunpowder and boxes of furniture caps. It was next to a bigger storeroom with an even heavier locked door. It took them a quarter of an hour, working with crowbars, to smash their way through it. When the door finally opened, Troy stepped in, holding the lantern high.

Boxes were stacked there, row after row of them, stretching from the floor almost up to the rafters. They walked to the nearest ones, still unsealed, and looked in.

The first one was filled with neatly packed brass boxes of bullets.

Sub-machine guns were in the next crate.

"Is this it?" Shaw asked. "What you were looking for?"

"It is. The machinery to manufacture these weapons, and the guns and ammunition as well. All in one place. It's almost too much to expect. But we must make the most of the opportunity." He looked slowly around. "We better get started— we have plenty of work to finish before the night is out."

"What are you going to do?"

"I thought it was obvious. Blow up the machinery. Burn this place down. Destroy it utterly. And when that is done we go after McCulloch. No more running away.

"I must find that man and kill him. This threat must be ended forever."

THIRTY-THREE

"If you really want to prevent this factory from ever operating again," Shaw said, "you are going to have a most difficult job."

"Why? Won't burning it down put it out of commission?"

"Only temporarily—if there are people who are really desperate to keep it running." He slapped the frame of one of the big presses. "These things are made of cast iron and steel. I've seen them taken out of the burned ruins of a collapsed building, dusted off and greased—and put back to work within twenty four hours."

"Then what are we to do?" Troy asked.

"We are to do what our French cousins call *sabotage*, an act of botching. We shall botch these machines beyond repair. The drawing presses that form the cartridges would be the best for us to work our mischief upon. They are the most delicate—and practically irreplaceable. Specially made to order in Scotland. A charge of black powder for each one should do the job well enough."

"All right. I'll make up the explosives and you can show me where to place them. We'll also lay black powder over the boxes of cartridges, make sure that they burn and explode. Which leaves only the guns themselves to worry about. They're rugged. Even if the boxes they are packed in are burned, we have no guarantee that they will be put out of commission. If they were cleaned up—and there is another store of cartridges someplace—this entire effort would be wasted."

"Then it's into the river with them. A few days in the water and they will be completely unserviceable."

"Right, let's do it. But it's not going to be an easy job. There must be thousands of them in these boxes."

"Then it is time we started, isn't it?" Shaw said, taking off his coat. "We'll see how many we can give the deep six before dawn."

It was an exhausting night's work. Once the charges had been placed on the machinery, they turned to the crates of sub-machine guns, breaking them open and carrying the guns out the side entrance to the river bank, hurling them out into the dark water. The work seemed endless and they still were not finished when the first light of dawn spread across the eastern sky. The rain had stopped, though the sky was still overcast. Troy dropped onto a box, gasping with exhaustion.

"Enough . . ." he said. "We have to lay fuse trails, think of getting out of here." He hesitated, looking at Shaw. "We must be well away from

here by dawn. I have sure knowledge that this rebellion is doomed. I tried to tell John Brown that
—but he wouldn't listen. Everyone taking part in
this raid, everyone who has not escaped, will be
killed. Of that I am absolutely certain."

"How do you know?"

"I can't tell you that now. Please, Robbie, take
my word for it. We must get away. We'll use the
rowboat since the land side of the building will
surely be watched."

They had been hearing sporadic gunfire for
some time now: there was no escape back the way
they had come.

"All right, let's do it. I have none of the love of
certain death that possesses our friend Brown."

Carefully, so as not to step on the grains of
powder and cause a premature explosion, they
trickled fine streams of gunpowder from the
remaining barrels. Joining the trails together and
leading a final trail out of the open door. The half-
empty barrels were placed on the last crates of
guns; then they were ready. When Troy put the
lantern down he saw the outline of the building
against the sky.

"It's time. We should be safe back against the
base of the wall here when the charges explode. As
soon as we are sure the place is burning well we'll
take to the boat. I'm bringing this with us." He
placed the saddlebags and the loaded Sten gun
under the front seat of the boat. "If we are seen we
may have to defend ourselves. This gun will even
the odds. If we are not attacked—it joins the
others in the river. We still have our pistols.
Ready?"

"Yes, do it."

They pressed close to the dressed stone foundation of the building as Troy broke the glass globe of the lantern, then thrust the burning wick into the trail of powder. With a soft burst of flame and smoke it caught and the crackling fire vanished through the door.

An instant later multiple explosions shook the wall against which they were leaning. Flame gouted through the windows as they exploded outwards with a crash of breaking glass. Smoke followed the flame, red-lit smoke showing that the combustibles had caught fire.

"That's done it!" Troy shouted over the roar of the blaze. "Let's get out of here."

They ran to the boat, jumped in and pushed it free. Troy seized up the single paddle and rowed hard, out into the fast-flowing river and away from the burning building. There was no one on the shore that they could see. Nevertheless, he rowed on with all his strength, until they were well away from the island and invisible from the shore in the dim grayness of dawn.

Troy was gasping, his arms burning with the effort, and was only too happy to let Shaw take over from him. They shared the rowing after this, turn and turn about, until they approached the black outline of the opposite bank. The rifle works burned brightly behind them; ahead of them the landscape was emerging with the first gray light of dawn.

"Can you see anything on the river bank?" Shaw asked.

"Nothing. Seems to be just meadows along here. But we're not too far from the road."

"Yet if anyone were there they should be visible by now. I think that we are in the clear."

It was quiet; the only sound was the splash of

the oar as they approached the shore. Then the
bow scraped against the bottom under the sloping
bank. A bird called plaintively in the dawn. There
were no other sounds. Shaw, sitting in the stern,
rowed hard to drive them up onto the shore. Troy
jumped out, holding the rope, and pulled the boat
further up onto the sand.

"All right," he said. "I'll hold it while you . . ."

Troy was looking at the Scotsman as he said
this, saw his sudden look of horror. His mouth
opened—

The shot blasted out. Shaw pressed both hands
to the suddenly bloody mask of his face and
dropped forward, unmoving.

Troy pulled at the revolver in his belt, turning
about, stopping at the sound of the voice above
him on the bank.

"If you try to draw that gun you will be just as
dead as your nigger-loving friend there."

Troy lifted his hands slowly into the air, turned,
looked up at the man who stood on the bank above
him. With his pistol leveled at Troy's head. It was
Colonel McCulloch. He spoke with cold anger.

"He has received just what he deserved. Robbie
Shaw accepted the hospitality of my home. Then
he betrayed me, brought you here to work against
me. He deserved killing ten times over."

"You didn't have to murder him," Troy shouted,
just as angrily. "There was no need. You're too
late to stop us. Do you see the flame? That's Hall's
Rifle Works burning. All your guns and ammunition, everything, all gone up in flame."

"Yes, I can see the flame. I saw it from the road.
Saw you outlined against it as well. That's the
reason why I am here. Here to kill you, black boy."

"The name is Harmon. Sergeant Troy Harmon. I

want you to remember that, colonel. Remember the name of the Black man who followed you here, followed you a hundred and twenty years back through time to destroy your insane plan."

"It isn't so insane, Harmon." McCulloch had his anger coldly under control now. "I still have the blueprints. The factory here, and the one in Richmond, they'll both be rebuilt. The men who helped me will aid me again. We'll find another site to manufacture the guns. This is only a temporary setback. There still is time . . ."

"Only until April of sixty-one—then your time runs out."

"I wouldn't bother about that if I were you. Your time has run out right now. You've caused me a lot of trouble, but that trouble is going to end the moment I pull this trigger. So you have just enough time for a quick prayer to your nigger-Baptist God. Let's hear you pray, boy."

Troy drew himself up, letting his arms drop slowly to his sides, coldly angry. When he spoke his voice was rich with contempt.

"You are a sick, mad, contemptible racist, McCulloch. A disgrace to your country and the uniform you wore. You think that the color of a man's skin—or his religion—makes him different from you. Makes you superior. I would love to spit in your face, but it isn't worth the effort."

"Big talk, nigger. If you beg for mercy I might not kill you . . ."

Troy burst out laughing. "You don't know *anything*, you ignorant redneck bastard! Shoot and be damned!"

McCulloch pointed the gun square in Troy's face, his thumb drawing slowly back on the hammer. In the coldness of certain death Troy was numb, beyond fear.

"Beg!" McCulloch said. "Beg for your life."

"I wouldn't give you the satisfaction. But I'll ask you to do me a favor."

"No favors."

"Just a small one. Tell me why you used the rifle works here at Harper's Ferry to manufacture the ammunition. After all, you knew about John Brown . . ."

His words were drowned out by the bark of the gun, the sound harshly loud in the stillness of the dawn.

THIRTY-FOUR

Troy could only stare, unbelievingly, as the bullets tore into McCulloch's body. The colonel folded forward, the revolver dropping from his fingers, tumbled and rolled down the slope to stop at Troy's feet. His eyes were open but unseeing. When he drew a last, shuddering breath there was the wet bubbling sound of air passing through the wounds in his chest.

"Who . . . who is John Brown . . ." he said. And died.

"Give me—a hand, Troy," Shaw said, slumped back in the boat. His face was a red smear of blood. He held the Sten gun limply against his body, too weak to lift it again.

The numbness left Troy and he was galvanized to life, jumping into the boat and seizing Shaw under the arms, dragging him ashore and placing him gently on the grass beside McCulloch's corpse. When he turned he saw that the boat was drifting away; he splashed into the water after it, seized the bow and pulled it up onto the sand. Then he climbed into it again to find the saddle-bags and rooted into them for his medical supplies.

"Scalp wounds, notoriously bloody," Shaw said as Troy wound the bandage about his head. "Stunned me when it bounced off my skull. I recovered consciousness face down in that wretched boat. Felt as though half my head had been blown away. But we Shaws have always been known for our thick skulls. Once I stopped feeling sorry for myself I was rather glad to be alive. I couldn't see very well, but there was nothing wrong with my hearing. By the sound of his voice I placed the mad colonel on the bank up above us—in the same place he had been standing when he shot me. The rest, as they say, is merely history. My hands were actually resting on the gun under the seat, although it took me some time to realize it. I did all the things you told me to do with it and they worked. Sorry to have taken so long—but I wanted to be sure all of his attention was on you before I made my move."

"I can't thank you . . ."

"Then don't." He was silent a moment, looking up at Troy's face. "I heard a good deal of what you were saying to each other."

"Did you?"

Troy rolled McCulloch's body over, pushed his coat aside and tore off a length of shirt that was not stained with blood. He took it to the river, dipped it into the water then wrung it out. He used it to clean the drying blood from Shaw's face.

"Was there any truth in what you were talking about?" Shaw said.

"Will it go any further, Robbie? Will you tell anyone else about what you have heard—or write it up for the newspapers?"

"It's a wonderful story, you have to admit."

"Would anyone believe you? I would deny everything, of course."

"There is that." Shaw sighed. "I wouldn't be believed—nor would anything be accomplished by publishing it. You have my word, then, Troy Harmon. I owe you my life, as you owe me yours, so there is this bond between us. But if I swear to reveal nothing, will you tell me the truth of the matter? Have you two—the both of you—have you really traveled here from the future?"

Troy hesitated, then slowly nodded, almost relieved to share this secret at last.

"And you followed him? That was a brave thing to do."

"Brave? I don't know. It just had to be done. He was bringing that gun here, to win the war for the slavers. To change history. That could not be allowed."

"War is coming then?" Shaw asked, his voice hushed. "You mentioned April of sixty-one."

"Don't ask me for dates, please. But the war will surely come—and hundreds of thousands will die. But the Union will prevail and slavery will end."

"Amen to that. But tell me—and you cannot deny me the question—what does the future hold for Scotland and England? You know it, don't you, know all the future?"

Troy stood and looked around, listening. It was quiet. They seemed to be safe for the moment. The gunfire may not have been heard.

"I am afraid to speak, Robbie. Afraid to tell you what is to come in fear that the knowledge, some action of yours, might alter it. It is not a bad future. There will be wars, but your country will remain sound and free. The world will change, physically that is, with machines everywhere. No beasts, the horses will vanish from the streets. The cities, all concrete and steel and pavings. But people will remain very much the same. Let it stop here, please. We must never speak of it again."

"But there are so many questions I burst to ask! I feel like the man in the story who is given three wishes, then is afraid to use them. The things that you know—that I never will!" When Troy did not answer he pushed himself up to a sitting position. "I'll try not to speak of it again—but it will be deuced hard!"

"We best think about moving on before we're found here. If McCulloch saw us from the road his horse must be tied nearby."

"What about the colonel?"

"His won't be the only corpse in the river this day," Troy said grimly.

He bent and quickly searched McCulloch's pockets, taking away his wallet and a large ring of keys. Then he pushed with his foot and the body toppled over the edge of the bank and splashed into the water, bobbed there for a moment before drifting slowly away. The colonel had come home, to the South he loved. Troy watched the corpse until the current took it and carried it out of sight. Then he climbed into the boat and gazed down at the gray form of the sub-machine gun, with a feeling of immense distaste. He seized it up and hurled it far out into the river, where it splashed and sank from sight.

They found McCulloch's horse tied up about thirty yards away under the trees. Troy gave Shaw a foot up into the saddle, then slung the saddle-bags behind him.

"Are you well enough to ride?" he asked.

"I think so. Other than a pounding headache I don't feel too horrible. Do you have a plan?"

"Yes. I have to return to Richmond. You heard what McCulloch said about the plans for the sub-machine gun. I must find them and destroy them. It is going to be dangerous, but it has to be done. I can't ask you to come with me."

"You're not asking, I'm volunteering. You don't think I would stop now, before this thing is finished? And there is the undeniable fact as well that you would never make it on your own. We'll keep to the back roads—I don't want to have to explain this bandage too often. We'll take it very easy. I doubt if the search for us will be carried on very seriously now. Not after this setback to their plans. And McCulloch's death."

By the time they reached the town of Culpepper they felt relatively secure. They were far enough from Harper's Ferry so that Shaw's injury was not associated with the uprising there. His explanation that he had fallen from his horse and injured his face was accepted readily enough. Troy held the horse while Shaw went into the general store to purchase supplies. He bought a newspaper as well. They did not open it until they were well away from the town. The raid on Harper's Ferry still led the news.

"It's all over," Shaw said, scanning the story. "The raid lasted thirty-six hours. Then a storming party of US Marines rushed the armory and took the survivors prisoner. The attack was led by Colonel Robert E. Lee of the Second Cavalry and a Lieutenant J. E. B. Stuart. I've never heard of either of them."

"I have," Troy said, grimly. "You'll be hearing more about them in the future."

Shaw hadn't been listening; he was reading the reports with a horrified expression. "This is terrible, it was just butchery. The whole thing turned into a shambles. The first person killed in the attack by Brown's people was a Negro—can you imagine that! And the raiders who tried to escape, the local people, they just slaughtered them. Poor Newby, remember him? The mulatto. He only joined Brown in order to free his wife and children from a plantation here in Virginia. His throat was cut, then his ears were sliced off for souvenirs!" Shaw hurled the newspaper from him and turned to Troy, his eyes deep with sorrow. "There will be more like this, won't there? This is just the beginning?"

Troy turned away so he would not have to answer, but his silence was answer enough. He retrieved the newspaper and later made himself read all of the details. He did not tell Shaw that John Brown and all of the survivors would be tried and hung. It would be months yet before that happened, but happen it would.

By the time they had reached the outskirts of Richmond, Troy had made up his mind about what he had to do. It was just before dark when they set up camp in a thicket some distance from the road.

"I have to get into McCulloch's house," Troy said. "There was nothing in his wallet or on his person that gave any clues where the plans for the gun are kept. But I know him well enough to believe that they must be in the house somewhere. I doubt if he would entrust them to anyone else. A couple of the keys on his ring were very impressive, possibly keys to a strongbox or a safe. You stay here, you'll be safe enough. I'm going to get in fast and out the same way. No one will see me. I'll be back before dawn."

"Good luck."

"Thanks. I hope that I won't need it. This should be a straightforward job of breaking and entering. I'll see you."

Troy took every possible precaution to be sure that no one saw him in the street during his circuitous approach to the house. McCulloch's servants were still in their slave quarters, but the house itself was dark. He watched for over an hour, but detected no movements or lights from the building. The moon was moving in and out of the clouds and he waited patiently for a period of darkness before he slipped soundlessly up to the front door. He found the correct key quickly enough, unlocked the door and went in—gun ready. The silent house had a musty, sealed-up smell. When Troy was absolutely certain that he was alone he tucked the revolver back into his belt and began the search.

It took him less than an hour to find the safe. Not that it was well hidden, he had just worked his way through the other rooms first before he reached the bedroom. The window drapes were heavy. He pulled them tight, then hung blankets over them for better protection. When he was sure that no light would be seen outside he lighted a candle and tried the keys on the safe.

On the shelves inside was a great deal of money, in bills and gold. And a single drawer at the bottom. Only when he had pulled the drawer open and actually had the drawings in his hand did he feel the release of tension. This was the last thing

that must be done. When these were destroyed,
McCulloch's scheme would be at an end. As he
took the plans from the drawer he saw the slim
form of the book underneath them. He wondered
what could be so valuable about this book that it
had been hidden here with the Sten plans and the
money. When he took it out and read the title he
felt a terrible chill.

Ordeal by Fire, by Fletcher Pratt. A short history of the Civil War. McCulloch's guide for his
plans to change history. But he had surely been
insane to have taken this book with him. It had to
be destroyed at once, along with the plans. But as
he held it, Troy's curiosity was aroused. McCulloch's dying words still preyed on his mind. *Who is
John Brown?* He flipped quickly through the book,
to the index in the back.

There was no mention of the attack on Harper's
Ferry. No mention at all of John Brown.

All at once it became terribly clear. McCulloch
had been an indifferent student in school, had
grown up in Mississippi, the state in the Union
with the lowest education standards. It was just
believable that in school he had never read about
John Brown, or if he had, had forgotten about it.
His knowledge of history must have been slight.
He had believed in an abstraction, a dream of the
old South. But when he wanted to alter the course
of history he had to learn more about the details of
the war itself. So he had bought a book, a history
of the Civil War. Never a scholar, one book had
been enough for him.

By some irony, some quirk of fate, some un-
guessable arrangement of the laws of chance and
of time, he had bought what was undoubtedly the
only history of the Civil War that failed to mention

John Brown's part in the tragic events of the last months leading up to that war.

With a convulsive spasm of his hands, Troy tore the book in two, disgusted with the realization that the incredible invention of a machine to move through time had been prostituted to such low purpose, by a man of this calibre. Enough! The matter was done with, it must be closed and finished and forgotten. He ripped a pillowcase from the bed, stuffed the book and plans into it, then turned back to the safe. What of the money? There was no reason to leave it here. With no one to claim it, the money would eventually go to the state of Virginia, to aid in the war effort. It would be of far better use turned over to the abolitionist movement. He dumped the gold and coins into the pillowcase, then relocked the safe.

The keys would go into the river, the plans and book into the fire, and that would be the end of that. End of McCulloch, end of his plans. End of his scheme to guarantee the future of the Confederacy.

But the cold winds of war were still blowing from the future, although it wouldn't begin for another eighteen months yet. There was more than enough time to see that this job was finished properly. With all of the loose ends tied up and his final report made.

THIRTY-FIVE

It was only after they had safely reached Washington City that Troy felt some of the tension begin to ebb away. They rested there, spent McCulloch's money freely to buy new clothes, to eat and drink expensively. Troy took his time and spent all of three days writing up a report on everything that he had done since he had arrived in this period of time. There was always the chance that this report might be found by accident so he was careful not to be too specific. He used the initial M. when referring to McCulloch and called the Sten gun simply 'the weapon.' It was a careful and detailed report, and after he had re-read it he was immensely satisfied. The assignment was ended, successfully completed, and as soon as delivery of the report had been arranged he would be free. He signed it with the initials T. H., dated it November 5, 1859, and carefully blotted it.

Experiments at a glass-blowers, had shown that it was impossible to melt shut the neck of a bottle without incinerating any papers placed inside it. Troy therefore settled for placing the report inside a whisky bottle, then corking the bottle tightly and fixing the cork firmly into place by covering it with layer after layer of sealing wax. Not satisfied with this alone, he had then put the bottle inside a stout wooden box which he had filled with molten pitch. When this had set hard the box was screwed tightly shut.

It was a balmy, Indian summer day, when they rode north out of the city. The sun was hot, the leaves splendid with their autumn colors. Troy had marked the spot well. They reached the rock soon after midday.

"If you tell me what you are doing I'll spell you on the shovel," Shaw said. Troy was digging industriously next to the wall of rock, hurling out a stream of dirt like a burrowing badger. He looked up, panting, running with sweat.

"All right, I'll tell you—but let's finish the job first. I want the hole dug, filled and covered before anyone comes by. This box must remain undisturbed for a very long time."

Shaw agreed and took his turn on the shovel. It did not take them long to burrow almost two yards down into the soft soil. Troy carefully placed the box in the bottom of the hole and settled it into place. It was not unlike a small wooden coffin. A coffin for what? McCulloch's plans for an independent South, perhaps. Troy crumbled a handful of soil and threw it down onto the box. End of McCulloch, end of his plans. Mission accomplished and report made.

Enough. He grabbed up the shovel and pushed a

stream of black earth down into the hole. It did not take them long to refill it. Troy stamped the mound down flat, then poured the excess soil into a burlap bag that he had brought along for that purpose. When they had scattered fallen leaves over the spot there was no sign of what they had done. Troy pointed to the top of the outcropping of granite.

"This is the spot where I arrived. This ledge of stone has been here, unchanged, for countless centuries. Nor will it be changed in the future. Some day they will build a laboratory up there, with more buildings all around here. I've made my report—it's in that box we buried—so my work is through now."

"You mean that they will dig here some day, in the future?" Troy nodded. "In order to find out what happened to you after you made your journey through time? My Lord, you are a conscientious fellow. You'll be long dead before your report is read."

"That doesn't matter. I've done as promised. Finished the assignment and delivered my report."

"I gather that there is no chance of your putting it under your arm and returning with it yourself?"

"None. This is a one-way trip. I knew that when I came. I have no regrets. I accomplished what I set out to do. I think it was worth it."

"I couldn't agree more. Though I'm not sure that I would have been able to make the decision that you did. But that part is finished. Do you know what you will do next?"

"I certainly do. I'm going to leave the South and head north, to New York City. That's my home town and I have an immense curiosity to see what it is like now."

"Sodom and Gomorrah," Shaw said distastefully. "A world unto itself and a pretty nasty one at that. The most corrupt and wicked city in the world. There is either a riot or a plague there every year."

"Sounds like home," Troy said. "Let's go look at it. Will you come with me?"

"Of a certainty. I plan nothing strenuous until my wounds are fully healed. If I must recover it should be in the lap of luxury provided by Mammon on Hudson. But no more horses. We'll take the train."

It was a slow and filthy trip, with greasy cinders leaking in around the windows and settling on everything. In New York they were more than ready to take a cab to the hotel and a hot bath. After three days of nothing more strenuous than eating large meals and sleeping late, Shaw ventured the opinion that he was fit enough to climb into a saddle again. They rented horses from a livery stable on Twenty-Third Street in Manhattan, then rode down to Houston Street to board the ferry across the East River. Except for the lack of bridges, Troy was amazed at how familiar the city was. No skyscrapers of course, and horses instead of cars, but the streets and the buildings on the East Side here were very much the same as the ones he remembered. Brooklyn was a warren of small homes, and it wasn't until they crossed into Queens that there were any marked changes. The houses gave way to farms and twisting country roads. They rode easily, stopping for lunch in a Corona inn, then carrying on.

An hour later Troy halted at the top of a hill that looked down upon the crossroads village of

Jamaica. There were farms all around, and beyond them the swamps and rushes of Jamaica Bay. He shook his head.

"I was born right down there," he said. "Grew up here. It was all small houses, the Van Wyck Expressway there, and the el along Jamaica Avenue."

"El?"

"Yes, the el train, the elevated railroad, you know."

"No, I don't, but it sounds like an interesting idea."

"Noisy. Cold as hell in winter when the doors open at the stations. Snow blows in. What am I doing here, Robbie? I don't belong here." Suddenly depressed, he pulled the horse about and dug his heels into its sides. "Let's get back to that inn. I need some strong drink."

Shaw galloped to catch up with him, then they slowed and rode along side by side. He looked at Troy, at his fixed gaze, and knew that he was not seeing the road and the trees ahead but was looking at a world forever lost, one he could never possibly see again. Shaw leaned over and placed his hand over Troy's where it rested on the pommel of his saddle. Troy turned to look at him then, and the depths of despair in his eyes were profound beyond belief. Then a trace of a smile touched his lips and some of the darkness slipped away.

"You're a good man, Robbie Shaw, and it has been my pleasure to make your acquaintance. Now let us get back to Manhattan and enjoy ourselves. We need a bang-up dinner with bottles and bottles of good wine. After that we are going to go to the theatre. We are going to celebrate and have a good time while we can. Because all of this is going to end soon. There is war over the horizon. A most deadly war of brother against brother that is going to tear this country apart. So now we are going to enjoy ourselves—and then we are going to part. I hope to meet up with you again, but I don't know where or when."

"You make it sound so final. What do you intend to do?"

"What I do best. I'm going to try to enlist in the Army. That War is coming and nothing will stop it. You and the other abolitionists fought your peace-time war against slavery, but that period is coming to an end. In the not too distant future the shooting war will begin.

"It is going to be a long, long time before it ends."

THIRTY-SIX

July 1, 1863

The water had been freshly boiled and was still warm when Troy poured it over his arm. It burned painfully as it washed the open shrapnel wound and started the freshly-clotted blood flowing again. The jagged cut wasn't deep, but it was painful, and Troy gritted his teeth as he swabbed it clean. His antibiotics were gone, used up on the wounded during the years of fighting, so the boiled water would have to do. The length of bandage had been boiled too, and he wrapped it around his arm until the wound was covered. This last effort on top of the fatigue of battle had brought him to the edge of exhaustion; he leaned back against the bole of the tree, eyes closed, arms draped limply across his knees, more asleep than awake as confused memories tumbled through his tired brain.

How quickly the years had gone by, yet how slowly as well. So much had happened since that day when he had said good-by to Robbie Shaw in New York. He had quickly discovered that his idea of enlisting in the army had not been as easy as he had planned. Black men were not wanted—except as servants or ditch-diggers. He would not settle for that. It had taken a year of hard work, and all of McCulloch's money, to organize the first Negro battalion in Boston, the First Regiment of Massachusetts Colored Volunteers. The amount spent lobbying and bribing the city fathers had almost been as large as that spent on equipment. But he had done it, that was what counted. When the war began they had been ready. And they had fought— oh how they had fought!—and died as well. Yet there had been no shortage of volunteers. In a little over two years of battle they had replaced over fifty percent of their number. Half their strength, gone. Dead men, faces now dimly remembered, names already forgotten. Troy nodded, half-asleep, his thoughts stumbling in endless circles through his brain.

"Sergeant, I brung you some vittles. Beans mostly, but if you look real close maybe you see some bits of the rabbit."

The voice startled Troy awake. He looked up, blinking at the big man with the lopsided grin; half his teeth were missing. He smiled back and dug the spoon from his pocket, reaching up for the tin plate.

"Thanks, Luther, I can use that." His fatigue was so great that Troy had not even realized that he was hungry as well as exhausted. He dug his spoon into the beans and chewed a great mouthful. Wonderful! When was the last time he had eaten? It was hard to remember, his brain still numbed by the day's fighting. Yes, it had been that morning, biscuits and acorn coffee. Nothing since. Except bullets and canister shot. But you didn't want to eat too much of that.

The evening was warm and dark. Up here on the hillside he could see the campfires of the Union Army spread out to both sides along the flanks of Cemetary Ridge; twinkling beacons in the night. The exhausted survivors of the day's battle huddled around them, cooking their dinners and trying not to think about what the morning would bring. They kept their backs turned to the night, not wanting to peer through the surrounding darkness to the distant lines of fires that marked the Confederate lines. There were an awful lot of them, stretching out on both sides of the little town of Gettysburg, Pennsylvania.

The rebel fox, General Robert E. Lee, was still alive after two years of fighting, and still attacking. And now the fox was in among the chickens. Driving north with his 80,000 men, he had taken the battle into enemy territory, past Washington and on into Pennsylvania. That is where they had stopped him today. He had not been beaten, but for the moment he was stopped, here at Gettysburg. The Union troops had fought all day under the concentrated fire of the Confederate guns, suffering the shock of attack after attack by those screaming gray files of soldiers. But they had held. Held all along the line, Troy had heard. That was the report, but it was like the report of some distant battle. His war had been here, among the wooded hills and valleys, the stone walls and winding creeks. The men of his regiment, the First Regiment of Massachusetts Colored Volunteers, had stood and fought—and won. No, not won, no more than any of the other Union regiments had won this day. But standing and fighting and withdrawing with their lines intact, that was a victory. A continuing victory since everyone, the officers included, had been sure that the black troops would run.

They never had. Since the war had begun they had stood up to everything thrown at them. Stood up to enemy gunfire and bayonets, dysentary and disease, the contempt of their own officers, the derision of the white soldiers. They had endured.

Troy finished the beans, scraping up every last drop and morsel. Then he licked his spoon off and put it back into his pocket. Everything was in order. The wounded had been sent to the rear, what food that he could find had been distributed. All of his men had full canteens, and he would make sure that they filled them again in the morning. He had done everything that he could for them. Now he looked to his own equipment.

He opened his patch kit and Lily smiled up at him from the battered photograph. He smiled back, still possessed of the warm memory of her love. After taking out a scrap of cloth he carefully replaced the photograph and sealed the case.

He was running the cleaning rod through his rifle when the messenger found him.

"Captain wants to see you back in the shebang tent, sergeant."

"On my way," Troy said, turning to the corporal sitting across the fire from him. "Finish this for me, will you Hank?"

"That is gonna cost you five dollars."

"Good. I'll pay you soon as the war is over."

Hank was a good man—they were all good men.

Troy had asked only because he knew that the
corporal would have done the job anyway the
moment his back was turned. They were a unit, a
family, the best men he had ever served with. They
were indeed brothers. He straightened his tunic,
buttoned the top buttons, brushed some of the
worst of the dust from the sergeant-major's
stripes on his sleeve, then turned and walked back
towards the tent in the hollow.

He always thought of the shebangs, the tents
and buildings of the U. S. Sanitary Commission, as
a combination Red Cross and PX. They helped
nurse the wounded, handled pension and pay
problems, even supplied some of the personal
items like soap and needles that made a soldier's
life in the Army bearable. If Troy thought that it
was a disgrace that the government had nothing at
all to do with the organization, that it was
financed by contributions and fund raising bene-
fits called Sanitary Fairs, he did not mention it.
The shebangs were there; his men needed them.

The captain returned his salute when Troy
entered the tent. He had been talking to two civil-
ians, a gray-haired man and an elderly woman,
and they all looked up when the sergeant came in.

"Sergeant Harmon, these are the representa-
tives of the Sanitary Commission in Boston," the
captain said. "They have raised a good sum of
money, specifically for this regiment, and we are
all greatly indebted to them. They will be leaving
soon, but they would like to speak to some of the
men before they go."

"If you please, I am a little weary," the woman
said. She was white-haired, in her eighties at least,
and had good reason to be tired after the day in a
wagon. "If you gentlemen will excuse me, I'll re-

main seated right here until we have to leave. If you will permit the sergeant to remain with me, I'm sure he can answer any questions that I might have."

"Of course, m'am," the captain said. "Remain here, sergeant, we won't be long." He held the tent flap aside to let the other men out ahead of him.

"Please be seated, Sergeant Harmon," the woman said. "We have some important things to discuss and very little time to do it in."

"Yes, m'am," Troy said, pulling up one of the camp chairs. The shorter this conversation the better. There was much to be done by morning.

"Do you remember me, Troy?" the woman asked, her words breaking through his thoughts. He looked at her closely for the first time.

"Sorry, m'am. Yes, you do look familiar. But I'm sorry, I just don't remember where from."

"From Washington," she said, smiling. "I'm a little older but it's still me. Roxanne Delcourt."

The words stunned him, he clutched the sides of the chair as though suddenly dizzy. Dr. Roxanne Delcourt! A visitor from another time, another age. The urgencies of battle had driven all memories of Washington from his brain. He was now so adapted to this world that he really had forgotten he had not been born in this age, but had traveled here from the future.

"Roxanne! I'll be damned, but it is you!"

"It is. Perhaps not the youngster you knew, I'm almost eighty-five now. But with the new drugs . . ."

"But you're not eighty-five, I remember that much, you must be closer to fifty-five. I don't understand. And what are you doing here? How did you find me?"

The questions tumbled out as long-forgotten memories returned. A distant world where he had once lived. Washington, D. C., the laboratory off the Beltway, the machine that had sent him here. He hadn't thought about them in a very long time. The pressures of war, of staying alive and keeping his men alive, these had driven everything else from his mind. Memory came rushing back now.

"But what are you doing here now?" he asked. "Your presence here, it can be no accident. And . . . your age, forgive me, it is all hard to take in at once."

She nodded agreement. "I'm sorry to be so abrupt. But it was the only way. My time is so limited. Let me tell you what happened after you left. We found the report that you prepared for us, thank you for that. We started digging for it the very next morning. When we cracked open the ancient box and saw the yellowed paper, the faded ink, I can't begin to tell you the impression that it made on all of us. I think it was then that we knew we had to do something to help you. We really began working in earnest, all of us. Admiral Colonne, he's retired now, but still strong, he helped. He sends his best wishes. And Bob Kleiman made me promise to say hello from him when I saw you. He was the one who was supposed to be here, not me." A shadow crossed her face. "Dead, cancer, over ten years ago. Or can we talk about time like that, subjective time?"

Her face was suddenly drawn, all of the years of her life in the lines scribed upon it.

"Roxanne," Troy said softly. "Thank you for coming. For caring that much about me."

She blinked and sat up straighter, returning his smile. "Someone had to, didn't they? The research went ahead after you left. Absolutely top secret. But everyone in government was so afraid of the possibilities that our hands were almost completely tied. They just didn't know what to do with us. Particularly with all the research restrictions that came in after the One-day War. After they discovered what McCulloch had done they actually stopped all experimenting for ten years. But eventually the program continued. We worked for almost thirty years on improving the machine. It sounds so strange when I say it like that. Thirty years of my time have elapsed, while— what?—it has been five years for you. But it took us all of those years of work to develop the means to both travel backwards in time and then return."

Troy's first confusion was over and he was beginning to understand what Roxanne and the team had accomplished. And why she had traveled back in time to this year, to seek him out.

"Do you mean . . .?"

"I do." Her voice was so quiet that he could barely hear it. "I've come to take you home, Troy. It's possible. It's no longer a one-way trip."

Troy was on his feet, pacing the length of the tent and back, unable to stay still. It was impossible, it couldn't be happening. But it was. Could it be true? He spun to face her.

"Return to *when?*" he asked. "To the time I left from—or soon after that?" She shook her head sadly.

"No, that is impossible. Or if it is possible— we just don't dare experiment to find out. Despite all of our work we still know so little about the real nature of time. I told you, it took us over thirty years to perfect the machine, and you never returned during that time. Therefore you didn't,

you couldn't. But we'll go back together. Things
aren't too bad in 2015. Though there have been
changes."

2015. The year was unimaginable. What sort
of world would it be? For some reason he
did not want to know. He spoke his doubts
aloud.

"But that's not my world. Now that you are
here, I realize that my world, the world I left, it
really is gone, vanished forever for me. I'll never
see it again—and I'm not sure that I want to. It
won't come into existence until long after I am
dead. It's the distant future from where we are
now—and it will be the distant past for you after
you return. But please don't misunderstand.
Thank you for coming, for making the effort to
help me. But, I am beginning to realize that this is
my world now. Those men out there are my people. Roxanne, you should get to know them. Poor,
but how proud. Less than half of them can read or
write—and I even have one boy who remembers
Africa, remembers being captured by slavers.
They are part of me now. I am grateful that you
came, that you have done this for me. But the
world that you live in now is no longer mine. This
one is. They need me here. And I guess, yes, I need
them."

His face was suddenly grim. "And I couldn't possibly leave, desert them at this time. We are going
to need one another tomorrow. This is the big one,
the big battle, the turning point of the war. And we
are going to beat the enemy. The South will never
rise again, will never regain its strength. This is
the battle that counts. Do you understand?"

Roxanne nodded, then opened her purse. "Those
of us who worked on this project, we were almost

sure that you would feel this way. We know the kind of man you are, Troy. We know what you did for us, coming back to this time with no thought that you would ever return. That is why we felt we had to do this, to give you the chance. Aren't you curious as to how we found you?"

"Why, yes, I suppose I am now that you mention it. Hadn't really thought about it. Army records?"

She shook her head as she took out a folded piece of paper. "No, they were worse than useless. But we did know where you were, that is one of the reasons we persisted with this line of research. You wrote that you would be going back into the Army. You probably know that this is the best re-searched war in history." She passed over the piece of paper. "This is a photocopy of a page, out of a history of the Negro regiments in this war. Read it, please. This is why I came."

Troy took it, read it slowly, these words from the future about the present. And, as he read, he could feel his heart beating louder and louder in his chest.

... the turning point of the war. The battle lasted three days and all of the Negro bat-talions suffered greatly. But they fought and their lines held. Much credit is given to Ser-geant-major Harmon who led the counter-attack on Culp's Hill that saved the day. Though the battle was won, Harmon was fatally wounded and died ...

His fingers were thick, and they fumbled with

the match box that he drew from his pocket. He struck a match, touched it to a corner of the paper, held it until the paper was fully aflame, then dropped it to the ground.

His voice was rough when he spoke. "It's not everyone who has the privilege of reading his own obituary." He ground the ashes under his heel.

"But it doesn't have to happen that way," Roxanne said. "Come away with me, tonight, everything has been arranged. You don't have to die."

"Don't I? But it's written here, isn't it? You wouldn't want to create a time paradox, would you?"

"We don't know. After all, you and McCulloch came here from the future, and nothing appears to have changed. Troy, I beg of you. Don't stay here and die. Return with me . . ."

"No, Roxanne, you know that I can't do that. It would be desertion. I think, even if I knew that I would have to die, I couldn't walk out on these men now. Don't ask me to. And please don't cry."

"Am I? I guess I am." She smiled and took out a lace handkerchief and touched it to the corners of her eyes. "All the time we were working I had the feeling that you would say this. But we had to go on. You really are something, Troy Harmon. Not once, but twice you've acted in a way that makes me glad I'm a member of the human race."

They were both standing and he had her hands in his, holding on hard. "Don't worry," he said. "Don't worry your head about me. Get out of here and get home safely and remember that we did meet again. If your machine has any value it let me see you one more time, let me hear that everything had worked out fine."

Voices came closer outside and he spoke quickly

now. "And I don't want you to be too concerned about me tomorrow. Your book could be wrong. History can be changed."

"I don't understand . . ."

"Forget about my report and think about the history books that you studied in school. Do you remember John Brown's attack on Harper's Ferry?" She nodded. "Well, what does your history book say happened there? The surviving raiders were captured and sentenced to death, is that right?" She nodded again.

"Do you also remember what happened to Hill's Rifle Works? The armory on the island?"

"The one that blew up during the attack? Of course. After reading your report we realized that you were responsible for that. The explosion stopped McCulloch's plan once and for all."

"Yes it did. But I can also remember my history books, quite clearly. I majored in history and was always good at dates. I remember distinctly that nothing was destroyed at Harper's Ferry. The raiders were taken and the armory remained intact. That is history as I remember it. And something else. I used McCulloch's money to organize a battalion of Negro volunteers in the year before the war started—he would have loved that! But in my history books there were no black battalions until much later."

She dropped his hands, raised hers to her face as she stared at him with sudden shock. "Then, what you are saying, is that history *was* changed by your coming here. That means that the theory of alternate worlds must be true. Events in one time cause a branching, the bringing into existence of parallel but alternate worlds."

"That's right." He smiled broadly. "And we

shouldn't be holding hands and be talking as if we were old friends. We've never met before. We're from different existences. I come from a world where there were no Negro battalions until years after the war began. This is not true here. In my world the raid on Harper's Ferry did no damage. Which means that my report was never received. When they dug beside the rock there was nothing there. But in your world the rifle works blew up. You found the report. Therefore I came to this age from a parallel existence, not yours, which makes us complete strangers up until this moment."

She was smiling now, too. "Then—that means that you may *not* die tomorrow. My coming here, telling you, may have altered history."

"Not may, *did* alter it. And now that I have been warned I will do my damnedest to stay alive."

"But you may still die . . ."

"Yes, there is that chance. But that is a chance that every one of us faces every day of this war. It was a chance I took when I used all of my antibiotics and medicine on my men. And I'm still alive. So there is also the chance that I may live to see the war end. I hope that I do. I like it here. It's a terrible existence in many ways, but it's mine now. I want to see the end of this war and I want to be there during the peace that will follow."

The tent flap opened and the captain came inside. Troy came to attention.

"I have to get back to the men now, sir."

"That will be all—if Miss Delcourt is through?"

"I am, captain, thank you. I have had a most enlightening talk with the sergeant. He has told me very much about the work we are doing and I shall return and report to the others the success of our efforts."

"Thank you, m'am," Troy said. "Please thank everyone for what they have done."

"I'll do that sergeant, believe me, I will."

Troy saluted, turned about and walked out into the night. The stars were bright above, the watch-fires spread out below. The year was 1863 and, despite the war, the possibility of death, it was a good time to be alive.

He whistled happily as he walked back to his men.

THE BEST IN SCIENCE FICTION

BEN BOVA

Buy them at your local bookstore or use this handy coupon:
Clip and mail this page with your order.

Publishers Book and Audio Mailing Service
P.O. Box 120159, Staten Island, NY 10312-0004

Please send me the book(s) I have checked above. I am enclosing $_____
(please add $1.25 for the first book, and $.25 for each additional book to
cover postage and handling. Send check or money order only — no CODs.)

Name _____

Address _____

City _____ State/Zip _____

Please allow six weeks for delivery. Prices subject to change without notice.